NO TIME TO RUN

A LEGAL THRILLER
FEATURING MICHAEL COLLINS

J.D. Trafford

Publisher's Note: This is a work of fiction. Names, characters, places, and incidents are a product of the author's imagination. Locales and public names are sometimes used for atmospheric purposes. Any resemblance to actual people, living or dead, or to businesses, companies, events, institutions, or locales is completely coincidental.

Book Layout ©2013 BookDesignTemplates.com

Ordering Information:
Quantity sales. Special discounts are available on quantity purchases by corporations, associations, and others. For details, contact the "Special Sales Department" at JDTrafford01@gmail.com.

No Time To Run/ J.D. Trafford. -- 1st ed.
ISBN-13: 978-1475280180
Book cover design by Scarlett Rugers Design www.ScarlettRugers.com

Other Books By J.D. Trafford:

No Time To Run

No Time To Die

No Time To Hide

To my wife.

—J.D.

CHAPTER ONE

Inches away, Kermit Guillardo's breakfast of hard-boiled eggs, marijuana, and salsa rode heavy on his breath.

"Rough night?" A small piece of egg dangled from Kermit's nest of a beard.

"Can you give me a minute here?" Michael pushed the empty Corona bottles away from his body, closed his eyes, and laid his head back onto the sand. It was a temporary respite from the Caribbean sun and a world-class hangover.

"Tin bird leaves in just a few ticks of the clock, *mi amigo.*" Kermit's head bobbled. His swaying gray dreadlocks mirrored the thoughts kicking around inside. "Next flight won't be 'til late, so you better rise and shine, maybe fetch yourself a clean shirt."

Michael didn't respond. His mouth was dry, and a dozen tiny screws were inching their way into the deeper portions of his brain.

"Andie called again." Kermit put his hands on his hips. "She's freaked out, man, very freaked out. Cops, like, won't talk to her, so she's just stirring in jail wondering what's goin' on an' all."

"What'd you tell her?"

"Told her you were flying out first thing. Didn't tell her you were passed out on the beach, though."

1

"I appreciate that." Michael sat up.

"No problemo, *mi amigo*." Kermit brushed away the compliment. "I've found that ignorance is often the key ingredient of a well-settled mind." He nodded, agreeing with himself, then his expression turned serious. "You really a lawyer? I know you said you were and all, but ... people say a whole lot of things down here."

"I was." Michael touched the small scar on his cheek. "And, I guess I still am."

Kermit nodded as his mind worked through the information. Finally, he said, "You don't look like a lawyer."

"Well I clean up pretty good. You'd be surprised."

With that, Kermit smiled wide.

"I bet you do." He leaned over and offered Michael his hand. Michael took it. "You know Andie's like a sister to me." Kermit pulled Michael to his feet.

"I know."

"Tendin' bar here and taking care of this little resort is the only job I've ever managed to keep, not that Andie couldn't have fired my ass, like, a million times by now ..." Kermit's voice drifted away with the thought, and then circled back. "She didn't do what they say she did, man. Not my Andie."

"I know she didn't."

"You gonna straighten it out?"

Michael started to answer, and then stopped. He had only been a lawyer six years before the incident that caused his premature retirement from the practice of law, but he had been asked that question hundreds of times by clients. Usually the answer was a hedge. He knew not to commit — the cops won, even when they shouldn't, and there were some problems that even the best lawyer in the world couldn't fix — but, this time was different. It wasn't a client. It was Andie, a woman who had stopped him just short of the edge. A woman he loved.

"I'm going to bring her back." Michael looked Kermit in the eye. His voice was steady, although everything else inside churned. "Whatever it takes."

CHAPTER TWO

He had sworn that he would never practice law again. Michael John Collins had quit his job. His Brooks Brothers' suits and silly striped ties were burned in a glorious back-alley bonfire, and he had given away just about everything else he owned. He had dropped out, and remained dropped out, living in the beautiful mess of shacks and huts, about an hour south of Cancun, that comprised the Sunset Resort & Hostel.

Listed in The Lonely Planet guidebook under "budget accommodations," the Sunset promised and delivered: "An eclectic clientele of backpackers, hippies, and retirees that is a little more than a half-mile down the road from the big chains, but a million miles away in every other sense."

It was just what Michael had needed. He couldn't really say whether he had fallen in love with Andie first, and then signed the overpriced lease agreement, or vice versa. But, either way, he had been an easy mark. Hut No. 7 at the Sunset Resort & Hostel had become his home, more than any place else he had ever lived.

As Michael finished gathering his toiletries and a change of clothes, he picked up the framed picture of his namesake. Growing up, his mother had hung three photographs above the dining room table in their small Boston apartment. The first picture was of Pope John Paul II. Next to it, there was a picture of President John F. Kennedy. And, the third, and most important, was a black and white photograph of the Irish revolutionary, Michael John Collins.

Michael had been named after him, and, when he was little, he would pretend that the revolutionary leader was his real father. The photograph was taken shortly before the Easter Rebellion against the British in 1916. The revolutionary was young at the time, in his mid-twenties, but the look on his face was hard and determined, with a glint of mischief.

Michael didn't believe in politicians. And his belief in religion came and went depending on the day, but the Irish revolutionary was a constant. He had kept the photograph after his mother had died of lung cancer during his senior year of high school. The picture gave him comfort, a thin tether to the past and loose guide for the future.

He wrapped the photograph in a few shirts and placed it in his bag, ready to do battle once again.

They were getting close, Michael thought. His two worlds, past and present, were coming together. Andie was somehow caught between. As he closed his knapsack, Michael looked around Hut No. 7 and wondered whether he would ever be back.

"You coming?" Kermit stuck his head through the open door. "We gotta shake a leg and head toward the mighty coastal metropolis of Cancun, my man. Tick-tock, tick-tock, tickity-tickity-tock."

Michael turned toward Kermit. "I'm coming."

He threw his knapsack over his shoulder, and took a last look at his sparse living quarters before walking out the door.

"You seem a little gray, dude, like a long piece of putty brought to life by a bolt of lightning and a crazy-daisy scientist or two."

Kermit reached into his pocket and removed a small plastic bag. As they walked past the Sunset's communal bathrooms, he held the baggie in front of Michael's face.

"Methinks you need a little somethin' somethin' to soothe your troubled mind."

Michael looked at the bag filled with a cocktail of recreational drugs, and then pushed it away. "You a dealer now?"

"No, man," Kermit said. "Dealers sell. I, on the other hand, give."

"That's deep." Michael walked past the Sunset's cantina and main office, and then to Kermit's rusted cherry El Camino. He placed his knapsack in the back, and began to open the passenger side door.

"Hold on there, young man." Kermit grabbed hold of Michael's shirt. "The doctor does not simply dismiss patients without providing some care." He retrieved two light blue pills from his baggie, and stuffed them into the front pocket of Michael's rumpled shirt. "Dos magic pills."

Michael looked down at his pocket and wondered what the jail sentence was for possession of two Valium without a prescription. Then, he got in and closed the door as Kermit walked around the front to the driver's side.

"Senor Collins. Senor Collins."

Michael looked and saw two young boys running toward them as the half-car/half-truck roared to life. Their names were Raul and Pace, the star midfielder and the star striker for the school soccer team. Michael was their coach.

"Senor Collins, wait."

"We have to go, *mi amigo*." Kermit shifted the El Camino into gear. "Time's wasting."

Michael raised his hand.

"Hold on a minute." He rolled down the window, and leaned outside. "Aren't you two supposed to be in school?"

The boys stopped short of the passenger side door.

"Heard you were leaving," Raul avoided the question.

"Wanted to say good-bye," Pace said.

"I'll be back." Michael tried to sound convincing.

"You are going to help Senorita Larone?"

"I hope so." Michael reached into his back pocket and removed his wallet. "I'm not sure how long I'm going to be gone, but I need to hire you two for a very important job."

The boys looked at each other. The smiles were gone. It was all business.

"This fellow over here," Michael nodded toward Kermit, "is going to need a little help running this place. Do you think you two can come over here after school and do what needs to be done?"

Raul and Pace nodded without hesitation.

"But you have to go to school and study hard. If I learn that you've been skipping again, then that's it. No second chances. Agreed?"

They nodded.

"All right." Michael handed the boys a small stack of pesos. "Be good." Michael turned toward Kermit and tapped the dashboard. "Let's go."

CHAPTER THREE

Inside the airport, Michael's nerves had grown worse. What little confidence he had shown Kermit that morning was in retreat as he made his way through one line, down a corridor, and then through another.

Everything was lit up by the bright, artificial glow of fluorescent bulbs. The light bounced off of the polished floors and tiled walls, giving the airport a disorienting hum. Parents and kids, honeymooners and college trust fund babies hustled from check-in to security, and then to the gate.

Michael's low-grade headache turned up a notch. The dozen tiny screws had joined forces. They were now working as one, drilling deeper into his head.

After getting his ticket and seat assignment, Michael floated along in the stream of passengers until he found a gift shop. He bought a pre-paid calling card, and then looked for a bank of pay phones.

Michael had what could loosely be described as a plan, but thinking about it turned the screws tighter and forced his stomach into a remarkable gymnastic routine.

He eventually found a payphone. Michael hesitated at first, and then picked up the receiver.

Following the instructions on the back of the calling card, Michael took a deep breath, and then punched in a series of numbers. He paused, and then finished dialing. A long time had passed since he had last called, and if asked, he probably couldn't say the specific numbers out loud, but his fingers remembered.

"Wabash, Kramer & Moore."

The woman who answered was professional with an edge of perkiness. It was a style that was pounded into all of the receptionists at the firm: be nice, not chatty; be quick, but act like you care.

"Lowell Moore," Michael said. The screws turned again.

"One moment." A new series of pauses and clicks ensued, and then finally another ring and a click.

"This is Lowell Moore's office."

"Hello," Michael said. "Is this Patty?" Patty Bernice was Lowell Moore's longtime legal assistant. She was a short, round woman who was considered by most associates in the firm to be a living saint. She took the blame for mishaps that weren't her fault, and often placed a blank yellow Post-It note on the side of her computer screen as a warning to all associates and paralegals that Lowell was in one of his "moods."

"Who is this?"

"Michael." He took a deep breath. "Michael John Collins."

Another pause, longer this time. "Michael Collins," Patty said. "It's been a while."

"It has. Too long to be out of touch," he lied. "Is Lowell around? I know he's busy, but I'm calling from an airport in Mexico and it's pretty important."

"I think so," Patty said. "Let me see if he's available."

There was a click as Michael was put on hold. He hadn't thought about what he would do if Lowell pushed his call into voicemail. He just assumed that the conversation would happen, but, the longer he was on hold, Michael began to wonder.

Minutes passed, and then Michael heard his flight number being called over the public address system. Pre-boarding had begun.

"Come on," Michael said under his breath. He looked at his watch, and started to fidget, then finally, a familiar voice.

"Mr. Collins." Lowell spoke with far too much drama. "A surprise. How are you? Good to hear from you."

"Good to talk to you too, sir." Michael's voice was higher now, and each word was distinct and clear. It was his bright-young-associate voice, and it shocked Michael how fast it came back to him. "Listen, Lowell, I know you are busy so I'll get to the point. I have a friend who's in some trouble up there, and I was wondering if one of the investigators at the firm could check it out."

There was silence.

Michael sensed the wheels turning in Lowell's head. Lowell Horatio Moore was the only one of the three named partners still working at Wabash, Kramer & Moore. Tommy Wabash died of a heart attack at age forty-seven. In the end, the 5'9" son of Protestant missionaries weighed in at a remarkable 287 pounds. Jonathan Kramer "retired" after a murky and rarely discussed incident involving a female summer associate, his sailboat, enough cocaine to jack up an elephant, and inflatable water toys.

"An investigator," Lowell said. "I don't know."

The firm's on-book investigators, meaning investigators that were officially on the Wabash, Kramer & Moore payroll, were billed out at $275 per hour. The off-book investigators were paid at least four times that much, depending on the information or task assigned to them. The off-book investigators were usually former FBI or cops. They weren't afraid to conduct business in ethical gray areas and that risk was rewarded. Most of the firm's cases were won or lost based upon what they found.

Michael knew his request would divert one of those precious billing machines from the paying clients with nothing in return, so he had to give Lowell something.

"I'm thinking about coming back." Michael said it with such earnestness that he almost convinced himself. "I'm not sure, but I thought maybe I could get set-up in the visiting attorney's office, do any extra work that you might have, and then handle this case for my friend, kind of a *pro bono* deal to get me back into the swing of things."

Lowell was silent again, thinking through Michael's offer.

The turnover at the 1,500-attorney law firm of Wabash, Kramer & Moore was incredibly high. It bled senior-level associates. Either they burned out and became high school teachers or went someplace else with a vague hope of having a life and seeing the spouse and kids, assuming the spouse and kids hadn't already left them.

"Sure you're up for that?" It was Lowell's attempt to sound concerned about Michael's welfare, but he couldn't disguise the excitement. His young protégé might be back.

"It's been over two years," Michael said. "I think it might be time."

Lowell thought for a moment. "Are you here now?"

"No, I'm at the airport." Michael looked at the line of passengers winding through a series of ropes, and disappearing through the gate assigned to his flight. "My plane's about to take off."

Lowell asked for Michael's flight information, and then told Michael that he was going to send a car for him when he arrived. "You can stay in my guesthouse."

"You don't have to do that."

"I wouldn't have it any other way." Lowell continued. Everything was a negotiation. "And what was the name of that friend of yours?"

"Andie Larone," Michael said. "She was arrested yesterday. Don't have many details because Andie doesn't know much herself." Michael felt his stomach flip. "When she asked for an attorney, the cops stopped talking to her. That's why I need the investigator."

"We can talk more about that when you get here."

Michael said goodbye, and just managed to get out a quick "thank you" before the chips, beer, and tequila from the previous night crept upwards.

CHAPTER FOUR

As Michael's ears popped at 28,000 feet. Noise filled his head. He was swimming in sounds — the rattling coffee cart, the coughing man in aisle 8, the snoring woman in aisle 17, and, of course, the bing-bing of the seat belt warning light turning on and off, off and on.

Michael raised his small plastic cup and rattled the remaining cubes of ice. The stewardess noticed him, gave a nod, and then worked the beverage cart back. With each step she smiled, then snapped a wad of gum, smiled, and then snapped again.

"Another rum and Coke." Michael handed her the cup.

"Just enough Coke to make it brown?" she asked with a Southern lilt.

"A very light tan." Michael opened his wallet and removed a few bills.

"This one's taken care of, sweetie." Her smile maintained, but Michael continued to hold out the money, expecting the stewardess to take it. "It's all paid for," she said, again. "That gentleman in the back already gave me the money." Smile, snap. "Said he was a friend of yours and figured you'd be a little parched."

Michael turned, and scanned the seats behind him with a lump in his throat. "Which man?"

15

The stewardess looked, initially maintaining her chew of the gum and perky demeanor, but quickly the smile faded.

"Now that's a weird 'un," she said; snap with no smile this time. "I don't see him no more." She shrugged her shoulders, handed Michael his drink, and then continued down the aisle with her cart.

The smile and snap returned after just a few steps, but for Michael everything became a little tighter. His seat became smaller. The row in front of him became closer. The ceiling dropped a foot, and the other passengers crowded in.

He got up and walked down the aisle. Michael looked for someone, although he didn't know who. Up the aisle, and then back again. Nothing.

Michael returned to his seat. A weight pressed down on his chest.

He reached into his knapsack, and removed the red envelope from the bottom of the bag. He stared at the large block lettering on the front of the envelope. It was addressed to him: Michael John Collins, Esq.

He had received the envelope two weeks earlier. It had been a lazy day, sunny and typical. After a morning of Hemingway and an afternoon of poems by Ferlinghetti, Michael had wandered back to Hut No. 7 to wash up and change clothes for dinner with Andie. A new Italian restaurant had opened up on Avenida Juarez in Playa del Carmen, and although it was hard for Michael to believe, he was actually excited to taste something made without avocados, lime or cilantro.

Michael hadn't seen it at first. The envelope was on his pillow, and it wasn't until he came out of the bathroom a second time that the envelope caught his attention.

Initially he thought it was from Andie or maybe even left by Kermit as some type of joke. Then he opened the envelope and thought otherwise.

It was the beginning of the end.

The front of the card was a picture of the New York City skyline. Inside, there was no signature or note, only the pre-printed message:

MISSING YOU IN THE BIG APPLE

HOPE TO SEE YOU SOON

Michael looked up from the card as the memory merged into the present. He put the card back inside the envelope, and then scanned the plane again for a familiar face. After craning his neck for long enough to make the people sitting around him nervous, Michael set the card down. He reached into his pocket and removed Kermit's two magic blue pills.

He popped them into his mouth with a chaser of rum and Coke. His ears popped again, and Michael's head filled back up with sound. He closed his eyes and decided to keep them closed until the captain announced their descent into LaGuardia airport.

When the plane touched down in New York, Michael waited for all of the people who sat behind him to exit first. He watched as each person wobbled down the aisle, hoping for a moment of recognition that never came.

Eventually, the smile-snap stewardess approached to inquire if there was something wrong.

"No," Michael said. "I'm going." He picked up his knapsack, climbed out of his seat, and walked toward the exit.

As he stepped from the plane onto the enclosed walkway leading to the terminal, cold winter air rushed through a narrow crack. He must have shaken, because the stewardess laughed.

"Might need to think about buying a jacket," she said.

Michael turned, couldn't think of anything witty to say, and so he turned back, continuing up the walkway.

With each step, the muscles in Michael's body became more tense. Nothing felt natural, and Michael had to remind himself to breathe. One foot in front of the other, he told himself, keep moving.

Michael stepped into the terminal. He half-expected to be rushed by thugs brandishing semi-automatic weapons or maybe a group of men in ski masks would throw a hood over his head and ship him off to a dark hole.

His eyes darted from one person to the next, but there were no thugs. There was, however, something worse: Agent Frank Vatch.

Agent Vatch was one of the meanest and nastiest paraplegics he had ever known, although Michael didn't know a whole lot of paraplegics. Rumor had it that Vatch's demeanor was caused by the origin of his disability. Some said he was paralyzed when a donkey kicked him at a petting zoo as a child, others said that he was snapped in half by his grandmother's malfunctioning La-Z-Boy recliner, and still others believed the paralysis occurred during his first sexual encounter.

Michael had his own theory about the agent's personality: Frank Vatch was simply born an asshole.

"Michael Collins." Vatch wheeled toward him with a crooked grin. His narrow tongue flicked to and from the edges of a slit, assumed to be his mouth. "A weird co-winky-dink running into you here after such a long absence." He wheeled closer. "If you would have called, I could've gotten flowers, maybe chocolates."

"A call would suggest I liked you, Francis." Michael knew that Agent Frank Vatch hated the name Francis.

He kept walking. He continued into the terminal's main corridor, putting his hands in his pockets, so that Vatch wouldn't see them shake.

"My sources tell me you are going back to the original scene of the crime." Vatch wheeled faster to keep pace with Michael.

Michael still didn't respond. He followed the exit signs. His eyes straight ahead, ignoring the chain restaurants, vending machines, and shoeshine stands.

"You couldn't need the money so soon," Vatch laughed, while Michael kept going.

Michael walked up to the customs desk, handed the official his passport, said he didn't have anything to declare, and was waved through.

Vatch flashed his badge and followed behind.

"Or could it be that you do need the money?" Vatch whistled. "Now, that would be something, burning through all that dough in just over two years. What was the grand total, again?"

"Don't know what you're talking about." Michael kept going. His head was cloudy from the Valium, and he wondered if he was really having this conversation. Michael knew that he would have to deal with Vatch at some point, but not like this, not so soon.

A man in a long, black coat stood in front of the door holding a white sign with Michael's name on it, and Michael remembered Lowell's offer to arrange for a car.

"Thank you, God," Michael mumbled under his breath. He pointed at the sign. "That's me. Let's go."

The driver hesitated as he noticed the man in the wheelchair ten yards behind giving chase and saying something about secret bank accounts.

"He's not with me," Michael said to the driver. "Just a crackpot."

"Fine, sir." The driver took Michael's knapsack into his hand, his eyes lingered for a moment on Michael's sandals, torn pants, and wrinkled shirt. "Gonna be cold," the driver said, and then started walking.

Michael followed him out of the terminal to a shiny black Crown Vic. The sun was setting, and everything was cast in an orange tint, even the inch of New York slush that had settled into the nooks and crooks of the otherwise cleared sidewalk.

The driver opened the door and Michael got in.

"See you, Francis." Michael closed the door, and Agent Frank Vatch flashed an obscene gesture. He also shouted something that likely went along with that gesture, but Michael couldn't hear it.

The driver put the key in the ignition, and started the car. He began to shift the car into gear, but stopped.

"You an internet guy?"

Michael thought about it, and then nodded.

"Yeah." He saw no sense in disturbing the only rational explanation the driver could think of for helping a thirty-something hippie escape in a limousine from an angry paraplegic.

"Lost my f'n shirt in the bubble," the driver said. "You mus' be one of the only ones left."

The driver reached down, and then pulled up a thick manila envelope. He handed it to Michael.

"Supposed to give you this."

On the outside, was the logo of Wabash, Kramer & Moore, and inside was a binder of paper with a cover memorandum written by some first-year associate summarizing the contents.

It was Andie's police file.

"Mind if we make an extra stop?"

"You got me for the night." The driver pulled away.

When they merged into traffic, Michael briefly looked up from the papers at a group of people standing in line for a taxi.

That was when he saw him. Michael couldn't remember the guy's name, but they talked once or twice when he stayed at the resort. He loved using big words, and always wanted to play Scrabble with other people in the cantina. He was odd at the time, but the beaches around Playa del Carmen were filled with odd people, particularly the Sunset.

Shaped like a barrel—six foot, maybe just over, balding, goatee— every part of his body - from his legs to his neck to his fingers - was thick. That was really the best description for him: Thick.

He must have been on the same flight as Michael, but how could he have missed him? Michael thought about asking the driver to stop, but then thought better of it. He didn't know what he would do.

Michael stared as they drove past. And then, at the last possible moment, the thick man looked at Michael, smiled, and waved.

CHAPTER FIVE

A djacent to LaGuardia Airport, ten mismatched buildings, collectively known as Riker's Island, sat on a small patch of land in the middle of the East River. They housed over 130,000 men and women who had been arrested, imprisoned or otherwise just plain thrown away. In the 1990s, the prisons on the island were so crowded that the mayor anchored a barge in the river to house another 800 inmates.

Riker's Island was Andie Larone's new home.

It had been almost ten years since Michael came to Riker's Island every week as part of Columbia Law School's free legal clinic, but the path through the island's maze of buildings and service roads quickly came back to him.

He directed the driver down one street and up another until finally arriving at the building they wanted, the Rose M. Singer Center for Women. It was a squat, concrete building put up in the late 1980s, and, as if to reflect the women who resided there, the outside of the building was a dirty, faded pink.

"I'm going to stay right here." The driver slowed the Crown Vic to a stop.

"Good," Michael said. "I'm not sure if I can even get in at this hour."

He collected the papers and put them back into the Wabash, Kramer & Moore envelope, and then took a breath. Michael tried to clear his mind, pushing Agent Vatch and everybody else to the side. He forced himself to concentrate on Andie. She deserved that much.

Michael got out and hustled toward the door. A hard wind came off the river and Michael conceded that the stewardess was right. He needed to buy a jacket.

The front door of the Singer Center closed behind him, and Michael walked up to the security desk. He told the large, male guard who he was and who he wanted to see, but the guard didn't move. He gave Michael a once-over and said, "Do what now?"

A half-dozen forms, four dirty looks, one condescending sneer, and a dismissive laugh later, he found himself in a small room set aside for attorneys and their clients. Michael sat in one of its two hard, wooden chairs. A three-by-three graffitied table was between the chairs, pressed against and bolted to the wall. A plastic pitcher of warm water and two dirty glasses rested on the table, daring someone to take a drink.

Sitting alone and waiting, Michael read and reread the file.

Andie Larone was the strongest person he knew, man or woman. Like Michael, she didn't have an easy time growing up. She was one of six kids, all removed by social services and shipped from one foster home to another. Some of the homes were good and some were very, very bad, but none were ever permanent. Andie learned to be independent before she learned her ABCs.

Even knowing Andie's strength, Michael wasn't sure how she would survive this. Seeing the case set forth in the police reports made Michael realize just how hard it was going to be to get her home.

Michael flipped through the papers and looked at the first two counts in the charging document: Count 1: First Degree Murder pursuant to Chapter 40 of the New York Penal Code Article 125; Count 2: Possession of an Illegal Substance with Intent To Sell pursuant to Chapter 40 of the New York Penal Code Article 220; Count 3, 4, 5, 6, 7, 8, and so on, fourteen counts total. Each one was a quick jab to his stomach, getting stronger and harder as he went. By the end, the charges had blurred into a rapid succession of punches until finally Michael had to set the documents down and push them away.

He glanced back at the door, wondering what was taking so long.

He looked back at the papers spread out in front of him. He looked for a mistake, something the police had done that tainted the rest of the investigation. A mistake that would allow him to prevent the prosecutor from using the evidence found in Andie's rental car at trial. In legal jargon, it was called "suppressing the fruit of a poisonous tree," but it was more like a "get out of jail free" card in Monopoly.

The door buzzed and a bell rang.

Michael looked up.

"Andie," he said, standing.

It had only been three days, but Andie looked pale. With no make-up, there was nothing to disguise the dark circles under her eyes. She hadn't been sleeping.

Then there was the necklace.

Andie's simple necklace with the four beads and burnt gold key was gone, probably tucked away in a plastic bag somewhere with the rest of her clothes. He had never seen her without it.

Walking slowly through the door, Andie stopped a few feet in front of him as Michael came toward her. She put out her arms, and then wrapped around him. She squeezed tight for a second, and then melted.

Nothing felt more right, and Michael let the guilt and anxiety that had dogged him since the airport fade away. She was his only friend, and he was going to stay in New York for as long as it took. "Save her or die trying," Michael thought, knowing it was a far more apt summary of the situation than he would ever admit to anybody, especially Andie.

CHAPTER SIX

In one of Michael's first cases as a lawyer, he and Lowell Moore had defended a surgeon in a medical malpractice case. The surgeon had been in his mid-50s, and had performed thousands of surgeries, some big and some small. He had been well respected in the medical community and had even served as an adjunct professor at Mount Sinai School of Medicine — a success. And then one day, he glanced at a chart too quickly and amputated the wrong leg of a man with diabetes.

When Michael had asked questions about it, the surgeon was unemotional. "I made a mistake," he had said, but there was no feeling in his eyes. There had been no remorse or empathy. Cutting people had become just a job; the unconscious body on the table was an inanimate object, not a father or a mother, or a grandfather or a friend. To him, cutting the wrong leg off had been the same as missing a meeting.

Michael sat across the table from Andie and felt like that surgeon. His emotions had been compartmentalized, and he went about his job, cutting and dissecting the facts presented to him and placing those facts within a legal framework. For the moment, he had convinced himself that it was the only way to help her. Although he knew, deep down, that wasn't true.

Michael let Andie speak. Every question he asked was weighed against the need for information. It wasn't about getting a complete record this time. It was about listening, digesting the facts. There would be time to circle back and fill in the holes.

"They showed me photos," Andie continued. "The cop called them the 'before' and 'after' pictures."

"Trying to shock you into saying something," Michael said. He was tempted to continue his thought, but held back. "Did you recognize the man in the photos?"

"I don't think so." Andie's eyes wandered away. "But I don't know."

"The file says that he came to the Sunset about five months ago, stayed four days, and then left."

Andie shook her head.

"Where'd they get that from? I don't know who comes and goes. I just scribble the names in a guest book; sometimes I don't even do that."

Andie closed her eyes. A tear worked its way down her cheek. She rocked back and forth, and then became still.

"This is bad," she said. "Isn't it? It's bad."

CHAPTER SEVEN

The dead guy in the photo was Helix Johannson, a drug dealer from the Netherlands who immigrated to the United States by stating that he would "invest" over a million dollars in the local economy, and of course, pay a nice fee to the federal government in the process. It was a legalized form of bribery and bias deep within the immigration code, where rich foreigners leap-frogged over the thousands of other people who had been waiting for years to come into the country.

All you needed was an affidavit, a bank account statement, and a cashier's check made out to Uncle Sam. God bless America.

Helix filed his papers in June 1989. A few months later he received his travel documents, a visa, and a brief letter from the State Department welcoming him to the greatest economy in the world.

To satisfy the immigration officials and the terms of his visa, Helix did invest. He set up a real estate company and bought properties in affluent neighborhoods in and around New York, Miami, Chicago, Dallas, Reno, and Los Angeles. They were the perfect tax write-off. They were also the perfect network of houses and apartments to distribute large quantities of pain killers, ecstasy, cocaine, and pot to his select clientele.

Helix wasn't interested in dealing to people in poor neighbor-hoods. He hated poor people, and there were also far too many cops floating around in those neighborhoods as well as too many small-time hustlers looking to avoid jail time by ratting out the next guy higher up in the chain. That guy would then rat out the next guy, who would then rat out the next guy, and on and on until they got to him.

Instead, Helix laid low. He kept the houses quiet, mowed the grass (which was all his new neighbors cared about anyway), and quietly serviced his growing list of customers.

They were, by and large, young rich kids who were killing time at college before landing a cushy job through a family friend upon graduation. They all had the cash-advance PIN memorized from daddy's credit card and a willingness to pay 35% above the street price, either because they didn't know any better or because they liked the convenience of on-campus delivery.

It was all going smoothly until last year when a campus rent-a-cop busted a kid urinating outside the Beta Chi fraternity house at Southern Methodist University in Dallas. The kid was so high and freaked out that he started rattling off the names and addresses of every one of his fraternity brothers as well as the location of one of Helix Johannson's properties.

The house was located in the nearby lily-white Dallas suburb of Highland Park. It was a two-story brick colonial with an im-maculate yard, two-car garage, and about a quarter-million dol-lars of marijuana and Vicodin in the basement.

The discovery of that house had led to the discovery of an-other, and then another. The FBI had been called in to help, and shortly thereafter Helix Johannson had become a priority target.

The FBI had thought they had a tight net around him. Then he disappeared. Seven days later Helix was found with five bullet holes in his chest. Michael found it hard to believe that the FBI had lost him, but that was what the report stated. It wouldn't be the first time that the FBI had messed up an investigation.

According to the police reports and the indictment, investigators believed that Helix Johannson had met Andie Larone at approximately 10:20 p.m. in an alley near West Fourth and Mercer by New York University.

An anonymous man supposedly witnessed the shooting from his apartment above, rushed down the stairs, and followed a "brown-haired woman" carrying two heavy suitcases to a Ford Taurus parked about three blocks away. The man called the license plate in to the police. The police tracked the license plate to a rental car company, and then to Andie Larone and the hotel where she was staying.

The police had gotten a warrant, the car had been searched, and inside they had found a gun and two suitcases filled with drugs and cash. As far as the police were concerned, the case was closed.

"Stop right here." Michael pointed, and the driver pulled over to the curb. "Last stop before I call it a night, I promise."

"Whatever," the driver said, "just get me home before two."

Michael grabbed his knapsack and got out of the car. It was nighttime now, and the financial district had lost its daytime hustle. The sidewalks were deserted, and it had somehow gotten even colder as gusts of wind howled down the empty avenues.

He crossed the street, walked up to the First National building on Vesey and Church, and then ducked inside.

When the large glass doors closed behind him, the sound of the wind was cut and Michael found himself in a silent, cavernous Art Deco atrium designed in the late 1930s by architects Harvey Corbett and D. Everett Waid.

Polished black stone shot up five stories with inlaid images of Greek gods and goddesses blessing a temple of commerce and the divine wisdom of unfettered markets. It was designed to inspire, and the architects were specifically instructed to ignore the stock market crash of 1929, the Midwest's transformation from farms to dust, and the 35 percent of the country who had become card-carrying members of the Communist Party.

Michael walked up to the security desk. A man and a woman dressed in blue blazers adorned with plastic badges looked him over. Their nametags read Cecil and Flo, respectively, although no formal introductions were ever made.

"Can I help you?" Cecil asked.

"We're closed for the night," Flo added.

"I know you are closed," Michael said, "but I was wondering if I could just ask you a few questions."

"Give you a minute," Cecil said.

"Maybe two," Flo added.

"Before we ask you to leave."

Michael took a breath, as he wondered whether Cecil and Flo had attended the same communication and customer service training as the guard at the Singer Center.

"I have a friend who came here after hours two nights ago," Michael said. "She's been accused of doing something, and I was wondering if I could look at your sign-in sheets."

"To show that she was here," Cecil said.

"Instead of there," Flo added.

"Exactly. She signed in, but the cops either didn't follow up or didn't care."

Cecil and Flo looked at one another, as if engaging in a telepathic argument regarding who would get up out of their seat to retrieve the daily log or whether they should both remain seated and do nothing.

Finally, Flo pushed her romance novel aside and with great effort began the process of extricating her body from the chair.

"What night you say?" Flo walked toward an unmarked door.

"Last Friday," Michael said. "Her meeting was at 9:30 p.m., probably arrived a little after nine."

Flo disappeared into a small back office that Michael had thought was a closet. He heard her shuffling papers, opening and closing file cabinets. Then he heard her sigh and say to herself, "Right here on top the whole time."

Flo came back and handed Michael a folder containing two dozen pieces of paper. They were stapled together. "These are all of them?" Michael asked.

Flo shrugged her shoulders. "It's what we got."

Michael flipped through the pages, scanning the various entries. Nearly all of them were visitors who had arrived before five o'clock. The last sheet contained the list of people who had arrived after-hours. There were only eight names. Andie Larone was not one of them.

"There's not another log?"

"That's it, sugar," Flo said.

"Who was she trying to see?" Cecil asked.

"Green Earth Investment Capital," Michael said. "A man named Harold Bell. He's a vice president there. Her resort was in trouble, and they were going to talk about refinancing and maybe bringing another investor to ..." Michael's voice trailed off, as Cecil and Flo shook their heads.

"Sure you in the right place?" Flo asked.

Michael told her the street address. "The First Financial Building."

"Right," Flo said.

"But no Green Earth here," Cecil said. "You can check the directory, but I never heard of it."

CHAPTER EIGHT

Lowell's house was exactly as Michael remembered: Huge. It was one of about four dozen such McMansions in a gated community about an hour outside of New York in Westchester County. There was no subtlety or craftsmanship. Each house looked like the other, and sat atop its own 1.5 acres of former farm land. They were designed for the single purpose of impressing upon visitors that those who resided there were rich.

Michael gave the driver a healthy tip, and then got out of the car. It was a little after midnight, and hard to believe that less than twenty-four hours ago he had been sitting on the beach getting drunk and watching the moonlit waves fall onto the white shore.

He lifted his knapsack onto his shoulder, and walked up the driveway toward the house. When Michael got to the front step, he noticed that all of the lights were on and loud rap music was thumping from inside.

Michael checked the numbers above the door, confirming that it was the right place. He rang the door bell and waited, but nobody came.

The rap music continued, with a thump-thump and a tragic tale of "bitches who been wronged by their nasty man, nasty, nasty man."

35

After a minute or two, Michael rang the bell again, waited, and then decided to try the door. It was unlocked and he went inside.

The front foyer was marble, a winding oak staircase rose up on the right and a formal sitting area was to the left. On the wall in front of him was a small line drawing of a fish in a bowl. The drawing was dwarfed by an elaborate and ridiculously large gold frame. The drawing was not an inspiring piece of art, but, in the corner, there was the signature of Picasso. That was all that mattered.

"Hello?" Michael took two steps into the sitting area. "Hello? Anybody here?"

The further Michael went into the house, the louder the rap music became. He walked through the kitchen, and then eventually to the source of the thumping.

It was a stereo in an entertainment room outfitted with a large plasma television, leather couches and chairs, and all of the audio equipment one could imagine. Three of the walls were filled with CDs and gadgets that Michael didn't understand, and the fourth wall was all glass. It opened up onto a dimly lit pool area that looked like a large greenhouse.

Michael walked through the sliding glass doors.

"Hello?"

A bleached-blonde woman in mid-dance-move turned toward him, a look of annoyance on her face.

She wore a small, red silk robe, which hung over a similarly small, red string bikini. The ensemble was completed with a pair of red high heels and a string of white pearls around her neck. This had to be Lowell Moore's new wife, Michael thought, but the two men standing behind her in matching Speedos were definitely not Lowell Moore.

"Excuse me," Michael said. "The door was open and I — "

The woman looked at her two companions and rolled her eyes.

"One minute," she said like a mother to her children. Then she walked toward Michael. She made no attempt to cover herself, and Michael couldn't help but notice that the woman's unnatural appendages remained firmly in place.

She leaned into Michael, and then softly and almost sweetly asked, "Did Lowell send you here to spy on me?" Without waiting for a response, she continued in a hushed voice. "You tell that man that if he wants a divorce it's gonna cost him, and if he still wants my ass to poke he better give me some damn privacy once in awhile."

"I just came into town," Michael said. "Lowell offered the guest house."

"Well, Lowell," she said, continuing her hushed tone, "didn't clear it with me, and since I'm here more than he is, that's a violation of my constitutional rights under God."

"Constitutional rights?"

"You know what I mean."

"Is Lowell coming back?" Michael asked. "Or maybe we could call him and get this straightened out."

"He had to go somewhere for some type of emergency legal crap." The woman looked Michael up and down as she teetered on her high heels. "But now I think he just wanted to set me up and send in his spy."

"I'm not a spy." Michael edged backwards toward the door. "Listen, I can go and stay at a hotel. It's not a big deal."

The woman crossed her arms in front of herself, sighed, and then looked back at the two muscular men standing by the hot tub. Her eyes lingered in certain places.

"If you could stay in a hotel for the night, I would really appreciate it." She twirled a strand of her hair and batted her eyes. "It's been a rough year, being newly married and all."

Michael nodded and turned away. "I'll see myself out."

The young and nubile Mrs. Lowell Moore responded with something like a thank you as Michael opened the sliding glass door and went inside.

As Michael walked back through the house, he noticed a leather jacket. It was draped over a chair in the dining room. Obviously the jacket belonged to one of Mrs. Lowell Moore's companions.

Michael picked it up. The jacket was black with a nice thick lining. Not really Michael's style, but the night was cold. It was no time to be picky.

He unloaded the pockets onto the counter, slipped the jacket on, and continued out the door.

There was a guard booth about four blocks away. It was unclear who the guard was protecting the residents from, since the "executive" development was isolated from the rest of society. Michael was, however, thankful for the residents' fear of the outside world.

He walked up to the door and tapped on its small glass window.

The guard was startled at first, and then waved Michael inside.

"I was just at Lowell Moore's place," Michael said. "Lowell offered his guest house to me for the night, but ..."

"Mrs. Moore wasn't in the mood for unannounced house guests this evening." The guard flashed a wicked smile, and chuckled to himself. "Looked like she'd gone off and already made some plans."

"Something like that."

"I'll call you a cab." The guard picked up the phone and dialed.

After a brief conversation with the dispatcher, the guard hung up. He turned back to Michael and said, "You come a few minutes ago in that black Crown Vic?"

"Yeah," Michael said.

The guard nodded his head and then looked in the direction of a forest green Jeep Liberty parked about a half-block away.

"Fella arrived about four minutes after you. Never got out, just sittin' there. Nothing necessarily illegal about sitting in your car, but I was thinking of calling the cops. Have him move along."

Michael stared at the Jeep Liberty. It was dark, but a nearby street light offered the silhouette of a bulky frame, probably the same man Michael had seen at the airport.

Before Michael could say anything, the Jeep Liberty's engine started, its headlights turned on, and it drove away.

CHAPTER NINE

Michael was asleep before his head hit the pillow. His sleep was hard and soon spun into flashes of light and images. The images were random, sometimes still and sometimes moving — : Andie and Kermit; his dead mother; the torn photo of his father, or the man that his mother claimed was his father; graduations and childhood birthdays celebrated by himself; purchasing his first suit and leather briefcase; his first day at the firm; and then the incident. It always ended with the incident: four shots, bang-bang, bang-bang.

Michael bolted straight up. His eyes were wide as he caught his breath. His heart pounded. For a brief second, a narrow stream of light cut across the dark hotel room. The door was open, just an inch. A hand reached through, fumbled with the chain.

The hand disappeared. The door closed, and everything went dark again.

Michael sat up, awake and still. He thought about grabbing his knapsack and running, somewhere in Europe this time — Eastern Europe, maybe Asia — a place far away from New York.

Then he thought about Andie. He would never forgive himself if he left her.

What would he have done if she had left him? There were moments in the beginning when she was scared. They had both been scared about letting the other get too close. The incident had still been fresh. The nightmares had been every night, and each dark corner had contained a threat.

Nothing had ever been said or reduced to writing, nor had there been any vows in the traditional sense. But a line had been crossed. Andie and he were simply bound together.

Michael leaned over to the nightstand and turned on the light. He waited for something else to happen, but it remained quiet. In the stillness of the room, he wondered if he had actually seen anything at all.

CHAPTER TEN

The morning came early. Michael had never really fallen back asleep. He started making lists of things to do in his head, and once that started, it didn't stop. The lists grew longer and longer. He prioritized and added detail, then he re-prioritized and added additional sub-tasks and sub-sub-tasks.

Anxiety pressed down upon him, until there was no choice but to get up and do something, anything, to keep from going insane.

It was a method of self-motivation that he had learned as a scholarship kid at Harvard who still needed to hold down a full-time job for rent and food. It came in handy during the run-up to finals at Columbia Law School, and it was a method perfected, if not abused, as a young associate at Wabash, Kramer & Moore.

Then, Michael would often go to bed at eleven o'clock at night, thinking of the lists, and then wake up at two, jumping out of bed, alert and ready to work, motivated by fear of failure.

There were some associates and partners at the firm that would deliberately send emails at three or four in the morning. It was a source of pride. They craved the off-hand remarks that such emails would generate about "late nights at the office."

The emails were documentation of their labor, memorializing their dedication, however fabricated.

Michael had never done that. He didn't need to prove how hard he worked, he just did it. Whether he was a sucker or a martyr, Michael didn't know. Two years after leaving it all behind, Michael still didn't know.

He wondered how life would have turned out if he had run away a little sooner. Nobody at the Sunset ever asked about his grade point average or even where he went to school. Nobody at the Sunset cared about the hip new restaurants and clubs that he frequented, or the fifteen-dollar mixed drinks he had bought for the girl of the week or the girl of the hour. And nobody seemed at all interested in knowing that he had been the highest billing associate at Wabash, Kramer & Moore for sixty-eight consecutive months.

Michael splashed a handful of water on his face, and then got dressed. He grabbed his knapsack, looked at his watch, and then poked his head into the hallway. When he saw that it was clear, he hustled into the elevator. Michael pressed the "close door" button about thirty times to ensure that he would be riding alone for the trip down.

A bell rang and the doors slid open. Michael walked out, checking the four corners of the lobby, noting the people sitting on the couches and standing around. Then he was out. Total time from room to cab was forty-five seconds.

The cab pulled away, and Michael's eyes scanned the front door of the hotel. Then, he looked at all the cars parked in front, coming behind them, or on the street. He waited for someone to follow.

"Where to?" The cabbie hit a button on the front of the meter.

"Chinatown," Michael said.

CHAPTER ELEVEN

S hopkeepers were busy cleaning the sidewalks in front of their storefronts and sprinkling salt on the ground to keep ice from forming. The fruit and trinket peddlers arranged and polished their wares for the inevitable onslaught of tourists, gawkers, and locals looking for a bargain. They would all arrive in the next few hours.

Michael got out of the cab. He walked three blocks down Canal Street, the main corridor running through the heart of Chinatown. On either side, a patchwork of varying buildings, signs, and buzzing neon lights rose above the street and provided a constant sense of energy. Even in the early morning, it kept the uninitiated off-balance.

Unlike the previous night, there was no wind, just cold. It surrounded him. Air burned his lungs as he took it in, and Michael lifted the collar up on his "new" leather jacket, shoving his hands deep into its felt-lined pockets.

Michael turned down Mulberry, and then ducked into a narrow, dead-end alley by a small noodle shop with perpetually steamed windows. The cobblestones beneath his feet were slick. The snow, piled high on both sides, made the alley seem even smaller the further he went.

Michael stopped in front of a battered metal door. There was nothing indicating that this was a place of business, but Michael knew that it was. He had lived in Chinatown during law school. When you live in a place, you hear things, especially when you can dispense a little free legal advice to somebody in trouble.

Hoa Bahns had been around for over a hundred years and never closed. There were always people in need of its services, regardless of the day or the hour. It was created before marketing and mass advertising divided the world into consumer niches, and business and pleasure were separated, regulated, and licensed. Modern rules did not apply to Hoa Bahns. Its only requirements were money and discretion.

The door opened.

The man standing in the doorway could have been a sumo wrestler. He looked at Michael with a sharp gaze. His arms crossed over his chest. He waited for Michael to speak first.

"*Ni hao,*" Michael said. How are you?

The man in the doorway still did not respond, nor did his expression change.

"*Dui bi qi, wo bu shufu an wo yao kan yisheng.*" I'm looking for a doctor.

The man stared at Michael for what seemed like an eternity, and then he stepped aside.

"*Xie Xie.*" Michael thanked him and walked past. The metal door closed with a loud clang, and he was inside.

Hoa Bahns was always dimly lit and smelled of incense, cigarettes, and whiskey. The tin ceiling was low. The floor was covered with tattered Persian rugs, and traditional Chinese music played in the background, soft and spare.

Michael walked past a sitting area occupied by two young prostitutes in silk robes, and took a seat at the empty bar. The bartender approached with a glass and a small bottle of San Pellegrino.

"Anything else, sir?"

"No. This is fine." Michael opened the bottle, poured it into the glass, and then waited. He knew it would take some time, and he tried not to look at the small camera perched above the bottles of whiskey. The camera pointed down at him. It was not a hidden camera. The proprietor wanted people to know that it was there and he was watching.

The camera transmitted an image to a monitor in a backroom where three men discussed whether or not Michael should be allowed to stay.

Michael sipped from his water and kept his head low. If people came or went, Michael avoided their eyes. Hoa Bahns was not a place to socialize or make friends.

He simply drank his water and waited, until he finally felt a slight tap on his shoulder.

"Mr. Collins."

Michael turned and saw a narrow man standing before him in a black business suit and white silk shirt.

"It has been awhile since you last visited, thus the delay." The man offered a slight bow.

"I understand." Michael followed the man around the bar to a door. On the other side, there was a hallway with a second set of sumo wrestlers and a stairwell.

"I think you will find everything in order."

"I appreciate that." Michael was led down the dark stairwell into another hallway.

They were probably twenty-five feet below Chinatown, but unlike the rest of Hao Bahns, this hallway was bright and sterile. Thick, polished stainless steel covered the ceilings and walls. A dozen closed doors lined each side, and each door had its own optical scanner and key pad.

Michael's guide walked to the third door, punched in a code, and then leaned over the optical scanner. The door buzzed. He opened it, and Michael was directed inside.

"When you are done, please press the red button and you will be escorted out."

"Thank you," Michael said, and then he was left alone.

The room was no more than six feet by six feet. Like the hallway, the walls, ceilings, and floors were covered with polished steel. On the wall facing east, for luck, were a series of safe-deposit boxes inset into the wall, each one with its own code. The only other objects in the room were a metal table and a large metal box that sat on top of the table.

Michael walked toward the box. Even though it was cold down in Hoa Bahns' vaults, Michael felt the sweat roll down his neck and then further down his back.

He unlatched and opened the box. Inside, the contents were just as he had left them over two years ago.

On top, there was his well-worn briefcase. A present to himself, purchased on the day he had graduated from law school. It was a dark, honey-brown leather with a small engraved nameplate near the handle. It wasn't the most expensive briefcase in the store, but it was his. Something he had purchased with money he had earned himself; something that he couldn't part with when everything else representing his former life had been burned or given away.

Underneath the briefcase, Michael looked at the remaining contents: three passports, each from a different country and bearing a different name; one double-A Glock 22; two full magazines for the gun; a box of bullets; and below that, five perfect rows of one-hundred-dollar bills, crisp and bundled, totaling 350,000 dollars.

CHAPTER TWELVE

Michael walked out of Hoa Bahns and took a long deep breath of fresh air. With his briefcase in hand and a wad of hundred-dollar bills in his pocket, he walked briskly out of the alley. He had left the gun and passports behind with reluctance, but it wasn't time for that, at least, not yet.

He turned the corner, and kept walking while he pulled one of two new cell phones out of his briefcase. The cell phones were fully charged, untraceable, and good for at least one week, according to Mr. Bahns.

Michael dialed the number for Father Stiles, and waited. The phone rang a few times, and Michael wondered what he would say. What could he say? The voicemail activated, and Father Stiles' calm and reassuring voice began the universal instructions for leaving a message.

Michael stopped walking as he listened, knowing that this was the right thing to do.

He waited as the tone sounded.

"It's me," he said. "I'm in New York. ... Long story." Michael looked up and down the street, seeing if there was anyone watching or listening. "I'd like to come by and see you. I hope that's all right."

Michael pressed a button, and the cell phone's screen went black. He put the cell phone back in his briefcase, and then walked another four blocks to General K's Haberdashery.

A small bell above the door rang as Michael entered, and General K appeared, bounding from the back before the door had closed.

"Hello, Hello, Hello." General K emitted a high girlish squeal. "You need to look proper. I see that you do." General K grinned, clapped his hands three times, and then squeezed between a glass case filled with cufflinks and gold watches, some real and some fake, and a rack of Hugo Boss knock-offs.

"Now, what can General K do for you?" Referring to himself in the third person.

"I need the makeover," Michael said, "but it has to be quick. I have a court appearance scheduled for this afternoon."

"So quick like bunny," General K said. "That I can do. Custom hand-made suit I cannot do in such short time." General K pretended to wipe a tear from his eye, then his smile was back. "But I make you look like man in catalog anyway."

"As long as I look the part."

The "part" was that of an attorney. And in a country that was supposed to be comprised of rugged individualists, its people kept pretty close to the script.

The costume attorneys were expected to wear consisted of a dark suit, striped conservative tie, white shirt, and polished wing-tip shoes. A male attorney had hair cropped short with no beard or mustache. Juries didn't trust men who had facial hair, it was said, because they seemed to be hiding something.

Female attorneys, if they were to be taken seriously, had similar dress requirements and were further required to have no sex appeal whatsoever: Boobs were to be strapped down and otherwise hidden at all times, hair should be pulled back and skirts were to come past the knee. That was how it was.

There were always people who strayed from the script of course, but they were not accepted at the hallowed offices of Wabash, Kramer & Moore or at any other large law firm. When a client paid between $300 and $1,000 an hour for the best legal advice he or she can afford, the Mickey Mouse ties and faded jeans stayed in the closet. The client paid for the sizzle as much as the steak.

Within five minutes, General K had marshaled seven suits to be hemmed and fitted. Six would be delivered later in the day by messenger to Wabash, Kramer & Moore. The seventh would be worn, which one of the seven didn't matter. Although they were all different shades of dark blue or black and maybe even contained a subtle pinstripe, from four feet away they appeared identical. That was what made them perfect.

Michael stood on a small wooden block in front of a mirror as General K measured his inseam, waist, neck and arms.

"Okay, Okay, I do these suits here." He took a pencil out from behind his ear and scribbled down the measurements in a small pocket notebook. "You go across the street, get haircut, come back, and we done."

Michael looked at the suits and nodded.

"Thanks for doing this." Then Michael turned and left the shop as anxiety and anticipation for the afternoon started to build. Lists, sub-lists, and sub-sub-lists scrolled through his head.

A few steps from the curb, he heard a familiar voice.

"Michael Collins, funny bumping into you here."

Michael turned and saw Agent Frank Vatch looking up from his wheelchair. The previous night's sneer had not gone away.

"I'm busy, Francis. I don't have time to chat."

Michael stepped off the curb and continued across the street to YiYu Hair Salon. Vatch wheeled off the curb, nearly tipping over, and followed behind him.

"Whoa there, don't you want to catch up on old times? Here you are back in the old neighborhood." Vatch continued to give chase. "Had an apartment over here during the law school days, correct?"

"I have an appointment to keep."

"Appointment? So busy upon your return, but your cutie girlfriend's arraignment isn't until this afternoon from my understanding."

Vatch's dark brown eyes, turned a shade darker. It took everything in Michael's power to keep himself from turning and punching Vatch in the face.

"Why don't we have a cup of coffee and talk?"

"There's nothing to talk about," Michael said.

"The agency seems to think otherwise."

"The agency doesn't think." Michael stopped in front of the door to the salon. "If you don't quit this, I'll sue you and the bureau for harassment. You've got nothing."

"Threats will get you nowhere, Collins, but honey will set you free." Vatch tilted his head to the side. His sharp tongue emerged out of the slit, and then just as quickly flicked and went back inside. "Or, in your case, maybe not."

Vatch laughed, and then opened his wallet, removed one of his cards embossed with the logo of the Federal Bureau of Investigation. He held it out to Michael. "Here's my number for when you want to talk."

"Save it."

"You're in trouble, Collins, and I think you know it." Vatch shook his head and smiled. "But it's going to be amazing when I arrest you. I really can't wait for that day."

"That'll be awhile, Francis." Michael turned away from Vatch and opened the door to the salon. As he walked inside, Vatch took his jab.

"Be careful, Mr. Collins, I've heard that hotel has had a rash of late-night burglaries and such." Vatch began wheeling away. "Some have even turned violent."

CHAPTER THIRTEEN

The trip to Brooklyn took about thirty minutes. After a transfer from the Orange line to the Green Crosstown Local, a voice announced the Myrtle-Willoughby station over the scratchy P.A.

Michael stood as the bell rang and the subway train jerked, screeching to a stop.

He walked out onto the platform, and then looked behind him. About a dozen others had also gotten off. None of them seemed familiar.

Michael stopped at the newsstand. He picked up a copy of the Post and threw some change in a tin can. The attendant grumbled.

As he walked, Michael glanced at the headlines. He had about a six-block walk to Saint Thomas the Compassionate Church near Tompkins Park. About halfway there, the sky started spitting ice so he slipped the newspaper under his jacket and walked a little faster.

It was the same walk he had made nearly every day after moving from Boston to New York. Sometimes it had been for a baseball or a football game with the other boys, but most often it had been to visit Father Stiles in the rectory.

Michael had never been turned away. Sometimes they would talk, but mostly Father Stiles had worked on his sermon while Michael had worked his way through every book in Father Stiles' collection of Catholic philosophers and thinkers — Aquinas, Kreeft, and Copleston.

He knew that Father Stiles had been disappointed when he had chosen to pursue law instead of the priesthood. He tried not to think about how much deeper Father Stiles' disappointment now ran.

Aqua light streamed through the Rose Window on the far end of the church. It filled the space with cuts of brilliant light. The window was titled, "Formless Creation," and was comprised of various shards of mysterious blue glass, some big and some small, radiating from a cluster of five hundred diamonds at its core. Each shard turned brighter and deeper, moving toward the outer petals. Underneath, a verse from the Book of Genesis:

And The Earth Was Without Form and Void and Darkness Was Upon The Face of the Deep … and God said, "Let There Be Light."

As he walked in front of the altar, Michael's hand moved up and down, and then across his chest in the sign of the cross. The gesture surprised him. Maybe it was a habit or done out of respect, but there it was without command. Automatic.

He turned the corner and stood at the base of a long, winding set of stone steps. Michael caught a glimpse of himself in the mirror — new suit, tie, hair cropped short — and paused. Shame and guilt roiled through his body.

Michael then took one step, hesitated, and then took another.

Eventually, he was at the top of the stairs, standing in front of a large wooden door leading to Father Stiles' personal office and library, which filled the upper floor of the rectory, an add-on to the backside of the church.

The door's heavy, iron knocker swung down.

"Come in."

Michael opened the door and stepped inside. The cluttered and cramped office had a distinct smell of vanilla candles, musty books, and microwave pepperoni Pizza Rolls (Father Stiles' favorite meal). The smell brought back a wave of memories. The hours spent in this room, thinking about himself and his mother, trying to come to terms with the fact that he didn't really care that she was dead. He was more angry than sad, and when he wasn't angry, he was hollow, driven to be somebody else.

Half-rimmed glasses perched near the end of Father Stiles' nose. "Michael." He closed a book. "Got your message." His tone was indifferent.

"Sorry." Michael didn't know why he said it, although there was plenty to apologize about. He walked toward Father Stiles, passing several full-size mannequins displaying Elvis Presley outfits from The King's later Vegas years.

"Still singing?" Michael looked at a white sequined jumpsuit covered in rhinestones.

"The kids love it. A chance to laugh." Father Stiles glanced at the same jumpsuit that Michael was looking at. "Not much to laugh about in the church these days, so it's something."

Michael walked over to the desk, and then picked a stack of papers off of the chair, placed them on the floor, and sat down next to the desk. He waited for Father Stiles to speak, but Father Stiles did not. Nothing was going to be easy.

"I'm sorry I disappeared on you," Michael said. "You deserved better than that."

Father Stiles tilted his head to the side, opened his mouth as if to speak, but then closed it again.

"I assume you've gotten the checks." A clumsy remark.

Father Stiles nodded his head. His eyes remained focused on the floor, then softly said, "Generous."

"I don't deserve forgiveness."

"God doesn't choose who is or is not forgiven. Everyone is forgiven, so sayeth the Lord."

Michael nodded, and then there was silence between them as his eyes took in every corner of the room.

"Did you hear anything?" Michael asked.

Father Stiles, a/k/a Father Elvis, wasn't just a priest. He was the most connected man in the city. Politicians, crooks, players, businessmen, everybody knew and talked to Father Stiles. If there was something, Father Stiles would have heard.

"I think you know the answer to that question." Father Stiles leaned back in his chair. "I've been concerned about you." He folded his arms over his chest. "Setting aside the disappearance and hurt I felt personally, I was concerned. Not sure what had happened to you."

"I ran."

Father Stiles let out a small laugh, picked up his mug of coffee and took a sip. "Figured that much out."

"I have a friend in trouble," Michael said. "I'm going to represent her."

Father Stiles nodded. He knew that already.

"It's a big case." Father Stiles turned toward Michael, shifting in his seat. "Been in the news when it happened and now with you it'll get complicated. It'll be in the news some more."

"I know."

"A risk," Father Stiles said. "Taking a risk for someone else is new." He took a sip of coffee. "Progress."

"I love her."

"Good," Father Stiles said.

"She didn't do it."

"You believe that?"

"I do."

They sat in silence for a minute, but it felt longer.

Michael looked at his watch.

"I don't want to keep you, but I'd like to see you again."

Father Stiles looked at him. His eyes managed to capture what little light there was in the room and sparkle.

"Whenever you want."

"Thank you."

"I didn't do anything," Father Stiles shrugged.

"You were here," Michael said. "You never had to be here, but you always were, always are."

"My job," Father Stiles smiled. "And maybe a little more than a job as it relates to you."

Michael stood and was about to leave, when Father Stiles raised his hand.

"There's something you should know." He opened his desk drawer, reached inside, and removed a small stack of papers clipped at the corner. "Got it yesterday morning."

Father Stiles handed the papers to Michael. It was a grand jury subpoena from the United States Department of Justice, In The Matter Of *The United States of America v. Michael John Collins*.

Michael looked down at the papers. A grand jury was the first step a federal prosecutor needed before issuing a criminal indictment.

They were coming after him, thought Michael. Vatch had to love it.

Father Stiles nodded toward the papers. "I had the lawyers from the diocese looking at it. Mostly what they want is privileged communication with a priest, but there are things they have a right to know."

"When are you going to testify?"

"Not sure." Father Stiles tilted his head to the side. "Next few weeks I suppose, timing is odd with you being here."

"Odd," Michael paused, and then handed the papers back to Father Stiles. "Thank you for telling me."

CHAPTER FOURTEEN

M ichael sat on a bench across the street from the New York Criminal Courthouse. It was a large building on Broadway shaped like a wedding cake covered with gray frosting. On a typical day the street would have been full of lawyers and government employees catching a minute of fresh air or eating lunch, but the temperature had dropped and the street was empty.

General K had included a long, wool trench coat and leather gloves as part of his overall makeover package. It was for a "very reasonable price," according to the General. "A very reasonable price for a super-special customer."

Michael sunk his hands further into the silk-lined pockets of his coat and tried to clear his head. The lack of sleep from the night before was catching up with him, and he couldn't quite get comfortable in the suit.

It hadn't felt like this before. The tailored clothes and ties had used to make Michael feel good. They had provided a little bit of confidence when he was unsure, but not anymore.

A series of bells rang from a nearby steeple, and Michael got up from the bench, crossed the street, and walked up the courthouse steps.

As soon as he was through the door, the winter calm gave way to mothers with crying babies, strung-out junkies arguing over cab fare, lawyers trying to sound smart, and cops looking tough. Some were just hanging out until their hearing, but most were moving through the metal detectors and security screen like bees returning to the hive.

Michael found what may have been construed as a line. Past a group of gangster trainees still not old enough to shave, he wedged himself in.

Each person in line did the security shuffle to the random beeps of detectors and wands. Michael followed their lead.

"Arms up."

Michael raised his arms out like a kid playing airplane, and then the security guard ran a black stick up one side and down the other.

"Okay." The guard gave a slight nudge. Michael stepped away from him to the conveyor, picked up his briefcase, and started walking toward the court administrator's office.

Everywhere he went, Michael felt like eyes were on him. Some of the people who passed were a little too clean or a little too dirty, or didn't seem like they were at the courthouse for any particular reason other than to steal a glance at him. Maybe he was being paranoid, but it wouldn't surprise him if Vatch had set something up. At least he hoped it was Vatch and not someone else.

Michael walked up a large set of marble stairs to the second floor. This was where the government clerks and record keepers processed and housed the thousands of pieces of paper that came through on any given day.

Past the service windows, there was a bulletin board with postings of the day's calendar. He was happy to see that it hadn't changed or been replaced by some computer terminal that cost three times as much and didn't work half as well.

Michael found Andie's name on the schedule, and then made his way to the courtroom on the fourth floor.

His mind drifted to Father Stiles. Michael wasn't sure whether he was glad to know about the subpoena or not. Grand jury proceedings were to simply evaluate a prosecutor's case and determine if the government had probable cause to press formal charges and proceed with a trial. Although the term "evaluate" suggests that a grand jury scrutinizes the evidence, in practice the proceedings were a rubber stamp. There would be no judge, no defense lawyer, and no testimony from the defense; just the prosecutor and the jurors alone. Michael knew that with that set-up, a good prosecutor could indict Mother Theresa.

Judge Christopher A. Baumann III looked over his courtroom with a wary eye. In a monotone voice, he called out the next case to be arraigned. Judge Baumann had been appointed to the bench in the early 1980s. He had been old then, and Michael couldn't believe that the man was still alive and looked exactly the same.

A door opened on the side wall to the right of the judge, and a black man in an orange jumpsuit, leg irons and handcuffs walked through with a bailiff close behind. A public defender directed the man toward his table and told the accused to remain standing while he tried to locate the right file.

The county prosecutor stood and began laying out the basic facts of the case and charges.

"How do you plead?" Judge Baumann asked.

"Not guilty, your honor." Everyone pleads not guilty, thought Michael.

"Bail?" the Judge asked.

"$5,000," the prosecutor said.

"Response?"

"We find that to be extremely high, considering the man has spent his whole life in the city. His family is here, and ..." Michael had heard all of the public defender's arguments before, and in the end, he knew it wasn't going to make any difference.

"Bail will be set at $5,000." The judge swung his gavel down. Paper shuffled from the judge's desk to his clerk, and then finally to a second and third administrator for filing and entry into a computer.

The black man in the orange jumpsuit was escorted out of the courtroom and the wheels of justice rolled on.

Other men in orange jumpsuits were led into the courtroom, and then out over the next hour. All were not guilty. And all of the public defender's arguments for lower bail were ignored.

Judge Baumann paused as he picked up the next file that was three times thicker than the others.

"*State of New York v. Andie Larone*, case file number CI-09-219375."

The young public defender and prosecutor sat down as Michael came forward.

"I'm Michael John Collins, Your Honor, representing the defendant in this matter."

"Mr. Collins, welcome to my world." Judge Baumann rolled his eyes. For the first time, he appeared to have an interest in the proceedings before him. "I believe that Ms. Larone will be out shortly." He looked at the door where the accused had been coming and going all day. "Could our distinguished guests on the other side now state their names for the record?"

Michael turned toward the prosecutor's table. He couldn't quite believe what he saw. The young assistant county attorney was now gone. In her place stood the top three law enforcement officials in the State of New York.

"I'm Shawn Kasper the New York County District Attorney representing the people of Manhattan in this matter, Your Honor. Also with me is the United States Attorney General for New York, Brenda Gadd, and the New York State Attorney General, Harold Frist."

The public defender had been packing his briefcase, but stopped. He swore under his breath. "Who the hell is your client?"

Michael didn't respond.

"Well, this is quite a surprise and an awful lot of legal firepower to handle an arraignment." Judge Baumann smiled. "Must be a press conference afterwards." There was some laughter in the courtroom, but Michael wasn't laughing. Something was about to happen.

The door opened and Andie Larone came out.

Just like the others, she wore an orange jumpsuit. Her hands were cuffed in front of her. A narrow silver chain attached one leg to the other. Michael wanted to take her into his arms and hold her, but he knew that he couldn't. All he could do was touch her shoulder.

Andie looked at his hand, and then at Michael. A tear rolled down her cheek. "Hang in there," he said. She nodded, and then turned to the judge with her head held high.

"Mr. Kasper," Judge Baumann said, "it's your show."

"Yes, Your Honor, thank you." The veteran district attorney of New York shuffled some papers in front of him. It was as if he hadn't been preparing for this simple arraignment all morning. Then he looked up.

"As you know, Your Honor, the charges against Ms. Larone are very serious. I have just found out that the federal government will be filing papers in order to initiate federal charges under 21 U.S.C. Section 848. Therefore, we would like to have this proceeding stayed and Ms. Larone held without bail until the federal case moves forward and Ms. Larone is transferred into federal custody."

"And then?" Judge Baumann asked.

"The New York District Attorney and the State of New York both consent to a stay of these proceedings until the federal prosecution is complete."

"The point being?" Judge Baumann asked, and then added without waiting for a response, "I'm not a federal judge, but our laws seem to be just as brilliant as the federal ones."

"Well, given our limited resources, it would only make sense to wait ..." Shawn Kasper paused, and then looked at the United States Attorney Brenda Gadd. He wanted her consent to continue with his explanation.

"Someone tell me what's going on, please?" Judge Baumann leaned forward, staring hard at the prosecutors. "Whether this woman ends up in some federal prison or state prison doesn't really matter. Bars are bars and cells are cells, assuming she ends up in prison at all."

A few more awkward seconds of silence, and then Brenda Gadd stepped forward. She was a career prosecutor who had made a name for herself putting away Wall Street brokers and analysts who had pumped up worthless internet stocks in the late 1990s.

"Yes, Your Honor, I believe I can speak to that." She folded her hands in front of her and waited to make direct eye contact with the judge. Gadd commanded the room with a pleasant, round, Mother Hubbard face that juries could trust. "The remedy that the federal government believes is appropriate is not available via the state court system. As you know, the state statute was found unconstitutional pursuant to state law, and therefore, it is in the people's interest to handle this case at the federal level."

Judge Baumann held Gadd's stare as he processed the information. Then he blinked when the pieces fell into place. "You are seeking the death penalty?"

"Yes, Your Honor, we are."

CHAPTER FIFTEEN

Andie threw the plastic pitcher of water across the room. What little liquid was in the pitcher splashed against the wall, followed by the empty noise of the pitcher rattling on the tile floor.

A guard opened the door, his hand on his gun, but Michael waved him off.

"It's fine." Michael stepped between the guard and Andie. "She'll be fine."

The guard eyed them both with suspicion, eventually leaving them alone. As the door to the small conference room closed, Andie looked at Michael with an intensity he hadn't seen before. She was caged and scared.

"Never even crossed my mind." Michael's voice was soft, calm; almost apologetic. "What they're doing, it isn't common. Usually the feds do their thing and let the locals do their own, but I guess that's changed."

"Why?" Andie asked, but Michael wasn't sure whether he should give her the answer: Him. He was the reason. Michael thought about the grand jury. The prosecutors were going to use Andie to get at him.

"There are actually two court systems in the United States, one is state and one is federal. The state courts deal with state law, and then the federal courts deal with all the federal laws. Most people don't know that."

"I don't want a civics lesson, Michael —"

"Just listen to me."

Andie folded her arms across her chest. "They're trying to kill me."

"But they can't," Michael said. "That's my point, the State of New York doesn't allow for the death penalty. In 2004, the appellate court found the state statute unconstitutional, and that's why the United States Attorney was here. She's a federal prosecutor, and she wants to take your case, because the federal government allows for the death penalty. They get to circumvent the state."

Andie took a step back, and turned away from him. She wasn't listening any more, but Michael continued.

"In the 1930s and 1940s, as the power of the federal Congress expanded into areas like employment, education, antitrust, gambling and drugs, the federal court system was forced to deal with all of these new federal laws, which often overlapped and sometimes conflicted with the state laws."

"I don't care."

"They say that you killed Helix Johannson as part of a drug trafficking enterprise," Michael said. "That violates both the traditional state laws and the federal 'drug kingpin' laws."

"Kingpin? I'm not a drug kingpin."

"I know," Michael said, "but he was." He took a step closer to Andie. "I'll oppose the transfer, but you saw what it's like in there. They're overwhelmed. Any judge would be happy to get this case off his desk."

"I didn't kill him." Andie's eyes focused on an invisible spot on the floor, her voice soft. The anger was gone now. Her tone was flat.

It was one thing for Andie to know in the abstract what was going to happen. It was quite another to experience it: the handcuffs, the jumpsuit, the guards, and the looks as you enter the courtroom and see that everybody is there because of you and everybody thinks you are guilty, because only guilty people are charged with crimes.

"We're going to have to work harder." Michael stepped toward her. "That's all."

They had been waiting for him, that much was obvious. Cameramen and reporters rushed toward Michael as he emerged from the courthouse. They had congregated at the bottom of the steps, and it took everything in Michael's power not to turn and run back inside.

But he didn't.

Michael took a breath, straightened his shoulders, lifted his head up, and decided to take the opportunity to educate the jury, whoever they would be. All he needed was a theme.

Every case was a story, and he needed to have one sentence, phrase, or word that would be repeated so often that every juror would know it by the end of the trial. Whether the juror believed it was a different proposition.

Ten more steps and the reporters had him surrounded.

"Aren't you too young to be handling this case?"

"Is it true your client has ties to the mob?"

"Did your client sleep with him? Were they lovers?"

"Have you ever handled a death penalty case before?"

"Is it true that Gadd is running for Senate?"

The questions came from every direction, some silly and some not. They baited him to respond, but Michael let the questions go unanswered. He stood there. His back straight and jaw clenched, looking as if he did this all the time and hadn't, in fact, woken up hungover on the beach just a day before.

Michael lifted up his hand, still unsure of what he was going to say, and the reporters stopped talking.

Michael waited another second more, and then decided to do something remarkable – he decided to tell the truth.

"Andie Larone was set up," Michael said. "I intend to prove it and in the process make these so-called 'protectors of the public' look like a bunch of asses."

When it was clear Michael was not going to continue his remarks any further, the questions came back at him even harder than before.

Michael raised his hand, and the crowd grew quiet once, again. "Thank you," he said. "That's the only statement I have at this time."

He began walking, and initially, it didn't look like the reporters were going to allow him to pass, but at the last moment a cameraman stepped aside.

Michael continued down the steps. His heart pounded, and his fingers tightened around the handle of his old, battered briefcase.

A few of the reporters trailed behind him with microphones and softer questions, but Michael wasn't talking. Finally, when he reached the sidewalk, a black Crown Vic pulled to a stop in front of him.

The car's driver got out and walked around the front.

"Mr. Collins." The driver opened the rear passenger door and ushered Michael inside.

"Thank you." Michael put his briefcase in front of him as the door was closed. Still a little shaken from the media onslaught, he was thankful to be hidden behind the tinted glass and have a moment to breathe.

"Hell of a first day."

Michael turned and saw Lowell Moore sitting beside him. He looked tan and fit. His balding head was bald no more. In the past two years, Lowell had gotten hair plugs. His teeth had been whitened, and the crow's feet around his eyes had been pummeled with multiple Botox injections.

"Thanks for bailing me out. It would've been embarrassing to try and hail a cab in that mess."

"It's just good to see you." Lowell smiled, extending his hand. "And good to have you back."

CHAPTER SIXTEEN

The elevator doors opened on the top floor of Hopper Tower in Midtown Manhattan.

"Just like you left it." Lowell winked. He allowed Michael off of the elevator first, and then followed behind.

They walked past the large, illuminated painting of a younger version of Lowell Moore and the firm's other two named partners, and then into the main foyer and reception area of Wabash, Kramer & Moore. The foyer itself was something of a legend. Over the years it had taken on a life of its own, as if it was a person rather than just the main entrance of a law firm.

There were rumors about the cost of the modern art that hung on the walls, and stories about the psychologist that the firm retained to advise the architects and designers on how to maximize the intimidation and awe that was supposed to overcome all who stepped foot in the place. There were other tales about the marble, which the founding partners had personally flown to Italy to select, and the furniture that had been designed and built exclusively by a husband-and-wife team in Greenwich Village – yes, that same husband and wife team who had designed and built the desk and chairs for President Clinton's home office in Chappaqua – and, finally, there were the rare teak panels harvested by hand from the Brazilian rainforests that framed every doorway and every window, set off by imported brass and ironwood accents from Zimbabwe.

When Michael had started at the firm, the foyer had represented his arrival. He had finally escaped the world he had grown up in. The government-subsidized apartment buildings and jobs involving either grease, dirt, cleaning detergents or all of the above were gone, replaced by the Wabash, Kramer & Moore foyer.

Even though his office had been on a different floor, he had looked for excuses to come up to the top and walk through on a daily basis. The foyer had kept his ego inflated, and had motivated him to work harder.

Michael looked around. It now seemed like nothing but a waste.

"You remember where my office is?" Lowell guided Michael past the receptionists and around the corner to the attorney offices that lined the outside of the tower.

It was set up like every other law firm in town. The higher the floor, the more important the person was to the firm, and each floor was a series of concentric circles that preserved a structured caste system. First, a ring of lawyers lined the outer offices with windows (associates in the middle and partners in the corners). Second, working toward the center, there was a smaller ring of offices with no windows. This ring warehoused the firm's paralegals, and scattered on the edges were cubicles for legal secretaries. Third, in the very center, there was a small ring of copy clerks and tech support. It was the legal world's version of Dante's Inferno.

Lowell pointed as they stood in the doorway of his office.

"Taking over Hooten's office was what really transformed this space. I was able to knock out a wall, creating more storage, and put in those French doors leading to the terrace for some occasional fresh air. Not a day goes by that I'm not thankful that old man Hooten finally retired." Lowell paused and turned to Michael. "Well, he didn't really retire. You know how that goes. Have to trim the fat sometimes."

"Trim the fat" was an expression used by the firm to get rid of partners who no longer generated enough revenue. In the old days, once an attorney made partner, he or she was untouchable. Unlike a typical employee, partners owned a piece of the firm and traditionally, it was difficult to get rid of them. That, however, was not the Wabash, Kramer & Moore way.

Each partner was expected to, personally and through their cadre of associates, generate at least $10 million per year. Failure to meet that goal two years in a row, and the partner could be fired by a simple majority vote of the five-member executive committee; a committee comprised of Lowell Moore's puppets.

The system kept every partner on edge. They were always looking for the next pay-off, whether it was a defective drug, boiler explosion, or airplane crash. The never-ending hustle was motivated by a fear of losing the penthouse on the East Side or the house in the Hamptons, the $300 dinners, and the $2,000 suits. If they lost the lifestyle of a Wabash, Kramer & Moore partner, then what would they do? Who would they be? The firm's paycheck and foyer were all they had.

"I staked a claim on the visiting attorney's office just down here for you." Lowell walked a little further down the hallway. "When you make your decision to stay, maybe I can convince the Executive Committee to let you keep it." He winked.

Michael nodded politely, as if the location of an office still mattered. He continued to follow Lowell around the corner to an office in the middle of the hallway. Three paintings by the portrait artist Chuck Close hung on the wall outside the door. They were three of his more recent paintings, but each was probably still valued at $350,000 to $700,000.

"Well." Lowell glanced at his watch. "I have to get back to work. Have a conference call at four-thirty. Maybe we could grab a bite to eat tonight? Catch up?"

"I think I have a lot of work to do," Michael said. "But maybe coffee tomorrow morning?"

Lowell smiled and nodded.

"That's the old Michael Collins I know. A 'prize workhorse' is what I told Patty the other day, not anything like these new attorneys straight out of school."

Lowell turned, took a step away, and then turned back.

"Val told me you came by the house last night." Although no formal introductions were made, Michael assumed that Val was the scantily dressed woman who had identified herself only as Lowell's wife.

"Yeah." Michael hesitated to say anything further. "It seemed like ..."

Lowell raised his hand, cutting Michael off.

"I love her." Lowell put his hands on his hips and shook his head. "Sometimes she can be difficult, and I'm not just referring to the credit card bills."

Images of Val Moore dancing around the hot tub with two other men popped into Michael's head.

"I cleared up any confusion she may have had." Lowell started to turn and walk away again. "But you can still stay in the guesthouse if you'd like."

"Thanks, but I should find a place of my own." Michael smiled. The lies came easy. He watched Lowell disappear around the corner, and hoped the man had a good prenuptial agreement, primarily out of pity. Then he turned his attention to his new office.

It was standard issue: the polished dark brown mahogany furnishings, the latest laptop computer, digital dictation device, a standard-issue BlackBerry PDA, one potted plant, and an array of office supplies (one black Wabash, Kramer & Moore engraved stapler, six Wabash, Kramer & Moore logo pens, twelve Wabash, Kramer & Moore notepads, three boxes of paper clips of differing sizes, one Wabash, Kramer & Moore tape dispenser, etcetera, etcetera) each neatly arranged in a row on the top of the desk, along with a box of business cards and personalized stationary.

Michael walked around the desk and sat in the large leather chair. It felt familiar, but a part of the past.

He turned and looked out the window at the jagged New York skyline, and then at the yellow cabs darting through the traffic below, little bumblebees returning to the hive. Michael closed his eyes and thought of the beach. He listened to the waves falling, and pretended he was lying in bed at Hut No.7 with Andie. There were no alarm clocks or schedules. They would get up when they wanted to get up, beholden to nobody. That was his life. That was their life.

Before guilt intruded, Michael took a deep breath and sat down behind his desk. He looked at his in-box. It was already filled with papers. There were orientation materials, internal policies, health insurance information. He picked up the top of the stack and started sorting.

There was a phone message from Rhonda Kirchner, another associate, inviting him to a recruitment dinner, and then underneath there were three thin, blue folders held together by a rubber band.

The color blue indicated that the folders contained research by one of the firm's private investigators. Everything at Wabash,

Kramer & Moore was color coded. Michael began to remove the rubber band and open the first folder, but stopped.

Michael set the files down and picked up the phone. He needed help, not with the folders, but with everything. He needed Kermit Guillardo.

God help him.

CHAPTER SEVENTEEN

The phone rang on Tammy Duckstein's government-issue desk. The desk was a classic piece of utilitarian furniture circa 1973, featuring dented metal drawers and a fake wood top. She glanced at the clock, 4:57 p.m. She hated these calls.

Tammy thought about letting it go. "But that's why they pay me the big bucks." She picked up the phone.

"This is Tammy Duckstein."

"It's me."

Tammy glanced at the thick file on the corner of her desk. Her pulse quickened.

"Yes." Tammy retrieved a pen from her top desk drawer and turned to a fresh piece of paper in her notepad. "I've been hoping that you'd call again. I've run into some –"

"He's back."

"When?"

"Just walked down the hall, I saw Collins sitting in his new office."

CHAPTER EIGHTTEEN

The transfer from the courthouse back to Rikers Island took over two hours. Eventually the white unmarked van came to a stop in the back of the Singer Center. The side door opened, and eight women in orange jumpsuits emerged from the vehicle in handcuffs. One by one, they hobbled out like clowns emerging from a funny car.

A guard lowered his black wooden baton in front of Andie Larone. "Not you, gorgeous." He tapped the baton against her chest. "Got something special for you."

Andie's hands balled into fists, and the guard smiled. "Let's go." He gave her a little push off to the side. Andie was led in one direction, while the others were led in another.

Inside, Andie and the guard walked down a pale yellow hallway that reeked of artificial lemon.

"Stop." The guard lowered the wooden baton onto Andie's shoulder. He then removed a set of keys from his belt clip and opened a door. "In here."

Andie didn't move.

"What's this about?"

"It's about nothing, sweetie, just go inside."

Andie took a step toward the guard, calm and steady.

"I'm not moving until you tell me what's going on."

The guard smiled.

"You've been hearing too many stories about lonely guards and lonely women." He laughed. "Now go inside and sit your ass down."

His hands shot forward, pushing Andie backwards into the room, and then another push.

Andie swung, but didn't land her punch. While she was off-balance, the guard closed the space and came around with his wooden baton. It struck just above the knee, and Andie collapsed to the floor.

As she held her leg, the guard knelt down next to her.

"Know your place, Ms. Larone." He leaned in closer, whispering. "I'm one of the nice ones."

The guard stood and walked away, closing and locking the door behind him.

Andie wiped away the one tear that had managed to escape and stood.

The walls were bare and painted the same pale yellow as the hallway. There were no windows, pictures, or graffiti, just a square fluorescent light fixture on the ceiling and two chairs.

Andie walked over to one of the chairs, and pushed it into the far corner of the room. It was as far away from the door as possible. She wanted time to move, next time there wouldn't be surprises. There'd be a fight.

She didn't have to wait long. When the door unlocked and opened, a man wearing a suit and tie and sitting in a wheelchair rolled himself inside.

"Agent Frank Vatch of the FBI." He extended his hand, and his tongue flicked out and back in. "Maybe young Michael Collins has mentioned me."

"No."

Agent Vatch puffed out his lower lip in a pout.

"I'm hurt," he said. "We go way back, Mr. Collins and I do."

"Since you know Michael, you know I've got an attorney."

"I do." Agent Vatch nodded with a half-smile.

"And so you can't talk to me, and I don't want to talk to you." Vatch smiled.

"I'm not here to talk about you and Helix Johannson. Well, not specifically." He reached into his pocket and removed an envelope. "Why don't you take a look at this?"

Andie took the white envelope. It had the seal of the U.S. Department of Justice in the corner. Andie paused.

"Well, go ahead, now, open it." Vatch was enjoying himself.

She slid her finger into a small gap in the back, and opened the envelope. Andie unfolded the pieces of paper and read.

"I don't understand." She looked up at Vatch.

"It's a grand jury subpoena for you." When Andie still didn't understand, Vatch continued. "It's about your boyfriend." There was little attempt by Vatch to disguise his delight, as he wheeled closer to Andie. "We need you to testify for the government against Mr. Collins."

Andie shook her head.

"Don't be so quick." Vatch's tongue flicked. "Your testimony could be very helpful to us. ... and to yourself." He removed a business card and handed it to Andie. "You need to get a new a lawyer, and have him call me at that number."

Vatch put his hand on Andie's thigh and let it roam upward.

"It might be the only way to prevent the ..." He made a buzzing sound, then rolled his eyes back into his head and jerked his body up and down, a crude attempt to simulate someone getting electrocuted.

Andie stood.

"Leave." She pointed at the door.

"Fine." Vatch spun his wheelchair around, and rolled toward the door. "You know, the death penalty isn't this nice, painless way to enter the afterlife," he said. "In your spare time, you might want to look up the case of John Evans. Poor fellow down in Alabama got electrocuted one, two, and then three times. Darn machine kept malfunctioning so they just kept at it until the boy was a piece of coal, charred and smoking." Vatch smiled and shook his head in amusement. "Then there was this other guy named Tafero down in Florida. Now he had a go with 'Old Hickory' and the sponges on his head lit on fire during the electrocution. Six-inch flames shot out – "

"Leave." Andie turned away from him.

"Problem is," Vatch continued, "folks don't care. In fact, the public says these fellas got what they deserve, hang 'em high."

"I said leave."

"Has Michael Collins ever told you about his last client, Joshua Krane, and how Mr. Krane met his maker?" Vatch knocked on the door. A guard on the other side opened it. "Or has Michael Collins ever told you how he got his money? Everybody needs money to live, and he isn't Bill Gates' long-lost son as far as I know. That question must have crossed your mind, Ms. Larone. Certainly it has."

Vatch wheeled out the door, and then turned around to face Andie once he was in the hallway.

"How about that little school near that resort of yours? Isn't it odd that soon after Mr. Collins arrived in your part of the world, the town built a brand new school with computers, new text books, supplies, everything? Doesn't your boyfriend coach that soccer team?"

Vatch laughed. "I don't think you know Michael Collins' whole story." He wheeled back into the room, and then stopped. "You're going to have to testify no matter what. Why not be a smart girl and get something out of it? Save that little bankrupt resort of yours. Or better yet, save yourself."

CHAPTER NINETEEN

It was well past dusk when Michael arrived at the New York Helmsley Hotel. He slid his key into the door, turned on the lights, hung his new clothes in the closet, and then crossed the room to the window and opened the curtains.

The corner room, which he had specifically requested, was on the second floor and offered views of both 42nd Street and Third Avenue. If someone was out there, Michael had convinced himself that he would see them coming. If he had to run, Michael figured that he could survive the jump with just a few bruises or maybe a sprained ankle.

The Helmsley also had the advantage of being relatively close to the office, and willing to rent a room by the week at a decent rate.

Michael sat down on the bed and turned on the television.

Channels flicked by as Michael searched for something decent. Two times through the dial, however, nothing interested him.

He checked the clock. It read 10:47 p.m.

Michael had worked later than he thought he did, filing a Notice of Appearance in state court, and then researching his opposition to the government's motion. He wanted to prevent them from stopping the state court proceedings while the federal case went forward. Unfortunately, all of his research indicated that he was going to lose. He was being forced to rely upon the "breakfast defense."

The "breakfast defense" was so named because it wasn't rooted in any law or legal reasoning. The defense and ultimately the decision itself were based entirely on the judge's mood as determined by what he or she had for breakfast. If the judge had eaten well that morning, he just might rule in Michael's favor.

Michael flicked through the channels again, this time looking for the local news or maybe the weather.

On Channel 3 he found what he was looking for. The Ken-and-Barbie anchor team worked their way through a story about a possible transit strike, a homeless cat that had brought a group of wealthy New Yorkers together, and then the weather.

Michael was about to turn the television off when Andie's picture came up on the screen.

"The murder trial of Helix Johannson began at the New York County Courthouse today, in what the local tabloids are calling the 'Kase of the Kingpin Kutie.' " The anchor held up a copy of tomorrow's Post, never known for its subtlety, which had the headline in large bold letters across the top of the front page.

Below the headline was a large picture of Andie wading out of the Caribbean surf in a bikini. The Barbie anchor smiled and shook her head, muttering something about "only in New York," while the Ken anchor continued.

"Here's our own Rachel Finn with more on the story that has local legal circles buzzing."

Michael watched shots of the press conference as another skinny blonde recounted the more salacious details contained in the formal charges against Andie. The local district attorney and New York Attorney General stood behind U.S. Attorney

Brenda Gadd as Gadd stated her intention to make New York a "perilous place for drug dealers to settle scores, no matter your race or gender."

Then, a quick shot of Michael standing on the courthouse steps. They used the "set up" quote because it was the only one they had, but it didn't sound as powerful as Michael thought it would. In fact, it sounded trite. He looked too young, and his promise to make the prosecutors look like a bunch of asses was unprofessional.

The age difference was going to be a problem at trial, Michael thought. The jury may not like Gadd, but they won't trust a kid.

He turned off the television and lay back flat on the bed. Michael stared at the ceiling and thought about the case. There were just too many missing pieces, things that didn't make sense. Andie's alibi was turning out to be non-existent, and how the FBI could have "lost" a drug kingpin under 24-hour surveillance was beyond him.

Michael got out of bed and walked to the bathroom, shedding his clothes along the way.

Stepping into the shower, he turned the water on and let the room fill with steam, then he stepped inside.

He took a handful of shampoo, worked it into lather, and then rubbed it into his scalp. The water washed the soap away. Then Michael did it a second time, and then a third. He closed his eyes, and his breathing slowed.

In these moments, these quiet moments, he could feel the bullet fragment still inside him, just a millimeter away from his spine. It felt alive, like a small worm burrowing further, moving ever so slowly to finish the job it had started.

Bang-bang; Bang-bang.

Michael touched the scar on his cheek, and then turned off the water. He took a towel off the rack, and walked out of the bathroom while drying himself.

As he picked a pair of boxers up off of the floor and slipped them on, he realized that the room had changed. There was a soft smell of cheap cologne and cherry tobacco. Some of the lights that he thought had been on were now off.

When Michael saw a dark movement out of the corner of his eye, he didn't wait. He grabbed a lamp, turned, and threw it as hard as he could. The lamp smashed against the wall, shards of glass falling to the floor.

Expecting a rush, Michael steadied himself. His hands were out, ready to strike anything that came at him, but nothing came.

He stood there, frozen. His eyes wide, searching.

There was nobody in the room except him.

Michael started to relax, thinking it was an overreaction. The smells could have come through the vents. Somebody could have walked down the hall smoking a pipe. He had seen something though. Hadn't he? Michael put his hands down.

As his breathing started to slow, the telephone rang.

The loud bell bounced off of the walls, and Michael jumped.

It rang again.

Michael walked across the room to the phone, and picked it up.

"Yes."

"This is the front desk. Is everything all right, Mr. Collins? We had a report."

"I fell." Michael looked at the scattered shards of glass. "Knocked a lamp onto the floor, but I'm fine."

"Would you like us to send someone up?"

"No, maybe in the morning." Michael's eyes drifted from the glass to the four dark corners of the room. "It's fine for now."

"Very well, Mr. Collins. Have a good night."

Michael hung up the phone, and walked over to his knapsack. He had just begun removing a pair of jogging pants and a t-shirt, when the phone rang again.

Somewhat annoyed, Michael walked back over to the phone and picked it up.

"Hello." He thought it would be the front desk.

"It's time we meet." The sound of the voice was not human. It was masked with a digital device, alternating from high to low with a long buzz trailing every word.

"Who is this?"

"Come down front. There's a car waiting." Michael walked over to the window with the phone still pressed to his ear. He pulled back the shade and tried to see the car.

The man or woman on the phone started to speak again. It was a question of some sort, but, before Michael could answer, he felt a prick in his neck: a needle. Then everything went black.

Michael woke up in the trunk of a car. He had no idea how long he had been out, and his head felt like it was filled with mud. Still wearing only his boxers, he could feel his toes and fingers turning blue from the cold.

He tried to move, but found that his hands and feet were bound with duct tape. Michael tried to scream, but the scream never came – a small ball, probably a golf ball, had been shoved in his mouth and then sealed inside with a thick, leather gag.

A series of bumps and turns lifted Michael up, and then threw him back down. The car slowed, jerked to a quick stop, and then continued in another direction.

The constant hum of tires on the pavement eventually changed into the crackle of tires on gravel. That sound continued for a short while and then the car stopped.

A door opened and closed, and Michael heard a man say, "Pop the trunk."

Michael heard a beep, a double click, and then the trunk opened. A small, white light fastened to the top of the trunk turned on, and Michael could see for the first time.

A thick man, the same thick man that he had seen at the airport the day before and at the resort earlier, looked down at him. It wasn't a menacing look, nor was it happy. The look was neutral, like that of a person who was doing his job.

"We have some items to discuss." The man grabbed Michael, and pulled him out of the trunk and onto the cold, wet ground without effort. The damp sank through Michael's thin boxers. He hadn't thought that he could get much colder, but a hard chill worked its way across and then under his exposed skin.

He tried to figure out where he was. Michael looked for landmarks, buildings, anything that could be traced later, but there was nothing.

They were in an open field.

About 200 yards away there was a hill, and below it, the field had been cleared, concrete had been poured, and a few spotlights illuminated another bland, market-tested subdivision that was in the process of being raised out of the wetlands.

The thick man took out a knife and cut the tape that bound Michael's ankles together. The gag remained in place.

"Stand. Don't run."

Michael struggled to his feet, while the thick man stepped back, put his knife away, and took out his gun in one smooth motion.

"The three questions often posed by people in your situation are as follows." He cleared his throat. His voice was gruff, but his words were clipped with clear articulation. He was a 250-pound college professor with a side-job of crushing concrete with his head.

"Please note that these are in no particular order and arguably elicit answers that overlap." The Professor cocked his head to the side. "Now, one, for whom do I work?" He paused. "Always a very good question, because it provides a framework for the situation in which you presently find yourself. For example, if I were to say, 'I work for nobody,' you will think that you can reason with me, plead to my better instincts and an abstract moral code. Or the fact that I work alone and for nobody, may also suggest that you could overcome me in a match of physical strength.

"That is, of course, ridiculous for I am quite large and you are quite," the Professor looked Michael up and down, "not large, but adrenaline does odd things to people. Certainly you would agree with that, Mr. Collins, and certainly adrenaline may justify otherwise irrational decisions by someone who considers himself or herself with no other choice.

"Thus, I must dissuade you from this notion, and direct your attention to the man in the front seat of the car. He is not my employer, nor I his employee, but, if for whatever reason you were to overtake me, that man will get out of the car and dispense with you." Michael looked over to the car and saw the shape of a second person, and then he looked back at the thick man whose face still revealed no emotion.

"Second question." The Professor continued. "Also a good one, I daresay, is, 'What do you want?' Implicit in this question, of course, is the idea that I want something, which I, personally, do not. The scope of my relationship with you and the tasks that said relationship entail do not vary. Success is a determination made by somebody else. I have a contract, and I comply with the terms of that contract."

"This second aforementioned question also suggests that you have some sort of bargaining power, which you do not. Not in the traditional sense. Bargaining, as that term is commonly used, connotes an arms-length negotiation between two equal persons or entities. That is obviously not what we have here. I am holding a gun, whereas, you are bound, gagged, and standing half-naked in a field." He smiled, and then just as quickly, the smile disappeared.

"Third question." The Professor reached into his pocket and removed a small metal tin and pipe. He filled and packed the end of the pipe with tobacco, and then struck a match.

The air filled with the smell of cherry pipe tobacco. It was the same odor that Michael had smelled in his hotel room. Now he knew the source.

The Professor continued to keep his gun squarely aimed at Michael's chest, while he puffed away, deep in thought.

"As I said, the third question is always, 'Why don't you just go ahead and kill me?' This is a logical question, but you can see by the manner in which it is often posed, that the question really is not an invitation to accelerate the events that may or may not occur in the future, but is actually another attempt by you, the captive, to obtain some sort of power over me, the captor.

"By suggesting that you are willing to die, I am supposed to fear that whatever it is that may or may not be wanted from you will never be had. This reasoning again assumes that I care whether or not my employer obtains what he wants from you, which I don't. Perhaps this is an argument in favor of commission versus a flat-fee method of payment, but I think that having a vested interest in the outcome of any endeavor such as this may cloud one's judgment. Thus, I always work for a flat fee."

The Professor walked back to the car, closed the trunk, and leaned against it while puffing on his pipe. He checked his watch, and then looked past Michael toward the construction site 200 yards down the hill.

When his tobacco had been smoked, he tapped the spent remains from the end and returned the pipe to his pocket. Then he checked his watch again.

"You have been very patient with me, Mr. Collins." The Professor began to walk around the car. "You are obviously quite cold, but there isn't much we can do about the weather." He turned and went to the front, spoke briefly and quietly with a person in the front seat, and then turned back to Michael.

"As previously stated, I do have an employer and I think you already know who it is. He asked me to deliver a message." The Professor took a breath, collected his thoughts, and continued. "He would like the money back. It's that simple."

The Professor walked up to Michael. He removed the gag, and Michael spat the golf ball onto the ground.

"I don't have it."

"He thinks you do," the Professor said. "Again, I don't have a vested interest, but if you don't have the money, then I will now take this opportunity to be bold and venture a suggestion. That suggestion is to obtain the ill-gotten gains from the person that does."

"You want me to get $500 million dollars?"

The Professor laughed.

"No." He shook his head. "Mario Deti wants you to give him back his $500 million dollars. I don't want anything, which I believe we have already discussed *ad nauseam*."

The Professor checked his watch, and then told Michael that it was time. The lesson was complete.

"Mr. Deti wanted me to do this. He, unlike myself, is not trained in the art of subtle communication and negotiation."

The Professor pointed down the hill toward the construction site.

"Let's go."

Michael didn't move, and the Professor fired a quick shot to his left. The loud sound of the gun filled the night and echoed back at them three or four times in return. Memories from two years ago flashed before Michael's eyes, and he steadied himself.

"Please." The Professor poked the gun into Michael's back. "I have certain instructions."

They proceeded down the hill together. The dead winter brush cut against Michael's legs, and his bare feet lost all feeling in the patches of snow and ice.

The Professor led Michael to the edge of a large hole that was still waiting for a cement foundation.

"And then, of course, you must take into consideration Ms. Andie Larone." The Professor pushed Michael closer to the edge. Michael could feel some of the dirt give way, sliding into the hole. "Prison can be such a nasty place, especially in the absence of her young, talented lawyer, which leads me to the details of your potential bonus."

"Bonus?"

"Mr. Deti has information that may assist you in your defense of Ms. Larone, and he may provide such information, if you cooperate."

"A deal?"

"No." The Professor sighed. "There are no deals here, Mr. Collins. He may give you this information or he may not. It is entirely up to him, but I assure you that he will not give you this information absent the return of what belongs to him."

"What's the information?" Michael asked.

"In due time," the Professor said. "Now, please look down." The cold steel of the gun pressed into the back of Michael's head, and Michael lowered it. Then another needle pricked his neck.

Michael felt his knees weaken, and then felt himself falling down into the hole as everything went black.

CHAPTER TWENTY

He woke up bruised and sore, but lying in the warm comfort of his hotel bed. The shards of glass from the broken lamp were no longer on the floor. The lamp itself had been replaced.

Michael thought about calling the police, but he had no idea where he had been or how he would answer their questions, and at the moment, Michael's head was so clouded that he wasn't even sure he had left the hotel room.

Michael looked at the clock on his nightstand. It was a quarter past noon.

He remembered his promise to have coffee with Lowell. Michael flipped back the comforter and sheets. When he was about to get out of bed, he heard the toilet flush. The noise shot a pulse through his body as the bathroom door swung open.

In the doorway, Michael saw Kermit Guillardo standing in front of him, delivered fresh from the Sunset Resort to New York. He had a lit joint in one hand, a toothbrush in the other and a towel wrapped around his skinny waist.

"*Hola, amigo.*" Kermit smiled, and then took a hit and let it go. "You gotta keep that door shut, man, anybody could just walk in here and start stealing shit."

###

After Michael got dressed for work, he and Kermit took the elevator downstairs and found an empty table in the lobby café. The manager eyed the odd couple, trying to figure out whether Kermit was actually an invited guest or just a panhandler harassing one of its fine customers.

"You two okay?" the manager asked.

Kermit looked up from the menu.

"After a venti dark sans the moo juice, I'll be a lot better," he shouted, even though the manager was less than a foot away. Inappropriate choice of volume was one of Kermit's bad habits.

The manager turned to Michael.

"And you, sir, are you sure you are okay?"

"Fine." As the one in the suit and tie, Michael's word was taken as final. The two were left alone while a tall, thin blonde started to work on Kermit's venti dark sans moo juice, which was otherwise known as a small dark roast coffee without cream.

"So here's some cash and a cell phone." Michael took a small stack of $20 bills out of his pocket and slid them toward Kermit, followed by one of Hoa Bahn's phones. "I need you to get some new clothes."

"Clothes?"

"Suit, collared shirt, tie —"

"Brother." Kermit held up his hands. "If you know where my dearly beloved amigo is, please release him from inside of you. What's a silk noose and geek pants have to do with busting Andie out of jail?"

"I need you to be my assistant — "

"Assistant?" Kermit leaned back in his chair and rolled his eyes. "I thought you said we would be like partners, man, you and me. I'm the Robin to your Batman. I'm the golden lasso to your – "

"We are partners." Michael put his hand on Kermit's shoulder. "But as my partner, I need you to act like my assistant."

"I don't know, man."

"We need to be able to go places together without drawing so much attention."

"Yeah, yeah, but there has to be another way." Kermit bit his lower lip. "One that allows me to continue being me, you know." He took a breath and then looked back up at the ceiling for an extended period of time, eventually he focused back on Michael. "After the jungles of 'Nam. ..." Kermit raised an eyebrow and held it high. "I swore off the machine and that includes the machine's dress code, if you catch what I'm saying."

"But you told me that you'd do anything to help Andie, and now you are saying that you'll only do certain things. I don't know how Andie'll feel about that."

"Andie wants me to do this?"

Michael nodded his head, although Andie had no idea Kermit was coming to New York. She would be scared if she knew.

"I need a partner who can be there with me at the firm, be an extra set of eyes and ears," Michael said. "Do the legwork that I can't do or don't have time to do."

The waitress arrived with Kermit's coffee. Kermit smiled, thanked her, and called her sweetheart.

"She's nice." Kermit watched as the waitress walked away. "Lots of pretty women in the city."

"Kermit." Michael snapped his fingers in an attempt to get back his attention. "I need you to do this for us, Andie and me."

Kermit eyed Michael's suit and tie.

"All right." He shook his head. "But I won't like it. You can't cage this bird." Kermit extended his arms and flapped twice. "You hear me, bro-ha?"

"I do," Michael said, "and after you get some clothes. I need you to do some internet research."

"Like Google?"

"Yeah." Michael nodded. "Like Google."

"I loves me some googley-doogley." Kermit laughed and took another sip of his coffee. "Then what?"

"Then come by the firm. I'm going to be there late tonight. Depending on how it's going, I might be able to take a break and we can go visit Andie."

"Cool." Kermit set his coffee down on the table. "Now what do you want me to ask Mr. Google?"

Michael leaned over, opened his briefcase, removed a notepad, flipped to a clean sheet of paper, and started writing.

"I need you to find out what there is on Green Earth Investment Capital and these other people. Might not be anything, but it's worth a shot."

The waitress then returned with the check. She set it down on the table, and Kermit eyed it. "After you pay, can I keep this?" He tapped the slip of paper.

Michael shrugged.

"I guess." He didn't really want to know what Kermit planned to do with the receipt, so he didn't ask.

CHAPTER TWENTY ONE

S he stared at the ceiling, alone with her thoughts. Questions popped into Andie's head, followed by doubt, followed by more questions, followed by more doubt. The cycle of questions and doubt dissolved into memories, running backward in her mind from near to past. First flickers of her life at the Sunset back to her decision to relocate to Mexico, and then back to her time in California, and finally settling in her childhood home of Australia and the month among the red sandstone monoliths, known as Uluru.

Even at a young age, death and pain were not new to Andie. She understood far too well what it was like to be branded with a curling iron and beaten to unconsciousness. She knew what it was like to wake up every morning hungry or alone. People floated in and out, but death and pain were constants.

So when Andie lost her footing and slipped, catching her arm in a long, narrow fissure while climbing alone on the western face of Ayers Rock, she didn't panic. Her head instead filled with cold calculations that were beyond her years.

How long would it take for the counselors at the camp for juvenile delinquents to realize she had run off again? What were the chances of another climber choosing to scale the western face, rather than staying on the more popular and safer routes to the top? How cold would it get when the sun went down, and how hot would it get when the sun was at its peak? How long could she last with just two bottles of water and a bag of granola?

Black ants canvassed her arm. Andie tried to shake them off, but there was no give. Caught just above the elbow, her arm was wedged deep into the rock. She had no leverage. Her arm couldn't move in any direction. The best Andie could manage was to flop her hand up and down, anything else simply made her already raw skin bleed even more.

Andie hung on the side of the stone monolith. Her water had run dry on the second day, and on the third Andie had begun to wonder if anybody at the camp was even looking for her. She hadn't seen any helicopters or planes, no spotlights or flares.

It was night, and Andie faded in and out of sleep. There was no way of knowing how long she had been out, nor how much longer until the sun would rise again. She was in a process she thought of as a "slow bake." Her neck and skin were burnt. Every time Andie licked her cracked lips, she tasted nothing but salt from the dried, collected sweat.

It was sometime before dawn when Andie decided that just surviving wasn't good enough. She was tired of surviving. Surviving was all she had done in her short life, and now she wanted to live.

Andie struggled, but she was eventually able to get a set of keys out of her backpack. Then she began scraping the stone. Little happened, but Andie didn't stop. When one key was dulled, she started with another. She planned to continue like that until she was down to the last key, and then she would stop trying to cut the rock and start cutting her arm. She wasn't just going to survive. She was going to live.

It took another day, before a fragment of rock came loose and Andie was freed. She took the dulled keys and threw them down the mountain, retaining the final one, a burnt gold key.

It was the key that would have gotten her off the mountain one way or another.

At the bottom of Ayers Rock, Andie didn't return to camp. She panhandled for bus fare, and went back to Melbourne where she enrolled herself in school, worked odd jobs to pay her own rent, and eventually got a scholarship to college. She worked. She hustled, and she saved. It allowed her to do something that she had never done before: live.

Andie reached for the burnt gold key that had hung around her neck for over twenty years. The guards made her take it off when she was processed and booked. The key was gone, but its meaning wasn't. She was stuck on that rock again, and had some choices to make.

Spread out around her on the bed were hundreds of letters, some opened and some not. The pile contained letters calling her a "whore" and a "bitch who deserved to die" and ultimately "burn in hell." The "burn in hell" thing was a popular turn of phrase. On the other end of the spectrum, there were letters that proposed marriage, or anti-death-penalty organizations offering counseling and legal help. A few, were even offers to purchase the Sunset Resort & Hostel, alluding to her future and offering just 35% below market value and a quick closing. They were all vultures, thought Andie, circling above her for their own reasons.

Swinging her legs over the side of her bed and standing, Andie picked up the white envelope from Vatch, and then walked over to the door of her cell. It was a solid metal door with a small, bulletproof glass window near the top. On the right side of the door was an intercom.

Andie pressed the button. The intercom beeped.

"Yes."

"This is Andie Larone." She looked down at the envelope in her hand, her palms sweating. The envelope contained the subpoena to testify against Michael. It was her only way out. "I need to make a phone call."

"Time for personal phone calls is over."

"It's not personal." Andie cleared her throat. "I need to find a new lawyer."

"Don't we all."

A beep and the door unlocked.

CHAPTER TWENTY TWO

It took Michael two hours of starting, stopping, and starting again, before the basics of writing a legal memorandum came back to him.

Alone in the office with only his law books and statutes, words eventually began to flow. In the brief pauses between legal incantations and citations, Michael remembered how much he loved the basic fundamentals of being an attorney, stripped of all its pretension.

Most attorneys hated writing legal briefs. For a poor Irish kid like Michael, the act of drafting legal documents was power – like lifting the hood of a car and knowing how the engine works. Nothing happens in court without something in writing: whether it was a lawsuit, a motion, or a final order of judgment. If a lawyer wrote well, the car could go very fast. If a lawyer didn't write well, the car might make it to its destination, but the car would sputter and spin and rely a great deal on luck.

Michael printed his memorandum opposing the government's motion for a stay. The memorandum was twelve pages long, but it was only the first draft. Before it's done, the document would be cut in half – the clock was always ticking, even for judges, and brevity was rewarded.

"Yo, ho."

Michael looked up, and Kermit swung through the door.

"How you like these duds?" Kermit spun around in a circle.

"Pretty nice." Michael appraised the beige khakis, tasseled loafers, and purple silk shirt. "No tie?"

"No tie," Kermit said, "but if absolutely necessary, I have a special arrangement with a certain street vendor on Mott." Kermit sat down in one of the chairs in front of Michael's desk. "This place is pretty nice, man. The front's a little nouveau riche, but all in all it ain't bad." Kermit looked around the room. "You think I can smoke up in here?"

"No, I'm pretty sure that's against firm policy," Michael said. "Did you do the research?"

"Internet café." Kermit continued studying the office as he spoke. "Hung with the other tourists. Met a nice lady from Iowa, you know how that goes."

"Not really," Michael said. "But the research, what'd you find?"

Kermit handed Michael a stack of paper about three inches thick.

"It's all there. Profiles of Brenda Gadd, that Attorney General guy, and the other lawyers. Found it on the state bar association website and some newspaper archives." He leaned forward and lowered his voice. "I also found a couple of articles on the Johannson dude, mostly after his death, and then a whole bunch of stuff on Mario Deti, who seems like one mean son of a bitch, BTW."

"BTW?"

"By the way." Kermit rolled his eyes. Michael was so un-hip. "After about his fifteenth or sixteenth mob assassination and criminal indictment, I stopped printing the stuff off. It was getting repetitive and the café was charging ten cents a page."

"What about Green Earth Investment?"

Kermit shook his head, snapped his fingers three times, and put a finger to his temple. "Forgot that one."

"Forgot?"

"I got a lot on my mind." Kermit stood up from the chair. "It's been awhile since I was in the urban jungle." He walked over to the window and looked down at the street below, studying it. "You hungry?"

"I am, but I got invited out to dinner by another associate. It's some sort of recruitment dinner. I got invited to it on the first day I was back, but had forgotten about it." Michael glanced at the small clock at the bottom of his computer screen. "Lowell Moore is going to be there. Since I missed coffee, I figured ..."

"So we're not going to see Andie?"

"You should go," Michael said. "Tell her that I'll come first thing tomorrow. I'm going to do this dinner, and then coming back here to finish up."

"Late night?"

"I guess."

"Don't get sucked back into the machine." Kermit's eyes went wide. "Its gears will grind you up, my man, take a lesson from me, *hombre*, I've resisted the lures of corporate entrapment my entire life." He walked back over to the doorway, and turned. "Sure I can't smoke up in here?"

"I'm sure."

"What about that lady I walked past on my way to you? Think I could go fetch some grub with her?"

"Patty Bernice?"

"That might be it." Kermit poked his head out the door and into the hallway. "Ms. Patty looks like she needs a good time."

"I don't know if you two would exactly fit."

"B.S.-imo." Kermit turned his attention back to Michael. "We'd fit perfectly. A ying and a yang, I can feel it."

CHAPTER TWENTY THREE

R ecruitment dinners were a fundamental aspect of big firm life. Wabash, Kramer & Moore was no exception. There were always people leaving the firm and other people wanting to get in. The dinner was an elaborate dance rooted in creating and maintaining a perception, wherein nobody lied, but the truth was shaded, mixed signals sent, and people heard what they wanted to hear.

When Michael walked in the door to Frazier's, he had to promise himself to bite his tongue and play along. He couldn't tell the recruits to run away like he had, albeit six years too late. He had to pretend that lawyers hung out at hip restaurants and listened to euro-techno jazz all the time.

"May I take your coat?"

Michael turned and saw a man in a black suit, baby-blue Geoffrey Beene shirt, and no tie. He was about 22, with slicked back hair and chiseled features. Model, thought Michael, or maybe an actor, or maybe both.

Michael slipped off his jacket. The model-actor handed him a numbered tag and took the jacket away.

Michael scanned the restaurant for his group. Beautiful people mingled by the under-lit bar, others spoke to one another over miniature versions of classic appetizers. Although the lighting was dim, his group in the far corner was unmistakable. In a restaurant full of young couples and singles on the prowl, Lowell Moore and his cadre of baby lawyers stood out.

"Ladies and Gentleman, Mr. Michael John Collins." Lowell raised his glass toward Michael as he approached. The recruits smiled and one actually clapped her hands.

"Thanks for the welcome. Sorry I'm running a bit late." Michael patted Lowell on the back, and then turned his attention to the two recruits. "And you two must be the guests of honor?"

The young lawyers grinned, and they told Michael their names, which he immediately forgot.

"Well, nice to meet both of you." Michael smiled and sat down. "And of course, I know you." He put his arm around Rhonda Kirchner. "Sorry I haven't dropped by sooner. Been a little crazy."

"Not a problem." Rhonda smiled, and then leaned in. "We need to talk sometime."

"All right, you two." Lowell tapped his butter knife against his glass. "No whispering at the table. Our bright, young dinner companions were just telling us why they are so interested in our little boutique firm."

Michael smiled and nodded politely, and for the next forty minutes each person at the table dutifully recited their respective lines: Wabash, Kramer & Moore was not like other large law firms; numerous *pro bono* opportunities existed and were encouraged; the firm may not be as diverse as it would like to be, but substantial efforts were being made; and of course, the focus of the firm was on producing a quality product for its clients and not just billable hours.

It was a dinner and conversation that Andie Larone would have walked out on. She didn't have time for small talk and pleasantries. Authenticity was the rule, which was why Michael could barely stand not telling her the truth. She deserved to know about Deti and the Professor.

Lowell took another sip of wine.

"And then there are, of course, high profile cases. Anyone can chase an ambulance or sue a doctor for this trauma or that, but, if you actually want to blaze new legal trails, this is the only place with the resources to do it and do it well."

Provided that you don't lose, Michael thought. Wabash, Kramer & Moore was all about blazing new legal trails, but if one of those trails turned out to be a dead end or cost too much money, heads rolled.

"I read about Mr. Collins' case in the newspaper, today," summer recruit #1 offered.

"Sounds fascinating," summer recruit #2 added.

"You don't really think she's innocent, do you? Don't get me wrong, I'm just not sure I could do it without knowing for sure."

With the last comment, Lowell Moore, Rhonda Kirchner, and the other recruit shifted in their chairs. The conversation had veered dangerously close to an actual discussion rooted in real life, ethics, and values. Such conversations were never to occur at a recruitment dinner.

"You don't have to talk about it, if you don't want to." Lowell's tone now far darker. "He's actually only been back at the firm a few days after some time off."

"Time off?" Summer recruit #2's eyebrows rose. "Like a sabbatical?"

"Kind of," Michael said, "A few years ago a client of ours was _"

"But he's back now." Lowell lifted his glass with a broad smile. He pretended to clink with an imaginary glass in front of him. "I believe it's time to look at a dessert menu." He took a sip, set the glass down, and shouted for the waiter.

###

The dinner wore on for an additional forty minutes. Michael and Rhonda had to suffer through another telling of Lowell Moore's favorite anecdote related to his first billing client. It was "back before the light bulb was invented. ... He had never seen a check as pretty as that one. ... Still have the client's check and the original billing statement framed in my home office, too important to keep unsecured at work."

They all laughed out of obligation. Then the waiter provided their bill, which Michael thought was the prettiest check that *he* had ever seen.

The bill was paid. Coats were collected, and the recruits were hustled into cabs and sent on their way.

Lowell, Rhonda, and Michael watched from the curb and waved. Then Lowell handed his ticket to the valet.

Rhonda looked at Michael, and then back at the restaurant.

"Lowell," she said, "I think I may have left my purse inside. It's a dark leather purse, medium size. Can you see if the host found it when they were clearing our table?"

Lowell grimaced at being requested to do anything by an associate, but the traditional roles of man and woman mitigated what would have otherwise been a flat rejection of her request.

"I guess." Lowell looked at the restaurant and calculated how much time he was going to waste on this endeavor. "Brown leather?"

"That's right." Rhonda attempted to look demure. "Sorry to ask, but you'll probably be taken a bit more seriously than me."

Lowell nodded in agreement with that assessment and turned. He walked back into Frazier's, leaving Rhonda and Michael alone for the first time that evening.

"I need to talk to you about Maltow."

"Maltow?" He hadn't thought about that case in years. Maltow was one of the last pieces of litigation Michael worked on before the incident. It was Maltow and Krane, with the Joshua Krane litigation being the more high-profile of the two cases that managed to dominate 97% of every one of Michael's monthly billing statements.

"We can't talk too much about it here." Rhonda's voice was hushed. "But I really need to –"

Lowell came through the door, shaking his head and looking even more irritated than when he went in.

"They don't have it. Are you sure you brought it? I don't remember you having a purse."

"I'm sure I did." Rhonda shrugged, trying to play it off. "Maybe you are right. Maybe it's still at the office."

Lowell looked at both of them, and turned his attention to the street.

"Where's my damn car? I don't have time for this." He rubbed his hands together, and then removed a pair of leather gloves out of his pocket.

He stepped a few feet closer to the curb, leaving Rhonda and Michael behind him, and looked down the street.

"There it is."

A black Suburban approached. It came to a stop in front of him, and the valet got out.

"You coming with us, Michael? I'm giving Rhonda a lift home," Lowell said. "I can do the same for you."

"No, you two go ahead."

Rhonda leaned in.

"I'll stop by sometime." Then she walked toward the SUV as Lowell opened the door.

Lowell looked at Michael, putting his hand on the vehicle.

"Sure?"

"I need to finish some things at the office," Michael said.

With that, Lowell looked at his watch and smiled. "Good boy. Stop by in the morning, and let's see if we can get you some files that actually pay the bills."

CHAPTER TWENTY FOUR

Vatch opened the front door of his two bedroom apartment in Hoboken, playing back the events of that evening in his head like a movie, careful that nothing got lost. He thought about Michael Collins, and then he thought about Frazier's and all the sleek-looking people who walked in and out of the restaurant while he watched from across the street, people that would never speak to him unless they had to, eating at a restaurant that he could never afford.

He shut the front door, turned the deadbolt, hung the latch, and then rolled his wheelchair across the small, spare living room to the second bedroom, a bedroom that he had converted into a study. Vatch turned on his desk light, and then flipped open a notebook.

He dated the top of the page, and meticulously wrote notes regarding everything that he had seen that day. Most of it was insignificant, but there might be something. He was coming close. For over two years he had tracked Michael Collins, and it was finally going to end.

Vatch looked at the framed picture of his dead partner, Agent Brenda Pastoura, on the corner of his desk. She was killed the same night that Joshua Krane, Michael's client, was murdered.

The FBI had placed Krane under 24-hour surveillance, fearing that the corporate executive would run.

Late at night, they followed Krane to the Bank of America building, watched him go inside and then get back into the car with Michael. A few blocks later a man on foot fired on the car, and Agent Pastoura chased after him. There was no way he could help. Vatch's wheelchair was in the trunk, and there wasn't time. He radioed for back-up, but it was too late.

In an alley two blocks away, both Agent Pastoura and the man who shot Joshua Krane were dead. Ballistics indicated that they had each shot the other, simultaneously, but Vatch wasn't so sure.

He looked from the framed photograph to the bulletin board above his desk. It was covered with photographs of Michael Collins as well as pictures of Michael's mother, his priest, his high school girlfriends. There were copies of key documents, and then there were bank account statements, wire transfers, maps, and letters. He knew that Michael was responsible for Krane's death, and Vatch was going to hold him responsible for Agent Pastoura's death as well.

He had almost given up hope of ever finding him, and then by chance, Vatch saw a photograph of Helix Johannson at a bar in Mexico. It sat with a half-dozen other photographs on the desk of another field agent. Vatch didn't even know why the photograph caught his eye as he passed by, but it did.

There sat Michael Collins in full color, staring back at him from a glossy 8x10. Collins was in the background of the photograph holding a beer; a woman was speaking with him. He looked so tan and rested, relaxed, like a guy who had gotten away with murder, which Collins had every right to believe.

Vatch smiled, reliving that day. Then, there was a rap on his window.

"Open up." A boy on the fire escape knocked on the window, again. "It's cold."

"Anthony." Vatch rolled back from the desk, irritated by the disruption. "Your mother know you're here?" He shouted as he rolled over to the window and opened it. Cold air flooded the room.

"She's working. You gonna let me inside?"

"It's late." Vatch pointed at the clock on the wall. "You should be in bed."

"Well, I'm up. Can I come inside or what?"

Vatch grumbled and allowed the eleven-year-old boy to crawl through the window.

"Shut it when you're in." Vatch rolled back over to his desk. "I'm working."

"You stressin' over that dude, again?" Anthony climbed inside, turned, and shut the window behind him. "Why you hate him so much, anyway?"

Vatch stopped writing, and turned toward Anthony.

"Because." He set his pen down on the desk and looked up at his collage of photographs and documents. "He represents everything that's wrong. That's why. That's always been why. It's the same reason I've given you a hundred times. That's going to be the answer every time you ask." Vatch picked up his pen, again, and started scribbling in his notebook.

"Got nothing to do with that pretty lady on the corner of your desk?"

Vatch looked at the photograph of Agent Pastoura.

"No."

"You want to play cribbage, then?"

"No, Anthony, I do not."

CHAPTER TWENTY FIVE

During the night, Kermit never moved. He was sprawled out on the floor wearing only a pair of jungle-print Jockeys. Kermit was also surrounded by two dozen cash register receipts. In his hand, Kermit clutched a small notebook that appeared to be filled with various mathematical equations.

Michael did not want to know why. If Kermit wanted to tell him, then Michael would listen, but he was afraid that the wrong question might send Kermit even further into his own world. Andie had told him that in the late 1960s, Kermit had been a Jakobs Scholar at MIT, and had nearly completed his dissertation in mathematics at Berkeley when the draft board called him up. The military taught Kermit Vietnamese and put him in the jungles to conduct interrogations and break codes. When he came back, his thoughts were unclear and the formulas didn't come as easy. He was a burnout at 21, bouncing around, and eventually ending up at the Sunset.

"He came with the resort," Andie had said. "An unwritten term of the purchase agreement."

Michael left a note for Kermit about lunch, and then got out of the hotel before the sun had an opportunity to rise above the wall of New York skyscrapers.

The air was crisp, and Michael walked a few blocks before catching a cab.

"Where to?" The cabbie punched the meter, and the numbers began to roll.

"Rikers Island," Michael said, "but with a little detour."

The restaurant in Little Italy was called Nicolias, but the absence of regular business hours, a full-time cook, or the availability of reservations resulted in a fairly unpopular and unprofitable restaurant. That, however, was irrelevant. The restaurant served another purpose.

The back room of Nicolias was one of the worst-kept secrets in New York. It was there that Mario Deti conducted his business, and that was all Nicolias needed to keep the lights on and its owners living comfortably in Phoenix.

The cab stopped.

Michael looked at the dark and worn-down façade of Nicolias Italian Food and Restaurante. Three large men stood smoking outside the front door. If Michael truly wanted to make a stand, this was where it would happen.

"I don't think it's open, man." The driver shifted the cab into park. "If you want the real tourist deal, I can take you up to Lombardi's just down the road here. They got this guy named Arturo that sits at this keyboard and just croons for the crowd, like all the Sinatra and Bennett tunes. Everybody sings along. It's a lot of fun. You should go there."

Michael continued to stare at the restaurant, running through scenarios in his head.

"Hey," the cabbie said. "You okay?"

"Fine." Michael turned back toward him. "Let's just go."

Once he arrived at Rikers Island, it took another twenty minutes before the door to the cramped attorney-client conference room opened and Andie was let inside.

"Look at you." Andie ran her hand down the seam of Michael's suit. "Still going all fancy on me." She pecked his cheek with a little kiss, and Michael turned red.

"You don't think I enjoy this?"

"I don't know," Andie said. "Close call. You're looking a little too sharp, but we'll see if you iron these new shirts." Andie nodded her head. "To iron or not to iron, that will be the ultimate test." She continued to play with him for a while, and then finally let Michael off.

"Any news?" She asked, and Michael was forced to admit that there wasn't any.

"I'll file my brief later this morning, and then who knows when he'll rule, maybe a few weeks."

"A few weeks." Andie's mood turned flat, and Michael decided not to tell her that "a few weeks" was a best-case scenario. Some judges took months to rule.

"I'm working on it."

"I know you are." Andie pecked his cheek with another little kiss, and then they sat down.

Michael thought about telling her about the Professor and Mario Deti's bonus, but instead, he kept that information to himself. She deserved to know, but the right words never came. The disclosure would lead to questions, and he wasn't ready to answer those questions. Not yet.

When he arrived at Wabash, Kramer & Moore, a stack of pleadings and legal research folders were piled on Michael's desk. Pleadings were in red folders, legal research in green.

On top of the stack, there were two notes from Patty Bernice. The first note was a phone message from Tammy Duckstein, requesting a return call. Michael had no idea who she was, and set it aside. The second note stated that Lowell wanted to meet at eleven for coffee and that he wanted Michael to start reviewing the file in preparation.

Michael checked his watch. It was a little after ten-thirty in the morning. Lowell wanted him to be fully up to speed in a half-hour. That wasn't going to happen.

He took a breath, and then tossed his suit jacket over a chair in the corner. As he sat down behind the large mahogany desk, Michael pushed Lowell Moore's precious files off to the side.

He needed to give the memorandum opposing the stay of Andie's case one more read-through and get it filed before anything else. That was more important than Lowell's research projects.

Michael printed a copy and started reading the memorandum out loud. He wanted to hear how it sounded. The final read-through wasn't just about catching a stray typo, it was also about flow.

He read, edited, and then read the document again. Half an hour quickly passed, and Michael was late for coffee with Lowell. He stood, and then there was a knock at the door.

It was Rhonda Kirchner.

"Hey." Michael reached for his suit jacket. "How are you?"

"Just fine." Rhonda's eyes darted from side-to-side, down the hallway, and then back at Michael. "Do you have a minute?"

Michael looked at his watch, and then picked a fresh notepad off of his desk.

"Actually, I need to go see Lowell. I'm already late."

"Oh."

"Something important?"

Rhonda's eyes ran the circuit a second time.

"We can talk about it later." She waved her hand as if she didn't care.

"Just shoot me an email, okay?"

"Yeah." Rhonda hesitated. "I could do that."

Michael patted her on the shoulder, and took a step out the door.

"Has Lowell said anything about me?" Her voice skipped.

Michael turned. It was an odd question.

"He didn't say anything to me." Michael figured that Rhonda had applied for partner.

"Nothing?"

"Nothing." Michael shook his head. "I'm going to grab coffee with Lowell now. Should I mention your name, see what happens?"

"No." Rhonda forced a smile. "Just come see me when you have more time." She gave a nod, and then turned and walked away.

Michael watched her go. It was difficult to believe that she was the same person he knew in law school. Rhonda Kirchner used to be confident and aggressive. She was editor of Columbia Law Review, Order of the Coif, and had already secured a prestigious federal clerkship when the other law students were still learning that a tort was a personal injury and not a puff pastry. Now Rhonda seemed pale, almost frail.

Michael turned away from her and walked in the opposite direction toward Lowell's office.

When he arrived, Lowell's door was shut and Patty wasn't at her cubicle. Michael took a red cherry Lifesaver out of Patty's candy jar, and then noticed the yellow Post-It note on the side of her monitor. A signal that Lowell was in one of his "moods."

Michael looked at Lowell's office. The door still shut, he wondered whether to just skip the coffee. Then, he heard the yelling.

Not quite able to understand what was being said, he took a step forward. Michael could tell that Lowell was angry. Patty screamed back at him, then Lowell came at her louder than before.

Michael got even closer, pressing his ear up against the door. He heard Lowell say, "It's a disaster. This is all a disaster." Then there was the sound of paper fluttering to the ground.

"It's not. Calm down."

"This is me," Lowell said. "My life, not to mention the reputation of the firm at stake, everything I worked for."

It was a rant that Michael was all too familiar with, and the worst part was that nobody ever knew when it was going to happen. Whether it was good news or bad news or no news, Lowell could go off at any time.

Michael had read somewhere that the way you train an animal to be subservient is not through a rational system of rewards and punishment, but by being erratic, constantly changing the rules without notice. Sometimes certain conduct would result in a whipping or a kick to the ribs, and, the next day, the same conduct would result in a gentle pet. The animal, never knowing when it would be hit, keeps its head low and always tries to obey, the moments of reward oddly becoming that much more important.

That was why Patty stayed. And that was why she had stayed for so long. She had been cast under the spell, seeking that rare moment of praise, a moment of feeling like the great Lowell Moore needed you.

"Think I don't know that?" Michael heard Patty say. "I've killed myself for this place from the beginning." File drawers slammed and papers fluttered, and then the door opened.

Michael stepped back, and Patty walked by him. She was calm, but tears streamed down her face.

Lowell started to chase after her, but saw Michael. He wiped the sweat from his forehead, and then forced a pearly white smile. It was a jackal's smile.

"Ready for some coffee?" His voice was calm.

"I am," Michael nodded, "if you are."

CHAPTER TWENTY SIX

After a long conversation with Agent Frank Vatch, Tammy Duckstein hung up the phone, checked the clock, and decided to straighten up her sparse government office before going to lunch.

Staff attorneys for the Attorney Disciplinary Committee rarely skipped lunch. They weren't paid enough to skip lunch, or come in on the weekends for that matter. Working past five was also rare, and everybody seemed to be okay with that. The people who worked for the committee had other interests. Some coached their sons' baseball teams and others ran marathons, and still others were active in their PTAs. The job was just that: a job, nothing more. Other attorneys around town had difficulty grasping that idea.

Tammy Duckstein tore the pieces of paper containing her notes off the pad, stapled them together, and then filed the notes with the rest of the *Maltow v. Jarvis Health System* file.

She didn't like this Vatch person. She didn't like him the first time they spoke, and the most recent conversation didn't change that opinion. She didn't appreciate being called "girlie," nor did she appreciate his demand for her to turn over the entire *Maltow* file. It was her investigation, not his. It was her informant, not his. And any cooperation between government agencies was wholly within the committee's discretion, not his.

Tammy Duckstein had been around long enough not to be bullied. If Agent Frank Vatch wanted a bureaucratic turf war, then she could provide him with one. For the past year and a half the *Maltow* file was the primary, if not the only, reason she came to work. It wasn't going to be given up that easily.

The other disciplinary files were simple cases. A lawyer showed up drunk to court or a lawyer made a racist joke. Occasionally, a lawyer was accused of stealing client funds, but the amounts were small and the cause was one type of mental illness or another. *Maltow*, however, was different.

A case like *Maltow* was why she spent all those nights at law school after the divorce. It was interesting, and she was finally able to match wits with some of the highest-paid attorneys in town. *Maltow* wasn't about a solo practitioner who had barely passed the bar. It involved the prestigious law firm of Wabash, Kramer & Moore.

Unless Vatch got a court order, the *Maltow* file was hers. She just needed Michael Collins to return her call. That's all she needed.

CHAPTER TWENTY SEVEN

A repeated thump, squeak, thump could be heard all the way down the hall. The Grateful Dead's "Uncle John's Band" provided the background vibe.

Michael saw that his hotel room door was open. Another few steps and he confirmed that his room was the source of the noise.

He walked inside and was engulfed by plumes of marijuana smoke. Distorted music blasted from a small clock radio on the nightstand. Kermit was on the bed jumping up and down with the beat. Black magic markers were in each hand; his head came only an inch away from the ceiling on each bounce.

Four large sheets of white poster board hung on the wall. Occasionally Kermit would bounce over to the board and write a number. Then he would reference one of the two-dozen receipts, also taped to the wall, and continue jumping.

"Kermit." Michael turned off the music. "Kermit," he repeated.

Kermit looked away from the poster boards and toward Michael in mid-bounce.

"Yo, chief." Kermit bounced, again, but, this time, dismounted the bed like a drugged-out version of the Romanian gymnast Nadia Comaneci.

"I was in the zone there, buddy." Kermit wiped a bead of sweat from his brow. "Sorry if I didn't see you." He walked past Michael to a table with an ice bucket containing several bottles of overpriced water from the wet bar. He put the caps back on his magic markers, set them on the table, and then removed a bottle of water.

"Want a sip?"

"Not really," Michael said. "Did you get the research done that I asked for?"

"Whoa." Kermit held out his hands. "Nice to see you too, my friend."

"Nice to see you too," Michael said, in a calm voice. "About the research—"

"Started it." Kermit pointed at the ceiling, and then at Michael. "Made serious progress, but then I ordered one of those fancy mocha java double espresso lattes with the whip cream and choco-sprinkles ..." Kermit looked back at the poster board, paused, and then shook-off whatever thought he had.

"And?"

"And I got this receipt for $4.62." Kermit pointed at one of the receipts taped to the wall. "Which was also served by Clerk Number 282."

"And?"

"And so I had to come back here and get to work." Kermit gestured toward the poster boards, as if it were all so clear.

At this point, despite a concerted effort to avoid knowing what Kermit was doing with the dozens of receipts he had been collecting since he had arrived in New York, Michael was forced to ask.

"I've become a follower of Dr. Moo Yung Song," Kermit explained. "You may have heard of him." Kermit paused, but Michael didn't respond and so he continued. "Dr. Song's birth name was Howard Carson, but that changed with the immaculate enlightenment, now its Dr. Song."

"Not ringing any bells with me."

"He is the prophet of numeric equilibrium." Kermit looked at the poster boards again, and then back at Michael. "I read about Dr. Song in the in-flight magazine coming up here."

"An article in an in-flight magazine?"

"Well," Kermit finished the remaining water, and set the empty bottle down on the table. "not exactly an article. It was an ad."

"In the back of the magazine."

"Correct-o." Kermit snapped his fingers, happy that Michael understood. "Dr. Song has a whole series of audio cassettes, CDs, MP3s, whatever your format, but they're pretty pricey. So …" Kermit paused and stared out the window for a minute, and then looked back at Michael. "I had to make do with the information provided in the ad." Kermit picked up a new bottle of water, and unscrewed the cap. "But from what I gleaned, it's pretty brilliant. An awakening for me, really."

"The ad talked about this?"

"Not exactly," Kermit said. "Dr. Moo Yung Song talks about how life is really a series of mathematical equations, and that we must bring the numbers into balance. Specifically, the number 100 is the ultimate sign of numeric equilibrium." Kermit took two quick drinks of water. "And so I thought to myself, what are the most common numbers we deal with every day?"

"I don't know." Michael checked his watch. He was ready to leave.

"Receipts," Kermit said. "And that's when I decided to commit myself fully to having the receipts equal 100 by the end of every day."

"Your receipts."

"Any receipts." Kermit smiled. "You take every digit on every receipt you have, and then you add them up, or subtract them, or multiply, or divide, and then. ..." Kermit spread his arms wide. "When you get another receipt the process has to begin anew because the whole numeric equilibrium has been thrown out of whack-o." His arms went wild, and then still just as quickly.

"That's why you had to stop researching for Andie." Michael looked at the dozens of equations covering the hotel room walls. "Because you got a new receipt."

"Not just any receipt." Kermit jumped up on to the bed and pointed at the first series of numbers at the top of a poster board. "A receipt with all even numbers, very rare."

"I see." Michael nodded. "Do you think you have time to break away from this important spiritual journey to try and actually get Andie out of jail?"

Kermit took in a deep breath, and then finished off the second bottle of water.

"I guess so," he said. "What'd you have in mind?"

The First National Bank Building was more open and airy in the daytime, but the large slabs of polished black marble still gave weight to the space. As they walked up to the security desk, Michael turned to Kermit.

"Just let me handle this, okay?"

"What about partners?"

Michael patted Kermit on the back.

"Just let me do the talking."

They stopped at the desk. Cecil and Flo both looked up at them. Neither had a smile.

"Sign in here." Cecil pushed a clipboard toward Michael.

"Then we can get you a visitor badge," said Flo, still no smiles.

"I'm actually not here to see anyone," Michael stumbled through an initial explanation. "Well, I am here to see someone, just not up there, if that makes any sense."

Cecil looked at Flo with a raised eyebrow.

"Don't make much sense to me," Cecil said.

"Me neither, honey."

Michael took a step back from the security table. He took a breath and started, again.

"I don't know if you remember me, but I came in here a few days ago. It was late at night, and I was trying to track down some information for a friend."

Cecil looked at Flo, again. The raised eyebrow was back.

"Anyway, I'm a lawyer. I'm going to serve a subpoena and discovery on the owners of this building. It's important that I talk to the building manager right away."

"Stop right there, Mr. Lawyer," Cecil said. "Subpoena you say?"

"You're an attorney now?" Flo asked.

"I am." Michael lowered his head, apologetically. "But, I just really need to talk to the building manager or whoever would know the contact information for the security guard that was working on the night of – "

"Well, he ain't here," Cecil said.

"Guy ain't ever here," said Flo.

"Works out of the main office uptown."

"Own forty or fifty buildings all over the country," added Flo.

"This is just one of them."

"Well." Michael was getting desperate now. "It would be great if you could help me out. Make a call for me?"

"Not on your life," Flo responded without hesitation.

"That's a negative," said Cecil.

"In our position, it's better to be seen," Flo said.

"And not heard."

Michael started to talk again, but this time Kermit cut him off.

"Perhaps you two are not aware of the teachings of Dr. Moo Yung Song. He was most recently featured in various in-flight magazines across the country."

Cecil looked at Flo, and Flo back at Cecil.

"No? Well, let me tell you a little something about Dr. Song, of whom I am a disciple."

Cecil leaned over to Flo.

"Call the police."

"Readin' my mind," Flo said back.

"If you could just hear me out," Kermit said as Flo picked up the phone and dialed. "Dr. Song teaches a lifestyle rooted in eternal balance of our earthly and solaristic energies, one that may be quickly summarized as a 'numeric equilibrium.'"

Kermit and Michael could hear the phone ringing.

"So to achieve this equilibrium, one must seek to have balance in their life, most often achieved by having even numbers, particularly 100. That is, at least, the sect that I am a part of." Kermit took Michael's wallet out of Michael's back pocket, and removed the cash. He handed the wallet back to Michael.

"This is First National." Flo eyed the money in Kermit's hand as she spoke into the receiver. "Thought we might have a situation, but I think it's taken care of." She hung up the phone as Kermit laid the cash in front of the two security guards.

"Now," Kermit separated the cash into two stacks, one for each. "Keeping in mind the teachings of Dr. Song, how can we help you reach your numeric equilibrium today?"

###

Flo led Michael through the doorway behind the security desk and into a combination office and break room.

"The guy's name who was working that night was Daniel Beale." Flo walked up to a cluttered desk.

She shuffled aside some empty fast-food containers and started digging through the sheets of paper underneath.

"We ain't exactly prepared for an audit or nothing." Flo pointed toward the circular break table. "Have a seat over there."

Michael walked over to the table, and removed a notepad from his briefcase.

"You said his name was Daniel Beale?" He wrote down the name.

"Yeah." Flo picked up a piece of paper, looked, and then discarded it. "Cool name, sounds like a ballplayer or something, but he certainly wasn't no ballplayer."

"He was new?"

"Didn't work here more than two months, before his supposed vacation."

"Supposed?"

"Yeah," Flo said, picking up another piece of paper to examine. "Didn't come back."

She sorted through more pieces of paper, and then finally pulled out a one-page memo.

"Here it is." Flo handed the paper to Michael. "Got all the addresses on there, home numbers, cell numbers, anything in case there was an emergency or you didn't show up for a shift."

"Can I use this?" Michael pointed at the telephone on the table.

"Doesn't bother me none."

Michael picked up the phone and dialed the first number for Daniel Beale. There was a pause, and then a choppy dial-tone followed by a recorded message. The number had been disconnected. Michael dialed the second number. Same thing. It wasn't a surprise.

Andie had stated that she arrived at the First National Building a little after nine in the evening. The security guard told her that she was expected, had her sign in, gave her a visitors' tag, and then led her up to the nineteenth floor.

The security guard unlocked a door marked, "Green Earth Investment Capital, L.L.C." The lights were on, and Andie was told that the person she was meeting with had just stepped outside for a quick, late dinner and would be back.

Andie sat down and waited for an hour, but the meeting never happened. Nobody ever came.

"Anything else you remember about Beale?" Michael set the receiver down and pushed the phone away.

Flo shrugged.

"Didn't really know him," she said. "I only work with Cecil, so we just run into the other guards when the shifts change over. And then it's usually nothing, just small talk – mostly weather."

"Did he work with someone else, like you and Cecil?"

"No," Flo said. "Everybody used to work with a partner, but not anymore. Me and Cecil are the only ones who still do, 'cause we been around so long."

Michael looked at the computer.

"Do you have a picture of him, like an ID badge or maybe video from the surveillance cameras?"

"Video would be taped over. Taped over every night, unless somebody grabs it and puts in a new one. ID badge would have been made right here." Flo pointed at a digital camera on a tripod that was shoved into the corner.

She turned on the computer and opened up Photoshop.

"Should be on here somewhere." Flo pressed a few keys, and a small hourglass appeared on the screen. "Thing is old, takes a minute."

"That's fine." Michael stood and walked across the room to where Flo was sitting. They waited until a series of thumbnail photographs started to dot the screen.

Flo clicked the mouse, and scrolled through them.

"Man," she said. "Lotta fallen soldiers in this bunch, here. I forget how many people come and go in this job. That's why I don't bother getting to know the others anymore." She scrolled further down, eventually stopping.

"Here we go." Flo double-clicked, and then sent the digital photograph to the printer.

An inkjet cartridge buzzed and jerked to life. Then, it ran back and forth on a piece of glossy paper. Both Michael and Flo stood in silence as the paper worked its way through the printer.

A few minutes later, the printer spat out a photograph and Michael pulled it off the paper tray.

One look, and he didn't need to ask Flo if she was sure that this was the man. Michael knew they had the right one.

"Let me ask you another thing." Michael folded the photo and put it in his pocket. "Then I'll get out of your hair."

"Sure thing." Flo bent over and turned off the computer. "Provided it's just one more thing. Otherwise, Cecil and me might need to recalibrate our equilibrium, if you know what I mean."

"This guy, do you remember if he liked to use big words?"

Flo's eyes widened.

"You know, that's right." A smile came across her face. "Few times I talked to him, he would just mammer-jammer on about this and that and whatever. Big Word Man, that's him."

CHAPTER TWENTY EIGHT

The Professor listed his home address as an apartment in New York's Alphabet City neighborhood, so named because the street names were various letters of the alphabet. Michael thought of the long-running joke that Avenue A, stood for you're all right; Avenue B, stood for beware; Avenue C, stood for use caution; and Avenue D, stood for you're dead.

Michael figured that "Daniel Beale" wasn't really the Professor's name, but it was another loose end that needed to be researched by either Kermit or one of the firm's investigators.

"What'd you see on the nineteenth floor?" Michael asked as the cab driver turned right on Avenue B.

"Nada." Kermit briefly turned toward Michael, and then back toward the window. Kermit watched the brownstones tripping by. "Empty offices, abandoned."

"No signs, no couches, no desks?"

"Nope," Kermit said. "Cleared out. What about this security guard? Anything important?"

"You might say we learned something important." The cab turned left on East 3rd.

"Like what?"

"Like he's a mob hit-man."

Kermit stared out the window, and nodded his head as the information processed through his clouded mind.

"Interesting development, *mi amigo*, very interesting."

The cab stopped in front of a four-story red brick apartment building. A green awning jutted out over the front door. The building was nothing special, but appeared to be maintained. Sidewalks were cleared of snow and ice, and only a few icicles hung from the gutter. On one side there was a small parking lot, and on the other there was a vacant lot with a fledgling community garden buried in ice and brown leaves.

Michael paid the cab driver, and he and Kermit got out.

Kermit walked about half-way across the street when he stopped, thoughts coming together.

"Mob hit-man, huh? Well, we'll see what happens when Kung-Fu Kermit unleashes his fists of fury." Kermit attempted a high kick, and nearly fell down. Shot both hands up to the sky, and then straight out.

"I thought you turned into a pacifist during Vietnam."

"Generally." Kermit started walking toward the apartment building, again. "But even Gandhi had to bust out the ninja moves every once in awhile. Seven deadly sins beware, man. Gandhi kicked ass."

Michael stopped at the front door to the apartment building, and then tried to turn the knob. "What does Gandhi teach us about breaking and entering?"

"Gandhi would say, 'go round back.'"

Michael and Kermit walked around the side of the building, and then into a small parking lot and alley. They looked up and saw a wrought iron fire escape zig-zagging down the middle of the building, from the top story to just above the back doorway.

"Get that trash can." Michael pointed at one of a half-dozen trash cans lined against the fence. Kermit grabbed a can and dragged it underneath the fire escape.

"You think you can reach it?"

"Don't know." Michael stared at the space between the trash can and the fire escape above it. "Only one way to find out." He walked over to where the trash can had been, and retrieved the metal lid that was lying on the ground.

Michael walked back and put the lid over the top of the can, smashing down the four bags of garbage that were inside.

"Steady this for me, will you?" Michael climbed on top and tried to stand.

The metal can groaned under the pressure and rocked side to side as Michael reached. He was still a good foot away from the bottom rung of the fire escape.

"You got it," Kermit said, "Just jump. I'll catch you if you fall."

"Seriously?"

"Do it," Kermit said. "Do it, man. On the count of three."

The numbers counted down, and Michael jumped as high as he could. Immediately the trash can fell out from beneath him, and then there was a loud crash as his fingertips touched the base of the fire escape.

He couldn't grab on.

Michael swore when he missed it.

"Catch me," he said as he fell, but Kermit had already run away.

On the ground, Michael was sure that his hip was broken.

He opened his eyes, and Kermit looked down at him from above.

"You really fell hard." Kermit squinted. "Looked like it hurt."

"I thought you were going to catch me."

"I was." Kermit's head bobbled from side to side. "Loud noises give me the freaks. You know how easy the K-man gets freaked."

"I guess I forgot."

"That's okay." Kermit reached down and pulled Michael off the ground. "How about a Plan B?"

"How about it?"

A young woman with purple hair and a piercing walked out the back door of the apartment building. Michael quickly moved toward the door before it could latch shut.

The woman turned and was about to say something when Michael shouted up the stairs. "Yeah, Johnny, when you want us to move your couch next time, how 'bout not locking us out in the cold?" Michael turned back to the pierced woman, and shook his head.

"With friends like these, right?" Then he and Kermit proceeded inside.

"Nice Plan B." Kermit closed the door behind him. "Now where's this guy's apartment?"

"Third floor." Michael bounded up the stairs.

"Any idea about what to do when we get there?"

"Knock," Michael said as he reached the top.

The third floor hallway was lit by two bare bulbs on either end. Walls were paneled with dark pressed-wood, and the carpet was a brown and orange shag. It was unclear whether that was the carpet's original color or if the unique patina had developed over time.

"302." Michael led Kermit down the hall to the Professor's door. He paused in front of it, and then knocked. Kermit readied himself in his patented Gandhi kung-fu stance.

Michael looked at Kermit, and then Kermit looked at Michael while still maintaining the stance. Another knock, and ... nothing.

Kermit straightened up. "Well, unless you can pick locks, *mi amigo*, I guess that's that."

"That's that." Michael nodded as he took a step back, stopped, looked at the door, and then kicked it as hard he could.

A crack and a pop, and wood splintered onto the ground as the lock bent backwards and the door swung open.

"We got two minutes." Michael ran into the apartment and Kermit followed behind. "Let's do it."

"Grab and dash." Kermit laughed. "Grab and dash."

"You got the kitchen and living room." Michael pointed. "I got bedroom and bathroom."

The bedroom was along the back wall of the apartment. The bed was unmade, and a few T-shirts were on the floor, but the dresser was empty and there wasn't anything left on the nightstand.

Michael moved into the bathroom and opened the medicine cabinet. Again, there was nothing.

"What'd you find?"

"Rotten milk and moldy cheese." Kermit closed the refrigerator door. "Dude's split."

Michael walked out of the bathroom and into the living room.

"Anything in the garbage? Bills, credit card statements, anything?"

Kermit looked. "Nothing."

"Then let's go," Michael said. They left the apartment without saying a word; their pace increased to a run by the bottom of the stairs.

Out the back door, they kept running until they made it to Bleeker station. As the train started to pull away, Michael and Kermit sat down together in an empty seat in an empty compartment.

Kermit looked at Michael. His breathing was heavy, trying to catch itself. He turned toward Michael and flashed a broad smile.

Michael looked back at Kermit, returned the smile, and then they both started to laugh. It was the first time that Michael had really laughed since coming back.

CHAPTER TWENTY NINE

With the advent of the computer, everything was supposed to be electronic. One look at Michael's desk, however, proved that a paperless society was far, far away. The stack of files and random pieces of paper had doubled while he was gone; a virus intent on consuming every bit of free space.

Michael took off his suit jacket. He slid it onto the hanger behind the door, and then sat down. Pushing most of the files to the side, Michael picked up two fax confirmation sheets. They indicated that his brief opposing the stay of Andie Larone's case had been filed and faxed to the court while he was gone.

Then he picked up the phone messages. The first was from the United States Attorney's Office. He checked the time, and then dialed the number for Brenda Gadd.

Her assistant answered.

"This is Michael Collins." He listened. Gadd wanted to meet with him after they received Judge Baumann's order. "Seems a bit formal." Michael looked down at the other messages, one from Father Stiles about dinner. Another from Patty Bernice, something related to Lowell Moore and "ASAP!!" underlined twice.

"Can't she just call me?"

The assistant continued, excuses were made and further reasons were provided. Eventually, Michael agreed.

"But, she's coming here."

He hung up the phone, and then looked at the last and final phone message. It was from Tammy Duckstein. Michael turned to his computer, and punched in her name for a quick internet search.

There were a number of hits related to "ducks" and German beer "steins," which were interesting, but not relevant. Michael clicked through a few more pages, and found a site related to the law.

Tamra P. Duckstein, Esq., worked at the New York Attorney Disciplinary Committee.

Michael clicked on the link, and then was routed to the committee's home page.

Ms. Duckstein was a staff attorney for the First Department Disciplinary Committee for New York and Queens Counties. The committee was part of the state court system, and heard any complaints or grievances about practicing attorneys in those counties.

Michael clicked out of the web page. He decided not to return the call. If a disciplinary committee wanted to speak with him, it wasn't likely to be good news.

He decided instead to prepare himself for a meeting with the great Lowell Moore. Michael picked up his legal pad and pen, but before he started, there was an unexpected guest.

"I heard you wanted to see me."

Michael looked up. There in his doorway stood the Professor. His hair was slicked back, face cleanly shaven. He wore the standard-issue attorney uniform, complete with striped tie and leather briefcase.

"Shall I shut the door?" The Professor took another step inside, closing the door behind him.

"How did you get in here?"

"I rode the elevator up to your floor, smiled at the lovely receptionist, and walked back to your office." The Professor sat down in the chair in front of Michael's desk and got comfortable. "You don't honestly think the receptionists know every attorney who works in this place, do you?"

"I've got nothing for you."

"Perhaps." The Professor surveyed the office's bare walls. "But then why were you looking for me, paying a visit to my former place of employment, breaking into a deserted residence in our beloved Alphabet City neighborhood?" He paused. "I know what you've been up to, Michael. There are a lot of eyes on you."

Michael started to respond, but the Professor raised one of his thick hands.

"If you may allow me the opportunity to posit a theory." He adjusted his tie, and then cleared his throat. "You were following up on Ms. Larone's — how do you say in Perry Mason-speak? — following up on Ms. Larone's alibi." When the Professor said the word alibi, he laughed, enjoying himself. "Anyway, you arrive at the First National Building, a truly magnificent representation of art deco design, and learn that the security guard that was working on the evening of Ms. Larone's arrest was one Daniel Beale, a man who bears a striking resemblance to the man seated before you."

Michael felt his grip tighten around his pen. He wished he had his gun.

"You also learn," the Professor continued, "that there is no Green Earth Investment Capital at the First National Building, and there never was, so you go to Beale's apartment with no real strategy other than to do something – strike that – do anything that would give you and that Cheech and Chong friend of yours the temporal feeling of progress."

The Professor leaned toward Michael, and then lowered his voice.

"Well, let me give you a little hint. You catch me and put me on the stand in your little trial, and you know what I'm going to do? I'm going to say I never saw your little girlfriend before in my life." His voiced went to a whisper. "It wouldn't be hard to hang your girlfriend, Mr. Collins, whether I'm on the witness stand or not." The Professor leaned back. "Unless, of course, you give Mr. Deti his money."

"I don't have it." Michael looked away. "How many times do I have to tell you that?"

The Professor shook his head.

"You know that isn't true. You can turn to that little computer, right behind you, log onto the internet, and transfer the money from your offshore account to an offshore account of Mr. Deti's choosing."

The Professor opened his briefcase and removed a sheet of paper. The paper was blank, except for thirteen digits printed across the top.

"Here's the account number." The Professor set the piece of paper on Michael's desk. "Things are changing, Mr. Collins. Perhaps you are aware of recent developments in the philosophy of natural process limits and chaos theory. If not, I would like to take a moment to enlighten you."

"If this has anything to do with Dr. Moo Yung Song and the numeric equilibrium, I'm leaving."

"Everything is a system," the Professor said, ignoring the comment. "There are problems within each system that can be internally solved." The Professor waited for his thesis to be absorbed and appreciated. "This is the classic case of cause and effect – you return Mr. Deti's money, and in return I go away. Cause and effect. But, when there are a series of simple cause and effect events, these events may trigger external issues outside the control of the internal system that we intended to develop."

"Could you get to the point?"

"Chaos." The Professor leaned his massive frame forward, again. "If you let this go any further, the grand jury is going to convene and you are going to be indicted. At that point, an external issue will have developed beyond the internal system that we intended to create. The grand jury is beyond my control, and certainly beyond your control. I'll be forced to accelerate things, and, shall we say, take a less diplomatic approach toward the retrieval of Mr. Deti's monetary assets." The Professor took a breath. "Mr. Deti has no intention of watching you go off to jail without getting his money. I want to be clear about that."

The Professor reached into his briefcase and removed a sheath of paper and a DVD.

"This is the bonus, Mr. Collins." He held the paper and the DVD up so that Michael could see them. "Something to incentivize conduct that will allow for a mutually beneficially resolution of this situation. The papers are a copy of the original sign-in sheets from the First National Building, which clearly bear the name and signature of one Ms. Andie Larone."

The Professor looked down at the piece of paper. "It says that she signed in at 9:03 p.m. and out at 10:20 p.m."

Michael swallowed hard. It took everything in his power not to jump over his desk and grab the papers out of the Professor's hand.

"And this is a DVD of the security video from that evening. It is, like all security video, time-stamped and dated. This video also clearly indicates the arrival and departure of your girlfriend at one location when she should, according to law enforcement officers and politically ambitious prosecutors, be across town killing a nasty drug-dealing Dutchman, pardon the alliteration."

Michael tested him: "What about the tip, the man in the apartment who called in the license plate?"

The Professor smiled.

"I believe that tip was anonymous, and I am also confident that the police will have a difficult time tracking that fine citizen down." He winked, and then stood, putting the DVD and sheath of papers back in his briefcase. "You have the account number."

He tapped his finger on the account number printed on the sheet of paper on Michael's desk.

"Transfer the money, get the bonus, and get out of here." The Professor turned and started walking out of the room. "I might even agree to testify, say that I offered the cops this information on the night of the Johannson killing, but they didn't want it. The cops told me they already had the case pinned on a little brunette cutie-pie, but I found that to be ethically wrong." The Professor put his hand on his heart and fluttered his eyelashes, a damsel in distress. "I will be morally compelled to testify."

CHAPTER THIRTY

Michael sat at his desk and stared at the account number in front of him. His heart and the thoughts running through his head seemed to be racing one another. Michael picked up the sheet of paper, reading the account numbers, again, and then glanced back at the computer. External issues out of their control were coming to a head. That much the Professor was right about.

The phone rang.

Michael set the piece of paper down, and picked up the receiver. It was Patty Bernice.

"Yeah," he said, "I got your message." Michael looked at the stack of untouched files on the corner of his desk. "I'll be right down."

He hung up the phone, and gathered a fresh notepad and pen. Michael got up from his chair, walked out of his office and down the hall, stopping at Patty's desk.

Noting that the yellow post-it note was gone, he asked, "Doing all right?"

Patty nodded.

"Got to have a thick skin around here." Her eyes were still bloodshot from crying. "Lowell's on the phone," she glanced at the red light on her phone, "but you can just go right in."

"Thanks." Michael put his hand on her shoulder, touched it briefly, and then walked into Lowell's office.

"We need to get to Slim Jim," Lowell barked. "He can push this thing right through the CPSC and it'll be on the shelves tomorrow."

The CPSC was the Consumer Product Safety Commission. Lowell waved Michael inside and pointed at the chair in front of his mammoth desk.

"Okay, talk to you tomorrow."

Lowell hung up the phone, and then looked at Michael.

"Corporate counsel wants to go through their congressman to get this through, and I tell them over and over that if you get the congressman involved, it's another layer of bureaucracy, another reason for delay, and we can short-cut the whole deal by going to Slim Jim."

Lowell's eyes were wide. Every word blurted out, as if there wasn't enough time in the day to get at all of the important and interesting tasks before him. He was a man who loved the fight.

"Slim Jim?"

"James H. Zimmerman," Lowell said. "He's head of the CPSC."

"What's the product?"

"Two-person Jumpin' Jacks." Lowell pointed at the papers in Michael's hand. "It's all in those files."

"Right." Michael glanced at the unread files. "So what's the problem?"

"Well, you know how babies love to bounce, right? And, there's a huge market for those things that hang off doorways and allow kids to spring up and down in a little chair that's hooked up to a huge bungee cord. Well, how great would it be if two kids got to do that at the same time? Brother and sister, neighbor and neighbor."

"Pretty great." Michael wasn't even coming close to matching Lowell's enthusiasm.

"Absolutely." Lowell nodded. "Our client's done research and there's a big demand for two-person Jumpin' Jacks, but some technocrat thinks it isn't a good idea. Nonsense about the strength of the spring and kids flying into walls and breaking their little necks."

"Right."

"So I need you to do a fifty-state survey of all the lawsuits related to the one-person Jumpin' Jack, and then in a letter say how the two-person Jumpin' Jack has addressed these concerns."

"Is there a paralegal or investigator that can help me?"

Lowell winced as the phone rang.

"Just you," he said, glancing down at the number on the Caller ID screen. "I need to get this." He picked up the phone. "Yes." Lowell listened. "Hang on a second?" He put his hand over the receiver. "We done?"

"When do you need it by?"

"Tomorrow it goes out," Lowell said. "Come by my house tonight, have dinner with Val and me, and I can go over the letter." His phone rang, again. There was a call on Lowell's second line. "Patty, who is it now?" Lowell screamed, and Patty screamed back. He looked at Michael. "I should get this too." Lowell punched one of his phone's many buttons. "I'll see you tonight."

The meeting was over.

Michael looked down at his empty notepad, unsure of how it had happened to him. Within sixty seconds and a flick of the hand Michael was dismissed with an enormous amount of work and his dinner with Father Stiles was summarily canceled.

CHAPTER THIRTY ONE

It was dark by the time they made it to Lowell's front door. Kermit hadn't been invited to dinner, but Michael thought his partner deserved a home-cooked meal after a day of bribing security guards and breaking into apartment buildings. Bringing Kermit also had the added benefit of minimizing the likelihood that Lowell would ever invite him to dinner in the future.

Michael knocked, and Lowell opened the front door. He held a glass of red wine, and wore a black Williams-Sonoma apron over his expensive tan pants and light blue cashmere sweater.

"I'm so glad you're here." Lowell smiled. "And if you don't want to go back to the hotel tonight, I really don't mind you staying in the guest house." Again with the guest house, Michael thought. The guy was obsessed with the guest house. "The beautiful Mrs. Moore decided that she would remodel and decorate it with only the finest accoutrements that the Northeast has to offer, and now that it's done ..." Lowell noticed Kermit for the first time. "And you are?" He held out his hand, skeptical of the tall, dreadlocked man standing before him.

"Kermit Guillardo, Michael's personal assistant." Kermit winked at Michael, as if his introduction had been incredibly smooth.

"I hope you don't mind. He's a friend."

Lowell paused, and then offered Kermit a gritted smile.

"Of course not, more the merrier." He gestured for Michael and Kermit to come inside. "As I was saying about the guest house, I figure you need to stay there for about fifteen years and pay me a couple thousand dollars a month in order for me to get a decent return on the investment."

Kermit looked at Michael and rolled his eyes, silently mouthing something about being trapped in the law factory. They followed Lowell through the living room. Then they entered the kitchen. It was all granite and stainless steel, the rich man's garage.

"Dinner is almost done." Lowell pointed at the pots simmering on the stove.

"Smells good," Michael said, as Val Moore got up from a leather chair in the entertainment room to see who had just arrived. She wore a red mini-skirt constructed of patches of recycled rubber tires and a tight red shirt, also rubber.

"Who do we have here?" she asked.

"Michael Collins." He extended his hand toward her. "We've met before."

Val shook her head.

"Don't remember." Then she looked at Kermit, her eyes brightened. "And who is this handsome man?"

"I am Mr. Kermit Guillardo, connoisseur of all things beautiful." He took Val Moore's hand and kissed it softly.

"Oh my." Val giggled. "I didn't know Lowell kept such interesting company. Shall I show you around? I give a fantastic tour."

"Bet you do." Kermit's eyebrows raised and his head bobbled with excitement.

"I'll stay." Michael looked at Lowell. "We can talk lawyer."

"Good." Val turned and began to walk away. "I don't want any of that during dinner." She and Kermit disappeared into the entertainment room. A few seconds later, Michael heard giggling, and then the sliding glass doors to the pool area opened and closed.

He pulled up a bar stool, and sat at the counter while Lowell continued playing with his toys.

"Wife #2 got me a culinary trip to Italy towards the end of our marriage." Lowell lifted the lid of a large stock pot. "We both knew that one of us was going to file for divorce in the near future, and in my better moments I think of it as our farewell tour of sorts, a very expensive farewell tour." He put the lid back down, and then picked up the open bottle of red wine at the edge of the counter.

Lowell poured a quarter cup over the golden chicken breasts. Steam rose up from the skillet as the onion and basil marinara sauce continued to simmer.

"My divorce attorney thought it was a set-up," Lowell said. "I hadn't exactly been Mr. Vacation. In fact, I can't really recall ever taking a vacation with her, not even a honeymoon. So he said I should take the trip because it might make me more sympathetic to the judge when we split, and her divorce attorney was probably advising her to just plan the trip and cry about me not going. An indication of all those years of neglect, you know the routine."

Lowell turned toward Michael, still holding the bottle.

"You want some?" Michael nodded, and Lowell located a second wine glass. He filled Michael's glass, handed it to him, and then refilled his own.

"So the trip was generally a disaster, which is a whole other story. But much to my surprise, I liked cooking. Lawyers, just think, talk, and listen all day. What do we have to show for it?

Maybe some paper, if we're lucky." Lowell shook his head. "Cooking is tangible—beginning, middle, end—but I don't get to do it as much as I'd like."

Lowell set his glass of wine down, picked up a sharp butcher's knife and crushed six large cloves of garlic.

"You get that letter done?"

"I e-mailed a copy to you." Michael took a sip of wine. "Figured that you could log on to the firm's system here and make whatever edits you need."

"Good. We'll do it after dinner." Lowell pushed some of the simmering chicken to the side and scraped a small mound of minced garlic off of the cutting board and into the empty space.

"That's a hotspot." Lowell pointed at the space in the pan now simmering with garlic. "You need to get the garlic just warm enough to release the flavors, watching for the caramel color. Most people just dump it into the sauce, but that leaves you with chunks of raw garlic, or they put it in too early and the garlic turns bitter."

He waited a few more seconds, and then Lowell dispersed the garlic in the rest of the sauce and returned the chicken to its place.

"Ready in about ten minutes." He turned the burner off and put the skillet into the oven. "Bread just needs to get warm."

Lowell removed his apron and hung it on a nearby hook.

Michael noticed, for the first time, that Lowell was slower than in the past. His hands were unsteady.

"Everything all right?"

Lowell turned, looked at Michael, and started to speak, but the words initially caught in his throat. He straightened up, trying to regain the authority expected of him, regain control.

"I need to apologize."

"For what?"

Lowell picked up his glass of wine and took a long draw.

"The first is Tammy Duckstein. Patty told me you got a message from her. Should've warned you, but I didn't want to pile a bunch of my problems on you in the first few days."

"What's the story?"

"Disciplinary committee," Lowell said, "The *Maltow* case. Remember that?"

Michael thought of Rhonda Kirchner. This was what she wanted to talk about.

"The patent case?"

"That's right." Lowell nodded. "Duckstein's investigating that."

"What for?"

"That's what I say." Lowell picked up the bottle of wine, refilled his glass, and then motioned for Michael's glass. "Somebody complained." He shook his head, while topping Michael's glass with wine and then setting the bottle back on the counter. "So anyway, I'm handling it. I can't tell you not to talk to her, because she could trump that up into some sort of obstruction charge, but if nothing happens, I think it'll go away. You understand?"

"I understand." Michael made a mental note to talk to Kirchner for the real story. "What was the second thing?"

Lowell took another sip of wine, and, Michael watched him. Despite the fake tan, hair plugs, and whitened teeth, the great Lowell Moore now looked rather old and tired.

Lowell turned off the oven, and then walked out of the kitchen.

"Follow me," he said.

As Lowell led Michael back through the formal dining and living rooms and up the stairs to the second level, neither said a word. Walking past a half-dozen doors on the second level,

Lowell turned into a large home office that was connected by an internal sliding door to the master bedroom suite.

Two of the walls had floor to ceiling bookshelves, holding legal texts and treatises. The third wall, directly behind the massive oak desk, was Lowell's ego wall. It was mostly a mosaic of photographs, featuring him. Some of the photographs were of him with the present and former Presidents of the United States, senators, governors; others were with third-tier celebrities; and then there were the photographs combined with awards and certificates from non-profit groups that had gladly accepted a portion of Lowell's wealth over the years.

Off to the side, there was Lowell's favorite.

Lowell loved bringing young associates before his ego wall and asking them which item they thought he would be most proud of. Inevitably, the associates would pick the picture of him with the president or one of his many "Man of the Year" or "Super Lawyer" awards. After enough time passed and the anticipation had been built to the appropriate level, Lowell pointed to a nondescript frame. It contained a yellowed photocopy of a check for $1,203.29 as well as a bill for legal services in that amount.

Lowell noticed Michael looking at the check.

"My most prized possession." Lowell walked around to the other side of his desk. "Proof of the first time I ever got paid for being a lawyer." Lowell shook away the memory. "But you've heard that story a million times."

"Yes," Michael said. "I think I have."

"Sit." Lowell pointed at a battered leather chair in front of his desk, and Michael bit his tongue and sat in the chair as instructed.

Lowell opened one of the desk's lower file drawers. He removed a green folder, set the folder on the desk in front of him, and pushed it toward Michael.

"I held some information back, because I was afraid you'd leave me again." Lowell shrugged his shoulders. He sat down. "Wasn't sure what I would do on my own." He looked at the green folder. "Open it."

Michael picked up the folder, opened it, and saw a half-dozen Polaroids and two greeting card envelopes.

"The first pictures are of my dog." Lowell leaned forward, providing narration as Michael worked through the file. "Never really cared for the mutt all that much. It was the wife's idea to have a pet, as usual, but freaked the hell out of me when I came home and found it like that."

Michael quickly flipped through the bloody pictures of the dog.

"The others are of my guest house."

Michael looked at the pictures. Curtains were torn down, furniture overturned, and the bathroom splattered with dark red paint.

"That's what really prompted the remodeling project," Lowell added. "Not just the wife's interest in spending money." He smiled at his own joke, but the room closed in on them, just a little.

Michael set the photographs to the side and picked up one of the envelopes. They were greeting cards, and Michael recognized the familiar large block writing on the front of the envelopes. There wasn't a need to look inside. Michael knew what they were and who they were from.

"Why you?"

Lowell shook his head. "I was hoping you could tell me."

###

With a pair of stainless steel tongs, Lowell removed two pieces of chicken and laid them on a bed of angel hair pasta; he then ladled the marinara sauce on top of it and added a handful of freshly grated parmesan.

"Here you are." Lowell passed the plate to Michael. Then he filled a plate for himself, and they both walked to the dining room.

"Should I get Kermit and Val?"

"No." Lowell shook his head. "They seem to be having a good time without us."

Michael and Lowell sat down next to each other at the table. Lowell sat at the head, Michael on his right.

"I suspected that you had been found by one of Mario Deti's men when you called about your friend, but I wasn't sure." Lowell picked up a knife and cut off a piece of chicken. "The dog was killed about six months ago. I got an unsigned sympathy card from them. That was nice. Then, the guest house was trashed. I got another nice card for that, and then about four weeks ago I got taken for a ride in upstate New York by some huge guy that sounded like he had a doctorate in philosophy from Oxford."

The Professor, Michael thought.

"That was when Mr. Deti revealed himself, although I figured it was him all along." Lowell took another bite of chicken, but his movements were slow. "I knew he was involved with Joshua Krane, you hear rumors and such. Doesn't mean I wasn't scared though, just means that I figured it was Deti."

"When I got my first card I tried to tell myself that it was some sort of joke," Michael said, "but as soon as Andie was arrested, I knew."

"She's leverage." Lowell pointed his fork at Michael, and he could see the wheels spinning inside Lowell's head. "Deti set her up."

Michael nodded, although it wasn't a question.

"Have you told her?"

Michael shook his head.

"I wouldn't know what to say."

"What about your friend out there?"

"Kermit?" Michael glanced beyond Lowell toward the pool area. "No."

Lowell nodded, and took another sip of wine, holding the glass to his lips.

When he set it down, Lowell looked up at Michael.

"I've been at a loss." He filled his wine glass again. "To be honest, even if I wanted to tell someone, there really isn't anybody."

Lowell sighed, surveyed his ridiculously large dining room, and took another bite of chicken, washing it down with a healthy dose of wine. At that moment, Michael couldn't tell whether he was being played or if Lowell was one of the saddest men he had ever seen. Maybe it was a combination of both.

Lowell held Michael in his stare. It was clear that Lowell was forming a question. He had seen Lowell do it countless times during depositions and trials.

Then, it came.

"I don't want to offend you, because I'm certainly no saint, and if I went through what you did, well, maybe I would be tempted as well," Lowell said, setting up the question. "But I need to ask, because the question needs to be asked – "

"So ask."

"Did you take Krane's money?"

Michael stared at Lowell, and, without blinking, said, "No."

Lowell paused, taking the answer in, nodded, and then started the "soft cross." Although in the movies and on television, lawyers were always filled with bluster and intimidation, the soft cross was the opposite and often more effective, taking every answer, appearing to accept it as true, and then pecking away until the original answer was revealed as a lie.

"Then what have you been living on?"

"I sold my BMW. I cashed out my retirement, stocks, 401(k), sold everything else. It adds up and goes a long way when converted to pesos." Michael took a drink of wine, and then set his glass down. "Besides, you'd be surprised at how little you need." A subtle jab back at a man whose monthly restaurant bills were more than most people paid each month in rent.

Lowell started to ask another question and then let it go.

"I guess that's it for us, then." He raised his wine glass, just as Kermit and Val walked into the dining room in their underwear. They were both dripping wet.

"I'm famished," Kermit said. "What are we having?"

CHAPTER THIRTY TWO

He woke up with a splitting headache from too much red wine and too little water. Michael and Lowell had polished off two more bottles, while Kermit and Val had decided to play water volleyball and partake in an illicit substance or two. Then everybody had decided that the guest house was, in fact, the best place for them.

Michael picked up the phone and arranged for a cab, but didn't move after he had hung up. He just sat on the edge of the large bed, staring at the floor in front of him and trying to muster the will to stand.

It wasn't just the headache that was keeping him down. He could feel every muscle in his body crying for a cold glass of water or anything that wasn't fermented in oak barrels.

Michael promised himself that he would never drink that much again. It was a promise he had made before, and it was a promise that never took too long for him to break.

"One, two, three." Michael stood up as quickly as possible, as if getting out of bed was the same thing as tearing off a Band-Aid. Once vertical, Michael steadied himself. He located a small bag of toiletries in a brass bowl near the bed, and then carried the bag across the room to the bath. His lists, sub-lists and sub-sub-lists scrolled through his head. He tried to figure out how to save himself, Andie, and now Lowell, but nothing came.

###

The flagstone path was ice, and Michael tried to keep his feet underneath him. He rounded a corner, and then walked into Lowell's large indoor pool area. When the glass door slid open, Michael was hit by a cloud of chlorine and the sound of Val Moore's voice.

"Quite a party last night," she said.

Kermit and Val Moore sat on two yoga mats with their legs pretzeled around their heads. Val Moore was in a very expensive red yoga outfit and Kermit was still in his underwear.

Val Moore smiled, unraveled herself, and stood.

"Too bad you didn't join us for a little swim last night."

"Too bad," Michael said. "Maybe next time."

"You mind if Kermie plays with me a little today?"

Kermit unraveled himself, and then stood next to Lowell Moore's wife.

"Just an hour or two," he said, "and then I'll get to work."

"Fine." Michael looked at the two, standing in front of him like two teenagers asking for permission to skip school. "Give me a call at the office. We can talk. I still need that research on Green Earth. Andie said they have a website, and I want to know who it's registered to. That's a priority."

"Consider it done." Then Kermit leaned into Michael. "If you could keep this one on the down-low, I'd appreciate it." He glanced back at Val Moore. "No need upsetting Ms. Patty."

"Patty Bernice?"

"That's right." Kermit winked. "You know how that goes."

CHAPTER THIRTY THREE

Tammy Duckstein's supervisor stood in the doorway of her office. "You're going to have to turn over the *Maltow* file." He placed his hands on his hips while his belly made a concerted effort to be free. "This is way above us."

"It's my file." Tammy looked at the stack of papers on her desk and moved them a little closer, a hen guarding her chicks. "It's the best case I've got; I've put hundreds of hours into it."

"And we appreciate that," the boss said, "but you are at a dead end, Tammy."

"Michael Collins will call me before he ever goes to Vatch."

"You don't know that."

"It's a mistake." Tammy's voice was a little too loud, and her supervisor looked down the hallway in both directions to see if anyone had heard. Then he took a step inside the office.

"It's a personal request from the U.S. Attorney for New York and we're going to comply."

"They're going to indict the wrong man," Tammy said.

"You don't know that."

"Lowell Moore is hiding something." Every muscle in Tammy's back tightened as she began to explain her reasoning, again. "After the *Maltow* case settled, the firm's CFO was fired and nobody has been hired since then. Two years have gone

173

by and Moore won't produce certified escrow statements or financials for the firm."

"He doesn't have to."

"Then we should get a warrant," Tammy said. "Get them to produce it under seal."

Her supervisor took a step toward her. He put both hands down on Tammy's desk.

"This conversation is done." He waited, making sure that Tammy was looking at him and listening. "This is Wabash, Kramer & Moore. You don't subpoena that firm, unless there's something solid. You don't have anything solid." He turned and started walking away. "Put the file on my desk by tomorrow along with a summary report for U.S. Attorney Gadd and Agent Vatch."

"It's a mistake," she said, but he had already left.

CHAPTER THIRTY FOUR

The cab idled in front of Nicolias restaurant. Michael examined every aspect of the building, from the peeling paint to the faded sign to the bars on the windows. Although he didn't like Lowell Moore, Michael felt guilty about bringing him into this. The swath of collateral damage was becoming wider, and Michael knew the confrontation with Deti was going to come sooner rather than later.

How could he trust Mario Deti? It wouldn't end there, thought Michael. It couldn't end there. Getting rid of Mario Deti wouldn't get rid of Vatch. Vatch wouldn't be satisfied until Michael was in an orange jumpsuit and chains. Then there was Andie.

Michael watched as two men emerged from the alley behind Nicolias, and walk around front. They huddled in close to one another, talking and smoking, occasionally looking across the street at Michael's cab.

"How long you gonna be?" The driver tapped the top of the dusty meter box.

"I'm good." Michael took a final look at the restaurant. "You can go."

The cab driver signaled, and then turned around. "You know, if you want a good one, there's a restaurant down the street."

"Arturo?"

"Arturo, yeah that's right." The cab driver accelerated into traffic. "He'll sing all the big songs. Great place to bring the family."

"I've heard that," Michael said, wondering how much that restaurant bribed New York City cab drivers every year for the unsolicited recommendations.

Michael worked on Lowell's two-person Jumpin' Jack project, and then researched the statute of limitations for a personal injury case that Lowell had down in Florida against a petting zoo. At eleven-thirty, he picked up the phone, called Father Stiles, and confirmed that they were still good for lunch.

Then he opened his electronic timesheet on his computer and entered his billable hours for the morning. When he finished tracking and justifying every breath he had taken that morning, Michael shut the computer down. He had just enough time to stop by Rhonda's office to talk about *Maltow*.

Michael walked past the inner offices, and ducked into a staircase. Down four flights of steps, Michael ran his security card through a black magnetic card reader, opened the door and stepped out.

He found Rhonda Kirchner's office in the middle of the floor, near the bathrooms. He knocked on the closed door, and then went inside.

The office was dark. Rhonda wasn't there.

He looked out the window, and then at the walls and bookshelves. On the top of Rhonda's bookcase there was a picture of her husband and two kids. It was from a ski vacation. They were standing on the top of a mountain, somewhere out West.

He and Rhonda had gone to Columbia Law School together, started at the firm together, and had gone to countless firm functions. He never knew she was a mother, much less a mother of two.

"Rhonda went home."

Michael turned and saw Patty Bernice in the doorway.

"Didn't know Lowell let you out of his sight."

"Sometimes." Patty held up a stack of papers in her hand. "Had some deliveries to make."

"Guess I'll just leave her a note then." Michael took an orange post-it note from the office supplies neatly arranged at the corner of Rhonda's desk, jotted down a message, and placed the note on her chair. "That should do it."

"I'm not sure when she'll be back."

"What do you mean?"

"Had her annual review today." Patty shook her head. "Didn't go well."

Regardless of when you went to the Belican, there was always an odd smell – a mixture of mold and chili. The mold was visible on a half-dozen ceiling tiles near the southeast corner of the room, presumably water damage. The chili smell wafted from a large pot in the back kitchen, a pot that was never emptied and never cleaned, just filled with more chili ingredients whenever it got to be about three-quarters empty.

Michael found a corner booth and sat down.

He hadn't waited more than a minute before Father Stiles, dressed as his alter-ego Father Elvis, came through the door. He wore a full white jumpsuit and bell bottoms studded with a thousand silver rhinestones. The back of his jacket boldly proclaimed in emerald green glitter: "Jesus Saves Souls From ROCKIN' In Hell."

"Must have a show," Michael said, as Father Stiles sat down.

"Two actually. One this afternoon at the Good Samaritan Old Soldier Home, and then another tonight at St. Bartholomew's on West 53rd."

"If any of the old ladies throw their underwear at you, I want to know."

"Always," said Father Stiles. "The King worketh in mysterious ways."

The waitress came over to the table. Not a word was said about the 59-year-old Elvis sitting at the table. The waitress had seen it all before.

Michael ordered a Coke and two chili dogs. Father Stiles checked his watch, confirmed it was past noon, and ordered a beer and one dog.

"What kind of beer?" The waitress held her pen and pad at the ready.

"Whatever's cheapest."

She rolled her eyes and muttered something about retiring as she turned away.

"Any more word about the grand jury?" Michael asked.

Father Stiles shook his head.

"Nothing." He was about to continue, but the waitress interrupted them with their drinks. She set a frosted pint down on the table in front of Father Stiles, and the glass of Coke in front of Michael.

"Dogs'll be out in a few minutes," she said, "the master chef back there needs time to work." They both nodded and watched as she walked back over to the other side of the room. Three sanitation workers sat vigil around two pitchers of beer and a bowl of free popcorn.

"So the attorney for the church talked to the folks who want me to testify." Father Stiles glanced around the room, again. "Seems pretty serious, Michael."

"I know."

Father Stiles pushed his beer aside and lowered his voice.

"I can't lie for you."

"I wouldn't ask you to."

Father Stiles leaned back. He took a drink of his Pabst, and then another.

"You have a lot on your mind."

"Andie," Michael said, "of course."

"She doesn't know, does she?" Father Stiles took another draw of his beer. When Michael didn't respond, he said, "You can't shut people out, Michael, that can't be how you go through life."

"Can't tell her everything, either."

"You can," Father Stiles said, "but you don't want to. There's a difference." He waited for the waitress to work the room, and then go to the kitchen to retrieve another order. "When do you see her again?"

"After this." Michael took a drink of his soda, and looked around the Belican. He looked for other eyes watching him. "I don't have a solution." His voice was quiet. "I can't tell her, and then not have a way out. I need to give her something."

"The truth is something." Father Stiles rubbed the back of his neck like he always did when he was thinking.

The waitress arrived with two baskets of chili dogs.

"Let the feast begin, boys." She tossed the baskets down on the table and walked away.

CHAPTER THIRTY FIVE

Every relationship follows a line, points when attraction be-comes flirtation, lust becomes love, dating becomes com-mitment, and two people are no longer separate, so it was sur-prising when Michael looked back and realized that a line had been crossed. Without realizing it at the time, he had become responsible.

Michael sat in the attorney-client conference room, and looked at Andie sitting across the table from him. He took Andie's hand in his own.

"I need to tell you something."

"So serious, what is it?"

Michael's grip tightened, and Andie looked concerned. Her eyes searched him for comfort that wasn't there.

"You're scaring me," she said.

Michael paused. He wondered whether he should just run. He could walk out that door and leave this behind. He could be on a plane to Bangladesh in less than twenty-four hours, or maybe the Falkland Islands. He hadn't been charged with any crime yet. He was a free man.

"When I came to the Sunset, you know how I was." The lump in Michael's throat grew. "I spent my days alone, away from everyone. I didn't care if I lived or died. My whole life was spent trying to obtain this goal, this idea of 'success' and I was so sure that all my problems would go away when I got there. ..." Michael shook his head. "Then I got there."

"What's going on, Michael?" Andie leaned in. Her eyes searched him for a clue. "You can tell me."

He heard her say it from a distance. You can tell me. He heard her say it while floating above himself, out of his own body. Michael watched himself sitting across the table from Andie, the one person in the world that he trusted and loved. He watched as they sat in silence, her waiting for him.

Michael then watched as he opened his mouth, and for the first time in his life words started coming out, uncensored, without filter.

"It was a little over four years ago." Michael looked down at the floor. "I was a 'rising star' at Wabash, Kramer & Moore, whatever that means. The great Lowell Moore had taken an interest in me. And I was focused on proving myself to those people. I believed that they didn't think I was worthy enough to be a lawyer and certainly not worthy enough to work at the firm. I thought my presence there was a mistake; that they would discover it was a mistake and it'd be over. I'd be back in the same housing projects where I grew up, a person on the margin.

"It was stupid. At the same time, Lowell Moore and all the other partners at the firm didn't exactly disabuse me of these notions. I was a little money machine, and they weren't going to mess that up. They were going to sow these seeds of doubt, a stray comment or joke here or there, so that I'd just keep on billing for them and never ask questions or complain."

Michael took a breath, and let the exhale out slow.

"So we get this client, and initially all I know is that he's from Boca Raton, Florida, which means to me that he is guilty as sin, because everybody who lives in Boca Raton is either skimming or scamming in one form or another.

"Lowell tells me that our client got served with a subpoena as part of a federal inquiry, and I'm told that I just needed to help him play defense. The client is supposedly the CEO and founder of this hazardous waste clean-up company that nobody has ever heard of, but handles basically all of the federal government's environmental disaster areas, Superfund sites, tornadoes, hurricanes. Anything that's blown down or contaminated; this company gets the contract to clean it up.

"So Lowell wants scorched-earth litigation. We have a rich client in serious trouble, who also paid the firm a huge retainer. Lowell wants me to fight the feds on everything, generate so much damn work and hassle that the bureaucrats get worn down. We figured they'd cave in eventually with a nice plea agreement like they always do.

"This goes on for about eight months. I never had the full file, because I didn't need it. Lowell was handling the client, and frankly I didn't care about the details. I was just cranking out the briefs and motions, billing the absolute shit out of that file.

"And then one day, I'm sitting in this bar and on the television screen pops up the picture of Senator Ted Faith of Rhode Island, the Chairman of the Senate Appropriations Committee and a one-time presidential aspirant. Then, the logo of Krane Engineering comes up on the screen, which I immediately recognize because this executive from Boca Raton is none other than Joshua Krane, the CEO and founder of Krane Engineering.

"Although Lowell and I had known about Senator Faith and Krane all along, we didn't know the feds had it all on tape. There it was: the good senator taking bribes from our client, Mr. Krane.

"In exchange for golf trips to Hawaii and private meetings with high priced D.C. call girls, the federal contracts would be awarded to Krane. All this juicy stuff recorded by the FBI, taped right there in a restaurant owned by a big-time K Street lobbyist.

"And, what makes this interesting to me is that Senator Faith is ratting out his colleagues in the Senate as well as Mr. Krane. That's a beltway first.

"The plea agreement with the senator changed everything, all of a sudden our leverage is gone because we can't really offer the feds a United States Senator anymore, since the senator already spilled his guts. Meanwhile the stock in Krane Engineering is tanking. At one point the stock was trading at $80 a share, and towards the end it was trading at $5 and then at pennies.

"The Securities and Exchange Commission is going crazy. You have thousands of employees at Krane Engineering who lost their retirement. There are major accounting problems at the company, and there are allegations that Mr. Krane not only gave bribes, but now there are rumors of mafia ties and that he embezzled close to one-and-a-half-billion dollars from the company over the course of ten years – a billion and a half.

"For Lowell and me, despite our publicly professed anger and outrage at the federal government for not revealing the whole scope of their investigation, we were privately ecstatic. Overnight, the case becomes front page news, which is great publicity for the firm, and the potential legal bills quadrupled. For me, that meant more billable hours, a bigger year-end bonus, and one step closer to partnership.

"So we go on for another year. I am only working on the Krane file and this one other case called *Maltow*, which was a separate deal. But, it was the Krane file that was my focus. It's us and the government lawyers, pissing back and forth. We do a ridiculous number of depositions and document dumps, and then finally the trial comes."

Michael stopped, took a breath, and then started, again. He felt the weight starting to lift away.

"Nobody wants to go to trial. At trial somebody wins and somebody loses, and no lawyer wants to lose after working on something for two or three years. So everybody is starting to get anxious to deal. The trial is scheduled to start on Monday, and on Sunday night the Assistant U.S. Attorney, who now happens to be U.S. Attorney Brenda Gadd, floats a nice offer. It's the first legitimate deal we receive: Ten years in prison, full cooperation with the investigation of the other senators, and the return of $750 million.

"We are all in Lowell's huge office. It's eleven o'clock at night, and Lowell is just hammering on Krane to take it. Finally, Krane looked up at Lowell and told him that he didn't have $750 million and Lowell said, 'Of course you can't pay $750 million, who has $750 million just sitting around?' And then Lowell asked how much Krane could pay so that we could do a coun-ter-offer.

"Krane shook his head, shrugged, and then said, 'Maybe $500 million.' There was a long silence in the room. Neither Lowell or I expected that much, maybe Lowell had an idea, but I didn't. Anyway, I was thinking that the guy may have stolen $15 million over ten years and had spent most of it, maybe had a couple million left. That's usually how it worked with the white-collar types.

"But Krane hadn't spent it. He had squirreled it away in a number of foreign bank accounts that only he knew of and the accounts were supposedly for the purpose of 'avoiding taxes' and 'eventual reinvestment in the company.' This was coming from a born-again Christian of humble means, who only months earlier swore under oath to God in a deposition that he didn't take a dime. I guess it depended on what your definition of 'take' was.

"Lowell got on the phone and in a matter of minutes a new plea agreement was faxed over by Gadd at the Department of Justice. Lowell told Krane that he needed proof of the money before the feds would accept the deal. Krane told Lowell that it was impossible, but Lowell kept at him.

"Finally, Krane divulged that he had the account numbers and recent bank statements in a safe deposit box at the Bank of America on Broadway. Although the safe deposit box was under his kid's name, he had the keys and access to get in there twenty-four hours a day.

"Lowell said that he was going to revise some of the language in the plea agreement, and that Krane and I should go down to the bank, get the account numbers and statements, and come back to the office so that the final details could be worked out and then we could sign the agreement that night.

"Krane protested, but Lowell said that we could redact the account numbers and locations from the statements and fax them to the feds as proof. Krane continued to resist, but eventually agreed. He was going to jail no matter what, and something told me that our wonderful client had another account floating out there, waiting to be tapped on the day he leaves prison.

"Krane and I took the elevator down to my car. I don't know why, but I volunteered to drive, maybe I wanted to impress Krane with my new little BMW roadster or maybe I just wanted some control, but I volunteered to drive and I think Krane liked having people shuttle him around. So we get inside, Krane puts his briefcase next to mine in the non-existent backseat, and then he gets into the passenger side and we go."

The words kept coming now, and Michael didn't stop. He was afraid to stop, afraid of what Andie might say.

"Krane gets out of the car, grabs his briefcase, disappears into the bank for about ten minutes, and then comes back out. I'm just sitting there waiting, right. He puts his briefcase next to mine in the backseat, and then we're off, as if picking up accounts and access codes for a half-billion is something we do every day.

"We're driving back to the office and talking about something, small talk, probably sports, and I stop at Broadway and West 23rd for a red light. I look over at Krane and finish whatever it was that I was saying, and then I look back at the light. I'm waiting for it to change, and then there's the first pop, then another.

"It was loud, and it felt like someone fired the gun right next to my ear. I know that's not true, but that's how it felt. All of the sound disappeared into a loud ring. Glass shattered, spraying across the dashboard. Another shot was fired into Krane. His head was half-gone, and a bullet to his chest jolted him like an electric shock.

"It happened so fast. I was looking at Krane. I never really saw the guy who did it. I mean, he was thin. I know that, or at least his shadow was thin. So he takes a step back and fires another shot. The next thing I know is that I'm in the hospital, it's five days later, and I have a bullet fragment about a millimeter away from my spine.

"That's it." Michael ran his hand across the thin layer of sweat that had built on the back of his neck. "After I got out of the hospital, I tried to go back to the firm, but it seemed ridiculous. So I went in late at night, cleaned out my desk, and called in my resignation. No letter or exit interview. It was over. I never intended to come back."

Michael allowed himself to breathe, leaning back in the chair and taking in his surroundings. "Then I met you."

Andie squeezed his hand, and waited for a few moments, and then asked, "Did they catch the shooter?"

"I guess you could say that. It was a Krane shareholder who had lost everything. The guy's mother said that he suffered from schizophrenia and depression. He had written about ten threatening letters to Krane leading up to the shooting.

"The FBI evidently had us under surveillance. So an agent chased the shooter and there was a confrontation in an alley a couple blocks away. The shooter's name was Reginald Thompson, I think. The agent fired and he fired, and they both went down. That's what they say."

"I'm sorry." Andie kissed Michael on the cheek. "I wondered … but the past was always the past with us." She looked away. "I liked that, actually. The past being the past."

Andie kept Michael's hand. She held it, and they sat for awhile.

"So … why am I telling you this now?" Michael touched her cheek. "Well," he said, answering his own question, "let's just say that my abrupt exit from the legal profession caught some by surprise. I don't know why. I had been shot in the face after all, but lawyers are forever lawyers or so they say. Rumors started about the settlement, the secret accounts, and about why Krane and I were going to the bank.

"Security cameras showed Krane entering the bank, getting an envelope out of his safe deposit box, and placing it in his briefcase. Security cameras also showed him getting into my car. So people think I took the account numbers and went to Mexico."

"They didn't find the papers in Krane's briefcase?" Andie asked, even though Agent Vatch had told her the same story that morning. She knew the briefcase had been empty.

"No," Michael said. "Krane's briefcase was found empty near Reginald Thompson's body. They looked in my briefcase, which was still in the backseat, and found no envelope, no codes or passwords, and no bank account statements."

"So maybe somebody took it from Reginald Thompson?"

Michael was about to answer with the truth, but he held back. He didn't know why. He had gone this far.

"I don't know." Michael shrugged. "A lot of this is just what I heard."

Andie shook her head.

"I guess I'm still confused. How does this relate to me?"

"Remember those mob ties with Krane Engineering?"

Then Michael continued his story.

CHAPTER THIRTY SIX

In the morning, Michael's computer beeped and a small envelope appeared at the bottom of the screen. He clicked on the envelope and read the message sent from somewhere in the inner-ring of the firm:

AN 18 PAGE FACSIMILE HAS ARRIVED FOR YOU FROM (212) 589-2938. CLICK HERE TO VIEW THE DOCUMENT. IF YOU HAVE TROUBLE OPENING THE DOCUMENT, PLEASE CONTACT MARIA, SYSTEMS SUPPORT, EXT. 1437.

Michael clicked on the link. The image of an hourglass flashed and turned, and then the document appeared in front of him.

He took a deep breath and read the order slowly, making sure that he understood every word. Such care, however, was not necessary. Judge Baumann had clearly and unconditionally granted the government's motion to stay the proceedings while the federal charges proceeded.

The judge had ordered Andie Larone to be transferred out of state custody upon the filing of a federal case. The state court proceedings would resume only upon the resolution of the federal case, and only if necessary.

Michael started to read the decision a second time, when his computer beeped again and another small envelope appeared at the bottom of the screen.

Michael clicked on the envelope and read the message:

A 2 PAGE FACSIMILE HAS ARRIVED FOR YOU FROM (212) 637-2201. CLICK HERE TO VIEW THE DOCUMENT. IF YOU HAVE TROUBLE OPENING THE DOCUMENT, PLEASE CONTACT MARIA, SYSTEMS SUPPORT, EXT. 1437.

Michael clicked on the link. The image of an hourglass flashed and turned, and then the document appeared in front of him.

His first appearance in federal court was set for the next day to determine Andie's bail and to set the trial schedule.

###

Patty Bernice called at four o'clock to tell Michael that U.S. Attorney Brenda Gadd was waiting in Conference Room 8701B with two other men. Michael straightened his tie, put on his suit jacket, and then picked up a notebook for the short walk down the hall.

When he opened the door, Brenda Gadd stood.

"Mr. Collins." Gadd held out her hand and Michael shook it. "This is Assistant U.S. Attorney Reed. I believe you know Agent Frank Vatch of the FBI."

"Of course." Michael shook Reed's hand, but simply gave Vatch a nod. "I thought this was an attorney conference."

"It is." Gadd looked at Vatch. "But he requested to be here."

Michael shrugged.

"It's your meeting."

"It is." Gadd and Assistant U.S. Attorney Reed sat down across the table from Michael.

Before she could begin, Michael unclipped copies of his motion and supporting memorandum.

"These are the motion papers I'll be serving tomorrow morning in this case." Michael passed the copies out. "I'm compelling you to turn over your file, all of your file. I can't believe that I haven't received anything."

"We have a box prepared and will give it to you prior to the hearing tomorrow," said Gadd as she thumbed through the papers in front of her.

"Is it everything?"

"Well, no," Gadd said, "but we'll make our arguments to the court."

"So what's this meeting about?"

"Your withdrawal from the case." A smirk escaped the corner of Gadd's mouth, but she recovered and continued. "I didn't want to embarrass you or your firm by bringing it up in front of the judge tomorrow."

"On what grounds?"

"There are many." Gadd folded her hands, taking it slow. "Chief among these grounds is your personal relationship with the defendant. You may also be called as a witness in the case, and then there are other reasons."

Vatch smiled.

"Mind sharing them?"

"Joshua Krane," Gadd said. "That was my case."

"I know that much, but I guess I'm not following you."

With that, Vatch laughed, and Gadd continued.

"We know about *Maltow*." Gadd paused. "And it makes a nice story. *Maltow* gives us motive and of course, you had the opportunity."

"I'm still not following you." Michael shook his head. "*Maltow*? What's this have to do with Andie Larone?"

"You can't be Ms. Larone's attorney in a death penalty case when you are also a defendant in another case," Gadd said. "A grand jury will be called later this week, and we're going to indict you. I've gotten plenty of indictments with less, and I'm confident your day will come."

The phone in the conference room rang.

Everyone stopped and looked at the phone, an intrusion from the outside world.

The phone rang again, and Michael got up and answered it.

"Okay," he said into the receiver. "I'll be right there."

CHAPTER THIRTY SEVEN

He was in the hotel hallway. Kermit's eye was bruised. A small trickle of blood ran from his nose. When he saw Michael, Kermit managed to raise his hand.

"*Hola, amigo.*" Then there was a fit of coughs, followed by a flurry of activity by several paramedics.

"What happened?" Michael knelt next to Kermit.

"Spent the morning with Val. I was going to meet Patty for dinner, but I had some time ..." Kermit looked at the hotel room door. "Came back to work on my equilibrium, and then, you know." Kermit closed his eyes and leaned the back of his head against the wall.

"Did you see who it was?" Michael figured it was the Professor. Who else could it be?

Kermit kept his eyes closed.

"No visual confirmation."

Michael placed his hand on Kermit's shoulder and then stood.

"They'll get you cleaned up, then we can figure things out." He walked the rest of the way down the hallway to his hotel room. The door was open and he walked inside.

Desk drawers had been pulled out and scattered on the floor. The mattress and bedding had been overturned, lamps broken, chairs turned on their sides, and drapes pulled down. It looked like the photographs that Lowell had shown him the night before of his guest house.

Michael walked over to the bathroom. He stopped in the doorway.

Every surface was either splashed or covered with a thick, dark red paint. The allusion to blood was not lost on Michael, not that it could have been lost on anyone. Mario Deti was not a man of subtle negotiation.

On the back wall of the shower, scrawled across the tile, there was a short message:

EXTERNAL FACTORS HAVE ARISEN

CHAPTER THIRTY EIGHT

When Andie Larone was little, one of the other foster kids would creep into her room at night. He'd do awful things. At first she fought and struggled, but the boy was bigger and stronger.

"Think of sunsets," he whispered in her ear, his full weight pressing down on her. "Think of rainbows and puppy dogs, anything but me. Don't look at me." It was a lesson in disassociation, separating from the present and escaping into oneself.

Andie found herself doing it, again, as her new attorney spoke in hushed tones, whispering instructions to her just like that boy so long ago.

"We need more information," he said. "They aren't going to be satisfied with that story."

"It's more than he ever told me before. You can't force it."

"You have to," he said. "A little. If you want out, you have to."

"I don't know."

"When are you going to see him again?"

"Tonight," Andie nodded. "He called and said he got the order from the judge this morning and I'll be transferred late this afternoon, so tonight."

"Then it has to be tonight." The attorney rapped his knuckles on the table, trying to get Andie's attention. "Andie, you have to understand that he's going to learn all about you at the hearing. You have to do it before the hearing."

"It's not true." Tears welled up in Andie's eyes. "Helix was part of the past, and I thought he might – "

"I've seen the photos, heard the tapes. As far as Michael is concerned, it's all going to be over after that hearing. He won't trust you after that."

Andie looked away, but the attorney continued.

"Find out if he took the money. That's what you have to do."

CHAPTER THIRTY NINE

The attorney-client meeting room in the federal Metropolitan Detention Center in the Bronx was no different than the meeting rooms at the Singer Center, which were no different than the meeting rooms at the city courthouse. The walls were dirty, and each room was furnished with a set of indestructible furniture.

Andie's hand ran across her neck as she felt for the necklace that wasn't there and the key that had represented who she had been for so long. She closed her eyes and thought about the resort, a business that she built from nothing, a place where she was in control. The Sunset was a place where she decided who would stay and who should go, who worked there and who didn't. It was hers, and, every day she was in jail, her independence slipped away. Every day, the business took one more step toward bankruptcy and foreclosure, and the government took one more step toward taking her life.

A vision of Agent Vatch laughing and pretending to have electric shocks sent through his body flashed before her eyes.

She needed to live. She needed to survive.

A knock, and the door opened. Michael came inside.

"Hey." He walked over to her, kissing Andie on the cheek. He tried to take a step away, but she wouldn't let go. Andie stood and kissed him long on the lips, their first real kiss since the arrest.

"I'm sorry I'm late." Michael stayed close to her, whispering. "There was some trouble at the hotel, and we had to figure out a new place to stay tonight."

"What happened?" Andie took a step back.

"Nothing you need to worry about." Michael looked down at his briefcase, and changed the subject. "I've got something for you." He took Andie's hand and led her back over to the small conference table.

They both sat down, and Michael bent over, opened his briefcase, and started to remove his tie.

"Now hold still." He wrapped the tie over Andie's eyes like a blindfold.

Andie laughed, and then said something about "being kinky."

"Now listen." Michael removed his small micro-cassette tape recorder and pressed play.

The sound of waves lapping against the shore filled the room.

"And how about a little Eau de Tourist." Michael took out a bottle of Cocoa Butter Sun Tan lotion, unscrewed the top, and waved the open bottle in front of Andie's nose. Then he squirted a drop in her hands.

"And then of course, the beach."

Michael took out a large Ziploc bag filled with white sand, and poured it on the table.

Andie ran her hands through it, and then clapped.

"More!" she laughed. "I want more. Take me away."

They sat together on the floor, holding hands, and listening to the waves. Andie refused to remove her blindfold.

"It's perfect." She ran her hand down Michael's cheek, searching for his lips, and then kissed him again.

"You know I've been getting letters," she said. "All these people, men mostly, who've seen the articles in the newspaper or stories on television."

"Anything good?"

"There are a few hot ones." Andie smiled. "Probably married." Andie shrugged. "And then there are some real offers, developers who want to buy the resort, partnerships, stocks."

"Do you want me to look at them?"

Andie shook her head.

"No," she said, "not now." Then she kissed him, again. "Do you love me?"

"I do," Michael said, without hesitation. "That's why this is so hard. ... I'm sorry, if I'm the reason that – "

Andie put her hand to Michael's mouth.

"We all have secrets." She kissed him again, and tried to decide who she was, or rather, who she wanted to be.

CHAPTER FORTY

The morning of Andie's hearing went by in a flash. Michael was busy sending courtesy copies of pleadings to the new judge, researching product liability laws in Kansas for two-person Jumpin' Jacks, and trying to prepare his oral argument for Andie's first appearance in federal court that afternoon.

"No Green Earth Investment, bro." Kermit handed Michael a copy of his research. "No filings with the IRS, the SEC, Department of Revenue or the Secretary of State."

"Phantom company."

"A ghoulish ghost of an un-godly sort." Kermit then noticed a Starbucks receipt on Michael's desk. "You gonna keep that?"

"Take it."

"Cool." Kermit picked up the receipt and examined it. "Some nice workable digits in here, no sevens. I hate sevens."

"What about Green Earth's website?"

Kermit snapped his fingers three times.

"That blew my mind." He put his index finger to his head, his eyes wide. "Absolutely blew my mind."

"What?"

"ICANN, that's the International Corporation for Names and Numbers." Kermit removed a folded piece of paper from his front pocket. "They let you look up the registrations and such for

203

who owns what on the triple-W." He handed the piece of paper to Michael.

Michael stared down at the sheet of paper.

"That can't be right."

"That's what it says," Kermit said. "The website's registered and owned by Ms. Andie Larone and the Sunset Resort & Hostel."

Michael put the piece of paper on his desk.

"Gadd's going to love that."

"Figure that somebody just registered it in Andie's name."

"Probably." Michael looked at the clock. "You having lunch with Patty?"

"Afraid not." Kermit shook his head. "Been acting weird lately, she won't return the calls or the e-mails. Maybe she found out about Val, but I figure if I let her wait, let absence make the heart grow fungus."

"Probably a good idea." Michael stood, and took the coat off of the back of his chair and slipped it on. "You going back to the hotel before the hearing?"

"I am." Kermit looked down at the Starbucks' receipt. "Got some thinking to do."

"I'll see you out." Michael walked around the desk, and they entered the hallway. They walked down the hall, through the magnificent foyer, and then to the bank of elevators.

Kermit pressed the down button. "You ridin' with me?"

"Just four floors." A bell rang. They got inside and Michael pressed the button as the elevator briefly descended before stopping again. "You're on your own. See you tonight."

"Then we go out and party." Kermit flashed the hang-loose sign as the elevator doors closed. "Always got to live it up – "

"Always." Michael turned and walked around the outside ring of attorney offices, looking for Rhonda Kirchner's nameplate.

He walked the entire circle, and ended back at the bank of elevators. He paused, checked the floor number, and then walked the circle again. Still nothing.

"Her nameplate is gone and her office is empty." Michael switched the cell phone from one hand to the other as he waived down a cab. "Do you know anything?"

There was a pause.

"Yesterday." Patty Bernice paused again, and lowered her voice. "Don't know if she quit or was fired, or if it was one of those, quit-or-you'll-be-fired sort of things. Why?"

"She wanted to talk to me about something." A cab pulled to a stop in front of him, and Michael opened the door. "Do you have her phone number?"

"I can get it for you. What's it about?"

"*Maltow.*" Michael covered the phone with his hand and directed the driver to the federal courthouse, then he brought the phone back up to his ear. "Do you know where I can find the file?"

"Storage, probably," Patty said. "But I can check on that too."

"Thanks. If I can get it right away …"

"I'll try."

CHAPTER FORTY ONE

The federal courthouse in New York was the opposite of the messy world of small-time thugs, prostitutes, crazy landlords, and parking violators over which Judge Baumann ruled. Where the state courthouse was old stone with a permanent patina of dirt, the federal courthouse was glass and iron. It rose high above a cold, granite square with dark, stone barricades disguised as abstract art.

Everything about the federal courthouse was formal. From its procedures to its staff to its extra security, the tone reflected the seriousness of the cases that were filed and adjudicated there each day. So it was a surprise when Michael entered the chambers of Judge Patti Sachs, and found her huddled in the corner with Brenda Gadd sipping tea and gossiping like two sorority girls outside the student center.

"Mr. Collins." Judge Sachs straightened, suddenly serious. "I'm glad you could join us."

Brenda Gadd set down her glass of tea. Her smile also gone.

"I thought you wanted to see us at one-thirty." Michael nodded toward Brenda Gadd, and then turned back to Judge Sachs. "I don't think I'm late."

"No you're not late, Mr. Collins. Brenda was a bit early, and so we decided to have a cup of tea and catch up with one another."

"Catch up?"

"Yes." Judge Sachs grinned. "Brenda was my supervisor when I was just starting out at the U.S. Attorney's Office." She looked at Brenda Gadd and smiled. "Haven't seen her since my son's wedding." She paused. "Our knowing each other isn't a problem, is it? I don't think it's a conflict, but I thought you should know."

Michael looked at Brenda Gadd, who offered only a straight face.

"It's fine." Although Michael did not think it was fine at all, there was little that he could do. According to the rules of civil procedure, a motion to remove Judge Sachs from the case would first be decided by her, and she obviously would rule against him.

With a subtle flick of her hand, Judge Sachs signaled that the issue was resolved.

She stood, walked to her desk, and then sat down.

"I think we have some motions to deal with." Judge Sachs picked up a copy of Michael's memorandum and other pleadings. "I need to issue a scheduling order, but I take it from all this paper that Mr. Collins has more pressing matters." She looked down at the stack of papers, and back at Michael. "You want to get discovery going, isn't that right, Mr. Collins?"

"Correct, Your Honor."

"You can sit down by me if you would like." Brenda Gadd patted the empty seat beside her, and continued in a patronizing tone. "I won't bite."

Michael thought of a million smart replies, but kept them to himself. Gadd was baiting him to make another remark like the one he made on the courthouse steps at the original bail hearing.

He walked over to the open seat and sat down.

"The government has no problem with discovery, Your Honor, but I believe that Mr. Collins asked for the information in seven days." Brenda Gadd shook her head. "Maybe Wabash, Kramer & Moore has the staff to put things together that quickly, but we'll need more time. It was a multi-jurisdictional investigation, and we have to coordinate and make sure we don't just dump a bunch of paper on young Mr. Collins."

Judge Sachs tipped her head to the side. Sitting behind her large desk in an even larger leather chair, Judge Sachs looked small, like a girl playing dress up. Her kinky black hair shot to either side. Her large red glasses crept down her nose.

"How about a month?"

"A month is very doable, Your Honor," Brenda Gadd said.

Michael tried to stop the inevitable.

"I don't understand why we can't do a rolling discovery starting in seven days. Certainly the U.S. Attorney's office has the resources to keep track of what they've sent and what they haven't sent, and I hope they had all the information on hand before they decided to pursue the death penalty."

"All right, all right, Mr. Collins." Judge Sachs raised her hand and leaned back, displeased. "No need to get all fired up just yet, no jury or reporters are present."

Brenda Gadd smiled, and Judge Sachs continued.

"I think a month is fine, unless you think these documents contain something that is going to make this case instantly go away." Judge Sachs waited for Michael to disagree with her, but Michael remained silent. "Good."

"We also have a box of documents to give to Mr. Collins, today," Gadd said. "Maybe that could be a compromise."

Michael was getting steamrolled.

"Perfect." Judge Sachs looked at the ornate oak-and-brass clock hanging on the far wall of her office. "When we go in there we can put some of these arguments and things on the record, and then I'll rule." The judge shuffled through another stack of paper. "And I guess the other issue is bail."

"No bail, Your Honor." Brenda Gadd sat straight, now. This was something that she cared about. "Ms. Larone is not a United States citizen, has no ties to New York, and at this point, has little to lose by running."

"Says the government," Michael said. "I know Ms. Larone and she has everything to lose by running. She'd lose her livelihood. As for fleeing, she couldn't go much of anywhere without getting spotted. And if you take away her passport, she couldn't leave the country."

"Passports don't seem to stop many people from coming in and out of this country every day, and I'm concerned that Mr. Collins' personal relationship with Ms. Larone may be clouding his judgment."

The last part got Judge Sach's attention. She looked from the papers in front of her to Michael. "Personal relationship?"

"She's a friend."

"Only a friend?"

"Yes, judge," Michael said, lying. "I'm fully aware of our Canons of Ethics, and I assure you that I know what they do or do not require of us."

Brenda Gadd let out a small, derisive laugh.

A stout bailiff stood near the door between Judge Sachs' chambers and her courtroom.

"All rise," he said, "federal district court for the Southern District of New York is now in session. The Honorable Judge Patricia J. Sachs presiding."

On cue, the door swung open and Judge Sachs emerged wearing her black robe. The large, clunky, red glasses were gone, replaced by smaller and more formal silver wire-rims. She walked behind the mahogany bench, and as she took her seat at the front of the courtroom, Judge Sachs directed the slew of attorneys, reporters, and gawkers to be seated.

"The court file number is CI-07-A85316, *United States of America v. Andie Larone*, please state your appearances for the record."

Standing, Brenda Gadd introduced herself and two Assistant U.S. Attorneys.

Judge Sachs nodded and wrote the names down on a notepad in front of her, as if it was the first time she had ever met Brenda Gadd.

"And for the defense."

Michael stood.

"I am Michael John Collins, Your Honor, representing Andie Larone." Andie got up from the seat next to him, and stood as well. She wore a black Nicole Miller suit with white blouse. If she hadn't been introduced as the defendant, Andie could have easily passed as one of the attorneys.

Her posture was straight. The tears that came so easily in Judge Baumann's courtroom were gone.

They sat back down. Michael leaned over and whispered in her ear.

"Here we go."

Andie turned her head, and mouthed the words: "I love you." But there was something about the way that she looked that made Michael feel uneasy.

"We have plenty of items on our agenda today. It's my understanding, Mr. Collins, that you will waive the reading of the indictment and charges and would like to enter the plea of not guilty."

"Correct, Your Honor."

"And, we also have a discovery motion by the defense," Judge Sachs said.

Michael nodded his head, and then repeated the same arguments that he had just made in chambers. He made each argument as if it was the first time, and pretended that he didn't already know the results. Brenda Gadd did the same.

"All right," Judge Sachs nodded. "Based on the memoranda filed by each party and the arguments made here today, I deny Defendant's motion. I will, however, issue a scheduling order requiring discovery to be exchanged in thirty days. It's also my understanding that Mr. Collins received a box of documents and that should keep him busy." Judge Sachs looked at her law clerk, and then back to the parties. "Next, we have the issue of bail. Perhaps the prosecution could begin."

"Yes, Your Honor." Brenda Gadd rose as Michael sat down. "The United States opposes any release, and respectfully requests that Ms. Larone be held without bail during the duration of these proceedings." Brenda Gadd paused, turned toward Andie and held her in a piercing gaze. "Looks can be deceiving, Your Honor, looks can be very de – "

Michael was out of his chair before Gadd had completed the sentence.

"Objection, Your Honor, this is ridiculous. Ms. Gadd is actually trying to use the Defendant's appearance against her – "

Judge Sachs raised her hand, a small smile escaping from the far edge of her mouth.

"To the extent that ridiculousness is a real legal objection, which I doubt, the objection is overruled. Please continue, Ms. Gadd."

"As I was saying." Gadd continued with her argument, cool and unflustered. "Looks can be very deceiving. Ms. Larone is not an innocent. As the prosecution intends to show at trial, Ms. Larone has quite a history and knew the victim in this case. Although this is not the time or place to make our opening arguments, it is fair to say that the prosecution is confident that the evidence will show Ms. Larone knew Helix Johannson, made arrangements to meet him in New York, and then took his life. Drugs and the murder weapon were all found in Ms. Larone's vehicle, and her purported alibi is unsubstantiated."

Brenda Gadd paused, letting her arguments sink in as Judge Sachs scribbled notes on the pad in front of her. After a moment, Gadd took a step to the side and began again.

"Ms. Larone has no connections to this community, no family, no children, and she is not a citizen of the United States." She let the last statement hang, as if the fact that Andie Larone was not born in the United States had been a criminal violation in and of itself. "There is no objective evidence of any ties to this community that our court and other courts look for in order to ensure a defendant's future presence. Therefore, she should be held without bail pending trial."

"All right." Judge Sachs continued to scribble notes, as Brenda Gadd sat down. "Mr. Collins, response."

"Thank you, Your Honor." Michael stood, waiting for Judge Sachs to look up at him. Judge Sachs, however, kept her head down. She continued to focus on the notepad in front of her, or, at least, made it appear that way.

"Holding Andie Larone without bail for the next two, three, four months, maybe even longer, doesn't make any sense.

From a practical standpoint, every day Andie Larone is in custody it is costing all of us money and resources. The jails are at capacity, and adding another long-term detainee doesn't help matters.

"Every day we release hundreds of people accused of similar or far worse crimes, and the percentage of those people who don't show up for trial or other hearings is miniscule. Despite the prosecution's optimism regarding their case, and that's all that it is at this point, Andie Larone is not guilty and under the law, she deserves that presumption."

Judge Sachs coughed, and without looking up from her notepad, began to speak in a flat tone.

"Fine public policy speech, counselor, but I didn't hear you dispute anything that Ms. Gadd stated regarding Ms. Larone herself."

"Yes, Your Honor," Michael continued, while a few reporters chuckled in the background. "In addition to an appropriate bail amount, each of those aspects of Ms. Larone's situation can and has been dealt with in the past by this court. She can surrender her passport. She can check in with the court periodically, and even be subject to surprise home visits. She can even wear a monitoring device." Michael, again, waited to see if Judge Sachs would respond to any of these suggestions, but she did not.

"Even if the allegations are true, which the defense vehemently denies, nothing suggests that Ms. Larone is a threat or that the crime will be repeated. This is a woman with no prior criminal record."

As soon as he said it, Michael saw Brenda Gadd rise out of her seat holding a stack of papers. He knew something was about to happen. Michael looked down at Andie, and she looked away.

"Your Honor, that simply is not true." Brenda Gadd raised a stack of papers in her hand. "Now I'm not trying to suggest that Mr. Collins is attempting to mislead the court, because I honestly don't believe he knows, but Ms. Larone certainly does have a criminal history."

Michael looked again at Andie, but she wouldn't meet his eye.

"Approach," Judge Sachs said, and Michael and Brenda Gadd walked toward the bench. The courtroom was quiet. Even someone who had never seen a hearing or heard a legal argument would know that Michael had just made a mistake.

Judge Sachs leaned forward covering the small black microphone in front of her with her hand.

"What do you know?"

"It's true that Andie Larone has no criminal record," Gadd said. "But Andie Larone is not her given name."

"She changed it?" Judge Sachs asked.

"About seven years ago," Brenda Gadd said, "her given name is Jamie Dask. While she was evidently living and going to college in San Francisco, she was pulled over for speeding and the police discovered a large amount of marijuana and some ecstasy in a duffle bag."

"Convicted?" Judge Sachs asked.

"Yes." Brenda Gadd handed the top piece of paper to Judge Sachs, and then another to Michael. "Charged with possession to deal because of the amount, but pled it down to possession for personal use. Given the business that Helix Johannson operated and what we now know, that plea agreement was a mistake, and we now believe that Ms. Larone was one of the many campus contacts in Johannson's network."

Michael looked back at Andie.

"Mr. Collins." Judge Sachs looked down at the record that Gadd had just provided. "I assume you did not know this."

Michael turned back toward the Judge, and tried to recover.

"No, Your Honor, and frankly this is the precise reason that I was so anxious about getting the discovery process started."

"I can't help that his client isn't being truthful with him, Your Honor." Gadd shrugged her shoulders, playing the innocent. "That can't be my fault."

Judge Sachs looked at Michael, and then back at Brenda Gadd.

"We'll continue." She waved her hand, dismissing them from her presence. She had already made her decision, and now it was clear that whatever Michael said would be of little difference.

He walked back to the table, thinking of how to spin his first major mistake of the case. Everything was about credibility – credibility with the judge, credibility with the jury, and credibility with opposing counsel – and, right now, Michael had none. He didn't even know who Andie really was.

Stopping at the table, Michael turned and faced Judge Sachs who, for the first time, was looking up from her notepad.

"Perhaps, the prosecution would have understood what I meant if they would have let me finish." Michael paused so that he could choose his words carefully. "Ms. Larone has no criminal record, meaning that she has no criminal record suggesting that she was capable of the type of violent crime alleged here. While there may be some 'history,' there is no history of violence."

Michael paused, praying that Brenda Gadd would not stand up again and prove him wrong. Even Judge Sachs appeared to be holding her breath, but the moment passed and Brenda Gadd kept the other surprises to herself.

"Bail request is denied." Judge Sachs slammed down her gavel. "She'll be held pending trial."

CHAPTER FORTY TWO

Michael set the box from Brenda Gadd down on the table and took off the lid.

"Let's see what other surprises we have." Michael started ruffling through the box.

Andie's new attorney told Michael to stop, but he continued.

"I think you need to leave," the attorney said again. Michael paused and looked up at the man. He was tall and thin, with chiseled features and his hair greased back.

Michael shook his head and looked down, continuing through the box.

"I said you need to stop."

"And who are you, exactly?" Michael asked.

"I'm Taylor Goss, Ms. Larone's new attorney," he said. "And I think you know that already, because Ms. Larone told you."

"Did she?" Michael looked over at Andie, but Andie wouldn't meet his eye. "I must've missed it." Michael continued his rough sift through the contents of the box, and eventually found an envelope. He took it out. Inside there were about a dozen micro-audiocassettes.

Michael turned the envelope upside down.

"It's weird." He let the tapes fall onto the table in a jumble. "I thought I was Ms. Larone's attorney. You see, it was me in that courtroom today and it's been just me this past week, busting my ass to get the motions filed and the arguments made."

"A notice will be submitted tomorrow making me the attorney of record in this case," Taylor Goss said, "accompanied by Ms. Larone's request that you withdraw, of course."

"Tomorrow?" Michael put on a fake smile. "That means right now, I'm still employed by her and, if you don't mind, I really need to review the contents of this box." Michael turned his attention away from Goss, and stared at Andie. "Because I just might find out who my client is."

Michael sorted through the tapes, each was labeled with the name of the agent who had made the recording, the date, and the length. He looked at one tape, tossed it to the side, and then another.

"I think Ms. Larone would like you to leave now."

"I haven't heard her say that." Michael picked up the most recent recording. "In fact, I haven't heard her say a word."

"You're being indicted," Goss said. His voice rose. "You know what that means. You're going to jail, Collins. You think you can handle a death penalty case from jail?" He took a step toward Michael. "You knew that Andie wasn't just some client you picked up off the street. You knew the grand jury was coming. Your eyes were wide open walking into this, so don't go playing the victim with me."

Michael raised his hand, stopping Goss from coming any closer or saying anything more. He then opened his briefcase and removed a micro-cassette recorder. He pressed a button, the small lid on its face opened, and he put the FBI's tape inside. Michael was about to press play, but then stopped.

He looked up at Goss. Calmly, he asked: "When were you hired?"

Goss didn't answer.

Michael looked at Andie.

"When did you hire him? It wasn't this morning. I guarantee that. You just needed to get a little bit more information out of me, right? So that you could cut a deal. That's how it went? That's the advice you received from Mr. Goss? Sell me out?"

Michael pressed play, and Andie's recorded voice filled the room, followed by Helix Johannson.

ANDIE: When will you be in New York?

HELIX: A few weeks, I have some business to take care of. Are you sure you can break free and meet me?

ANDIE: I'm sure.

HELIX: Your little boyfriend won't be mad?

ANDIE: He's not my boyfriend.

HELIX: Sure about that?

ANDIE: You are my one and only.

HELIX: That's my girl.

ANDIE: Love you.

HELIX: Love you, too, beautiful.

Michael shut off the tape player. He looked up at Andie or Jamie or whatever her name was.

"Should we all listen to it again, since we're all on the same team here?"

"I can explain." Andie came toward him, but Michael held out his hand. "I was hoping he could give me money, money for the resort – "

"I trusted you."

"I didn't do it," Andie said. "I was meeting with Green Earth. That was true. I wasn't there when he got shot. I swear to God."

"I'm leaving." Michael ejected the tape out of the player, and put it back on the table.

"That man had the proof," Andie said. "You told me he had the building's logs and the security tape, you saw it. I wasn't – "

"Enjoy the rest of your attorney-client conference." Michael picked up his briefcase, and put the player inside. "I'll send the file over to your office in the morning."

He walked over to the metal door, knocked twice, and the bailiff, standing outside in the hallway, let Michael out.

Michael left the room and started walking toward the elevator, but remembered the reporters and television crews that were in the courtroom. They were probably waiting for him out front. The working headline: Kingpin Kutie's Kounsel Kraps Out.

"Excuse me." Michael got the attention of a passing woman. She wore a courthouse staff identification badge around her neck, and clutched a pack of Kool cigarettes while carrying the burdens of all low-level bureaucrats throughout the world on her shoulders. "Is there a back door or stairwell where I could smoke?" Michael asked. "I'd go to the front, but my boss has been on me to quit. You know how that goes."

Initially the woman looked at Michael with suspicion, but when he got to the part about his boss hassling him to quit, solidarity formed.

"The other clerks and me go to the delivery dock. Take the main stairs to the second floor, and then there's a smaller stairwell next to the men's bathroom. That'll lead you to an exit door. It says an alarm will sound when opened, but ..." she flashed a guilty smile, "somebody may have disabled it."

"I understand."

Michael thanked her and turned toward the stairs. Following the clerk's directions, he found the emergency exit two floors down.

He paused at the door. Even though she told him it was disabled, the warning signs for the alarm still caused concern.

Michael took a deep breath and pushed.

The door swung open. Cold winter air surrounded him. He waited, but no siren sounded.

A trio of courthouse staff turned. They were huddled at the end of the concrete loading dock near a larger double metal door, sharing their misery and likely complaining about all the arrogant lawyers they had to deal with on a daily basis. They looked over at Michael. He was not one of them.

Michael gave a slight nod, and they returned to their cigarettes and conversation. He hustled down the concrete stairs, through a narrow puddle-filled alley, and finally to the busy sidewalk on the east side of the courthouse building.

"Making your escape?"

Michael turned toward the voice and saw Agent Vatch sneering up at him.

"I figured you wouldn't want to comment on your amazing performance in court today," Vatch said. "And then I thought to myself, 'What does young Mr. Collins do whenever he's in trouble or things don't go exactly his way?' And then I said to myself, 'Well that's an easy question, Agent Vatch, Mr. Collins runs for the nearest exit and never looks back, like a rat on a sinking ship,' not that I'm calling you a rat or anything like that, but you know what I mean."

Vatch's tongue flicked twice.

Michael shook his head, turned, and started walking away, ignoring him.

"You're going to have to deal with me at some point," Vatch followed behind. "The grand jury is coming, and I believe your girlfriend is going to be a star witness."

Michael continued walking, but Vatch continued with even more taunts.

"Is she still your client? Must've been a lover's quarrel of some sort after that hearing; a real shocker. Jamie Dask, who would've known?"

He kept following.

"You know what's surprising to me?" Vatch asked. "Not that she lied to you about who she really was. That didn't surprise me so much, but what really got me ..." Vatch wheeled himself closer to Michael. Once on his heels, Vatch continued. "What really got me was how fast that little whore sold you out, but I bet – "

Michael turned, exploding on Vatch. He had heard enough, been through enough. The rage came from every part of his body, pent up for so long, finally it came out. His calm, his detachment, his calculation, all of it suspended while he moved at Vatch in a blur.

His briefcase dropped to the ground. Michael's left fist connected with Vatch's jaw. His right fist drove into Vatch's nose. Snap. It broke. Blood started to flow. Vatch screamed in pain, but Michael didn't stop. His left fist drove into Vatch's nose, again, and then his right, until Vatch finally folded onto himself, cowering, covering himself with his arms.

Michael still didn't stop. He hit Vatch, again and again until he heard a woman say, "Somebody stop that man before he kills him." He didn't know why the woman's voice managed to cut through the noise in his head, but it did.

Michael took a step back from Vatch, staring down at his hands. They were covered in blood. He was shaking. His rage began its descent into shock, as the crowd of passersby formed a circle around him.

Vatch cried. His body in a heap; still folded onto himself in his wheelchair.

Michael took a step toward him, but, when he reached out, Vatch's crying slowly turned into shallow laughter. Vatch unfolded himself. Sitting upright, he stared at Michael. The entire lower half of his face painted red from blood. His narrow slit of a mouth bent into a smile.

"I think you just assaulted a federal law enforcement officer." Vatch's tongue licked the blood from his lips. "And I'm placing you under arrest."

Michael shook his head, staring at Vatch, never blinking.

"No. Not today."

Michael turned and ran, bursting through the circle of onlookers.

"You see, now, that's just rude," Vatch said. Then he pointed at Michael. "Stop that man. He's under arrest."

Michael ran faster, darting between and around other people who were on the sidewalk.

"Stop that man!" Vatch tried to follow, but distance grew. "He's under arrest! Somebody stop that man!"

Michael heard sirens in the distance. They were coming for him.

He came to a quick stop in the middle of the block, and turned.

"Good-bye, Francis."

Michael cut across the street. On the other side, there were stairs leading down to the subway, but he only got halfway.

A white delivery van barreled toward him, accelerating. Michael waited for it to pass, but, instead, the van screeched to a halt in front of him. Its door slid open, and a man in a ski mask jumped out. There was only one man built like that. It was the Professor.

"Get in the van." He grabbed Michael by the coat, but Michael fought. He landed a couple elbows to the Professor's ribs and a kick to his shin, but the Professor easily threw him into the side of the van. Then he tried to get Michael inside the door. "Come on."

Michael thrashed in the Professor's arms, kicking and punching, occasionally landing a shot as car horns sounded and traffic backed up. The police sirens sounded closer.

"Hurry up, hurry up." the driver screamed. It was a woman's voice. She sounded familiar, but he couldn't place her. "Get him inside. We have to go."

A gun shot rang out.

People on the sidewalk fell to the ground. Then there was another shot, and the Professor tossed himself and Michael to the pavement. Michael looked back. It was Vatch. His gun was drawn.

Still on the ground, wrestling with the Professor, Michael only had one more chance.

He drove his knee as hard as he could into the Professor's groin and broke away as the Professor screamed. Michael rolled his body underneath the van, and then over to the other side just as Vatch fired a third and fourth shot into the side of the van.

Michael looked back. The Professor was too big to follow. The van was low, and the thickness of the Professor's body would never allow him to get underneath.

"We have to go!" the driver laid on the horn. And Michael saw the Professor pull himself up and climb inside.

As the van peeled away, Michael entered the temporary safety of the subway station.

CHAPTER FORTY THREE

The picture on the small television strained to find a signal, flickering in and out of clarity. The periodic buzzing and static, however, did not mean that people weren't watching. The dinner crowd at the Round-the-Clock Diner on 9th couldn't turn away. They watched the news report about gunshots at the courthouse and the man who fled the scene as if they were all at risk and the city was under siege.

"That's great television." Kermit stole one of Michael's fries. "I mean really freakin' good T.V., possible regional Emmy material or maybe national, assuming, of course, there isn't a huge natural disaster." Kermit took another handful of fries. "You can't compete with the natural disasters, you really can't."

"Well, let's all pray for a year without hurricanes, then."

"Pray, indeed." Kermit took a sip of soda. "You need me to go with you?"

"No," Michael shook his head. "Better if I fly solo from here on out." When he said it, Michael caught his reflection in the mirror. The mirror ran the entire length of the diner's back wall in a desperate attempt to create the illusion of space where none existed.

Michael's hair was shaved off and bleached white, an earring in both ears. His suit and tie were gone, replaced by baggy jeans, a black New York Yankees jersey, and a ridiculously puffy North Face jacket.

While the van pulled away, Michael had disappeared into the rush hour crowd beneath the city. Within twenty minutes, he had shed the suit and found new clothes. Within an hour, he had platinum hair and his ears sported gold rings.

"Here's your bag." Kermit passed Michael's green knapsack across the table. "Ms. Patty sure wanted to know where you were, but I played it cool, man, nothing to worry about."

Michael looked in the knapsack. It contained his toiletries, some clothes, and most importantly, the photograph of his Irish revolutionary namesake that had been hanging in his office at Wabash, Kramer & Moore.

He probably shouldn't have called Kermit from a pay phone and asked him to retrieve the photograph for him. It seemed like a needless risk, but Michael felt better having it with him. Unfortunately, his briefcase was gone, left on the street with Vatch.

"So you got in and out of the office without much of a problem?"

"Smooth as silkworms in a bubble bath, *mi amigo*." Kermit finished his soda. "It was in the door and out, all in, like, a minute or two."

"But Patty saw you?"

Kermit nodded, pushing his empty glass inside and grabbing the last of Michael's fries. Michael didn't mind. His thoughts were elsewhere.

"Not much I could do about that, man, she was like in your office, going through your stuff."

"And what did you say?"

"I said, 'Hey pretty lady, come here often?' and she was not amused. Then I said you had some things in there of a personal nature, things that were yours no matter what happened."

"She accepted that?"

Kermit shook his head.

"No, but what's she gonna do?" Kermit finished drinking the rest of his soda. "The love thing was probably never going to happen between us anyway, different worlds, you know? But still, the look she gave me as I took the picture off the wall ..." Kermit shook his head in dismay. "It was not a soft look, let me say that."

A waitress appeared at the table. "Anything else for you two?"

"Nothing for me," Michael said.

"Have any chocolate shakes?" Kermit licked his lips.

"Of course." The waitress nodded.

"Hand dipped?"

"Of course."

"Vanilla ice cream and chocolate sauce, rather than just chocolate ice cream all mixed up?"

"Yes."

"Then I'll have one of those." Kermit watched her jot down the order and run it back to the kitchen, and then turned back to Michael. "So I've been thinking about this security guard thing, and I'm starting to think that – And don't say I'm crazy here – but I'm starting to think that maybe Andie was set up and the guard had something to do with it."

Michael stared at him, silent.

"What do you think?" Kermit asked. "Crazy or does the theory have legs?"

"I think the theory had legs about two days ago when I told you that was the theory."

"Oh." Kermit looked down at the gold Formica tabletop in front of him. "So we each get, like, half-credit for the theory if it all works out?"

"You understand that I'm no longer Andie's attorney."

Kermit raised his eyebrows.

"When did that happen?"

"This afternoon, when ..." Michael's voice trailed off. It wasn't worth the effort, explaining what had happened with Andie or that a person who has assaulted a federal law enforcement officer and is soon-to-be indicted for stealing $500 million is not in the best position to represent someone in a court of law.

He needed to move. He needed to get out of the city, and Kermit had stopped paying attention. Wheel Of Fortune was on the diner's television.

"That dude has got to buy a vowel in a big way." He took a sip of milkshake without taking his eyes off of the screen. "Buy a vowel. Buy a vowel. Buy a vowel." When the show went to commercial, Kermit turned back to Michael. "What were you saying?"

"Nothing."

"All right." Kermit shrugged. "Say I'm pretty beat, how about you? You want to go see Andie, and then hit the hay?"

"Probably not a good idea right now." Michael glanced at the door, expecting a SWAT team. A family walked inside from the cold, instead. "You know you haven't said anything about her, yet."

"What about her?"

"You were at the hearing, right?"

"Yeah."

"And you don't have anything to say about Andie not really being Andie."

Kermit put his head down and fiddled with his napkin.

That was when Michael realized.

"You knew." Michael shook his head. "Of course you knew."

Kermit remained silent, while Michael watched. For somebody who swore that he wouldn't ever trust anyone, Michael couldn't believe that he had been so naïve.

For his part, Kermit kept his head down. He wanted to tell Michael how much Andie loved him, how torn up she was about keeping her past from him, how she didn't want Helix Johannson back, but she needed money for the resort.

"You gotta understand Andie's situation." Kermit continued to look away. "She was in a rough spot, that's all."

He waited for Michael to respond. When Michael didn't, Kermit continued. "You have to understand the circumstances. The numbers were off. The equilibrium was all whack-o."

When Michael, again didn't respond, Kermit finally looked up, but Michael had already gone.

CHAPTER FORTY FOUR

The conference room adjacent to Brenda Gadd's office had been converted into a makeshift war room. Maps of New York City covered the walls, dotted by colored thumb tacks indicating each subway station where Michael may or may not have gotten off or transferred. Three televisions on carts had been rolled into the corners of the room, broadcasting live news reports, and young men in pressed white shirts, loosened neck ties, and rolled-up sleeves darted in and out, delivering reams of paper.

"This is it?" Vatch shook his head. "All we can confirm is that about one hour and forty minutes ago a man who may be Michael Collins may or may not have been seen exiting the Green Line on Spring Street?"

"I saw the tape," a young agent said. "It looked like him, but it was black and white, grainy. I'm 99 percent."

"Get out of here," Vatch barked, touching the narrow white bandage across the bridge of his nose. Every minute that went by made it less likely that Michael Collins was going to be caught.

"Where did he go?" Vatch turned to Tammy Duckstein. "Where'd your *friend* go?"

Tammy looked up from a sheath of reports listing every neighbor and co-worker Michael Collins had ever had.

"I don't know," she glared. "And he's not my friend."

"Sure he is." Vatch rolled his wheelchair out from under the table, crossing to the window overlooking Foley Square below. "Maybe if you would've gotten us the Maltow file a little sooner …" Vatch shook his head. "Maybe I could still breathe through my nose."

"That's not fair. I was trying – "

"Enough, children." Brenda Gadd entered the room. "Everybody out except Duckstein and Vatch. We need a minute."

Vatch had never seen agents, clerks, cops, and Assistant U.S. Attorneys clear a room so quickly.

Brenda Gadd shut the door, walked over to the televisions, turning each one off. The conference room soon became silent and still.

"We can play the blame game tomorrow, all right?" She glared at both of them, Vatch still with his back turned and staring out the window. "Any word about our little helpers in the now-bullet-ridden white van?"

"No word," said Duckstein. "Disappeared. Nobody got a license plate. We think it didn't have any."

"What about our runaway attorney?" Gadd asked Duckstein, and then looked at the map of New York City. "I assume from your silence, you've got nothing." She turned back toward Duckstein and Vatch. "Well, I haven't told the media about the $500 million that Collins has hidden away somewhere. So far, everybody's kept quiet about the pending grand jury indictment. That might leak eventually, but not by me. There are political implications to raising the stakes. If we can't find him we look incompetent and we don't need another story about incompetent federal agencies at the moment."

Or when contemplating a run for the United States Senate, Duckstein thought.

"Right now," Gadd pointed at Vatch, "the story about attacking a handicapped federal agent in broad daylight is all the motivation anybody needs to hunt this kid down and keep the story going on television."

Vatch's jaw clenched at the description of him as a "handicapped federal agent."

Brenda Gadd walked away from the maps, and over to the conference room table. She sat down.

"Agent Vatch, come over here," she said. "Please join us."

Vatch grumbled, but even he knew not to disobey the United States Attorney for New York.

When Vatch was at the table, Gadd looked at both him and Tammy Duckstein.

"I want this guy" Gadd said it as if she was revealing a secret. "The case against Joshua Krane was the only one that ever got away from me. Agent Vatch has his own motivations." She looked at Vatch, and Vatch nodded, thankful that Gadd hadn't mentioned his dead partner. "This kid was responsible, one way or another. I think we all agree on that, don't we?" Gadd looked directly at Tammy Duckstein, waiting for a response, but none came.

"So where is he? Where is he going?" Gadd waved off the maps. "Forget the subway stations and finding security video, we don't have that kind of time. You two know him best. Where did he go?"

Tammy went first.

"Gone. If he took the money as you say, which I don't think he did, he has the resources to buy a plane ticket and fly anywhere in the world."

"He won't use his own passport." Vatch adjusted the bandage across his nose. "I know he has access to fraudulent papers."

"Know this for a fact?" Gadd asked.

Vatch's narrow slit of a mouth turned into a crooked smile as he thought about shaking down the proprietor of Hoa Bahns.

"I have excellent information," he said. "I'll pass the boy's aliases on to the border patrol so that we can be notified if he tries to get out of the U.S. Let's leave it at that."

"Well, I can't leave it at that." Gadd paused, thinking. "There has to be somebody in his life."

"Andie Larone was one," Vatch said. "But she's out, so that just leaves us with our beloved priest. That's it."

"Then that's where we'll go. Find Father Stiles as soon as possible and stay close, but I want the agents in plain clothes. SWAT and helicopters on standby. I can't have them circling and spooking this kid away."

"Isn't that all a little much?" Tammy asked.

"No." Vatch wheeled back from the table and started toward the door. "Sounds just right to me."

CHAPTER FORTY FIVE

The outer edge of a winter storm, still days away, kicked stray pieces of paper down the sidewalk through quick bursts of cold wind. Michael turned the hood up over his head, and adjusted the green knapsack that hung over his shoulder. After a quick visit to Hoa Bahns, it contained several alternate passports and three credit cards issued under other names. Two hundred thousand dollars in cash also kept the picture of Michael's revolutionary namesake company.

As for the gun, he had left it behind. By morning Michael would be on a plane, and, the last time he checked, airlines didn't appreciate armed passengers.

He turned another corner and stopped, scanning the street for windowless vans belonging to the FBI. He looked for people just sitting in their car, neither coming nor going, anything that would be out of the ordinary for Friday Karaoke and Trivia Night at Saint Thomas church.

He saw nothing.

Michael cut across the street and joined a family of five walking toward the side door of the church. He stayed close, as a group of teenagers fell in behind. Michael walked with the pack down the sidewalk, through the door, and eventually down into the church's basement.

As usual, the darkened room was filled with happy families enjoying free baskets of chips and popcorn. The kids had small cups of pink Kool-Aid, while the parents drank 3.2 keg beer donated by McSweeney's Liquor on Columbus. Although there was never any doubt, the presence of alcohol confirmed that Saint Thomas the Compassionate Church was a Catholic institution, not Baptist.

A seventeen-year-old girl belted out her version of the classic rock tune, "These Boots Are Made For Walking," while Michael skirted the outside of the room. He avoided eye contact and moved with purpose. It was an attempt to dissuade others from engaging him in casual conversation.

Michael stopped, waited, and then continued on, moving closer to Father Stiles. The priest stood on the side of the small stage watching the future pop princess work up to the song's final refrain. His pompadour was combed high and back, and his crushed blue velvet jumpsuit and cape hugged every inch and bulge of Father Stiles' body.

"Father." Michael spoke in a hushed voice, barely audible over the music.

Father Stiles looked around, not knowing who in the audience had called for him.

"Father." Michael casually and briefly raised his hand.

The priest met Michael's eye. He squinted, then a look of recognition.

The song ended and the young girl put the microphone back in the stand. Father Stiles looked at the girl, then the audience, and finally back at Michael. He mouthed the word, "Office." Then he trotted over to the microphone with a large, silly grin.

"Thank you, Miss Sandy." It was a smooth, southern drawl. "Father Elvis thanks you, thanks you very much."

Then he began talking up the next performer, thirteen year-old Stuart Capri. He would be singing George Strait's "All My Ex's Live in Texas (That's Why I Hang My Hat in Tennessee)." Classic karaoke.

Michael turned from the stage and walked over to the bar. There was a temporary lull in the usual run on beer, and he had the space to himself.

He looked around.

Nobody was coming; the volunteer bartender had his back turned. He was restocking the sodas and filling the cooler with ice. Before the bartender could notice, Michael reached into his knapsack and removed three large stacks of one-hundred dollar-bills. Michael slipped them through the slit of the offering/tip box on the corner of the bar.

Then he walked away.

Surrounded by the musty theology and philosophy books that he had devoured as a young man, Michael waited in Father Stiles' office. The smell of recently microwaved pepperoni Pizza Rolls still filled the room, reminding Michael that Kermit had stolen much of his dinner. He hadn't really eaten since lunch.

Lunch now seemed like a long, long time ago.

There was a knock at the door, a warning, and then Father Stiles entered the room. He locked the door behind him, and then took his place behind the large cluttered desk.

"Not a big fan of the hair," he nodded toward Michael's new platinum crewcut. It was meant to be a joke, but Father Stiles' tone and expression were flat. He knew what was happening.

"I've got to go."

Father Stiles nodded.

"But you wanted to say goodbye?"

"I did," Michael said. "You deserve that much, and I regret that last time ..." Michael shrugged his shoulders, and then took a deep breath. "I've been a little ..."

Father Stiles raised his hand.

"Now isn't the time for punishment, either self-inflicted or by me." Then he cocked his head to the side. "There'll be lots of time for reflection, Michael." The conversation was heavy and stilted; both wanted to say more than they could.

"I don't know if I'll be back."

"You'll be back," Father Stiles said.

"I don't think so." Michael shook his head. "Not this time."

"You're going to want this thing resolved one way or another. All things must be resolved in time, and you, in particular, are not satisfied with running away. I know that's what you've done and what you are doing, but I also know it isn't who you are."

There was a knock at the door.

Father Stiles looked at Michael, and then at the door.

"Yes?"

"It's Graydon Horner." The person on the other side of the door knocked, again. "There's a man here that wants to see you, Father, says it's important."

Father Stiles stood.

"I'm coming." He and Michael embraced, holding close. "Take the stairs through the house," he said, and then Father Stiles took a step back. "Father, are you coming?" Graydon Horner continued from the other side of the closed door.

"Yes. I'm coming. I'm an old man now, you know."

When he got to the door, Father Stiles glanced back at the stairs leading out of the rectory's attic to the second level of the attached house. Michael was already gone.

"Can I help you?" Father Stiles asked, after he had unlocked and opened the door. Graydon Horner stood before him with a blank expression, while a man in a wheelchair shouted at Horner to get out of the way.

"Where is he? Who were you talking to in here?"

"And who are you?" Father Stiles was forced to step aside as Vatch nearly knocked Graydon Horner down as he wheeled past. "Excuse me, who are you?"

"You know who I am." Vatch wheeled further into the office. "Where is Collins?"

"I believe that I have a right to see some identification, if you are claiming to be a law enforcement officer of some sort."

Vatch turned to the priest.

"I'm pretty close to tossing you in jail for obstructing this investigation and harboring a criminal." Vatch looked around the office. "So where is he?"

"I was just meeting with a parishioner. Last time I checked, a conference between a priest and a parishioner was confidential."

Vatch wheeled to the desk, and then to the back stairwell.

"Really." Vatch looked down the stairs. "When was this so-called parishioner here?"

"The parishioner was here when I got up to answer the door."

"Good." Vatch smiled. "That was helpful, Father, very helpful." He took out his phone and pressed the speed-dial.

While peering down the stairwell, Vatch pressed the phone against his ear and strained to catch a glimpse or hear a sound of Michael.

"In the house." Vatch turned off the phone, and then turned back to Father Stiles. "You're a real man of the cloth, Father, a real man of God." Vatch wheeled toward the door and the church's old rickety elevator just on the other side. "The government of the United States thanks you very much."

CHAPTER FORTY SIX

Taking the stairs three at a time, Michael was down one flight in four steps and a leap. He righted himself at the base, and then kept going. He ran through the second-story hallway until he reached another flight of stairs. Michael tried to take a hard right, but the momentum pushed him forward, and he crashed into the wall. Two framed pictures fell to the ground. The glass shattered, cascading down the steps along with him until he finally reached the main level of the rectory where Father Stiles had lived for over twenty years.

Michael was breathing hard, now. They may have found him, he thought, but they weren't going to catch him. This was his neighborhood.

He sprinted out the front door, not bothering to close it behind him, just as two helicopters, maybe three, appeared out of nowhere.

They circled overhead. Their spotlights crossed back and forth, searching for him. Michael ducked down between two parked cars.

He waited.

There was activity at the far end of the block, people meeting, and then spreading. Car doors slammed closed. Michael knew the circle around him was forming. They were moving in.

A woman in jeans and a navy blue windbreaker ran down the street toward the rectory. She held a walkie-talkie to her ear, listening, and then shouting back into it.

"I'm twenty yards away, fifteen, ten ..." Michael edged further between the cars, as she turned and ran into the house, her gun drawn.

Two men came up to the house from the other direction, also with their guns drawn. A helicopter passed directly overhead, its spotlight missing Michael by only a few feet. He didn't have much time.

Michael took a breath, counted down from three, and then darted across the street, staying low.

Once across, Michael again ducked between two parked cars. He waited, his eyes wide, his heart beating faster than it ever had before. Michael listened. He heard more agents and police officers running toward the house. Could they see him? He couldn't wait.

Michael ran across the sidewalk, and then into a narrow space between two sets of row houses. There was barely enough room to move. The arms of his jacket scraped along the brick exteriors on either side; catching and then coming free.

"I thought I saw something over here. Give me your light." Beams from an agent's flashlight streaked the space as Michael made it to the end. He threw himself around the corner, and fell to the cold, wet ground.

"Did you see that? Did you see that?"

"I didn't see nothing."

"Hold it right there, Collins. Don't make me fucking run."

Michael picked himself up off of the ground. He had fifteen seconds, maybe less.

He ran to the far side of a dumpster, only five feet away, and pushed it as hard as he could. At first, the dumpster didn't give, but then the wheels underneath righted themselves and the dumpster lurched an inch forward.

Michael pushed, again, and the dumpster rolled in front of the narrow space between the two sets of row houses. The men giving chase must not have had time to stop, because Michael heard them crash into the dumpster as he ran down the alley toward Tompkins Park.

CHAPTER FORTY SEVEN

The park was abandoned and dark. It had been over ten years since the city bowed to the pressure of the increasingly gentrified neighborhood residents, and started barring homeless people from sleeping there.

Michael ran northeast, past the 1890s monument to Congressman Cox and toward Temperance Fountain. The simple stone drinking fountain at the center of the Tompkins Park was one of fifty such fountains built by temperance crusader Henry Cogswell in the latter part of the 19th century. From a distance, the fountain appeared to be a simple squat column. Surrounded by four taller columns that supported its roof, the fountain's only adornment was a bronze statue of Bebe, the mythical carrier of water.

About fifteen yards from it, Michael ducked off the path and into an old grove of elm trees. In the center, there was a small, concrete slab with a rusted metal grate. There were two hinges on one side and a padlock on the other, giving the appearance that the grate was secured.

Michael, however, knew better. The bolts supposedly keeping the hinges together had been removed. Attempts were periodically made by the city to "fix" the grate, but the bolts always managed to disappear a short time later.

249

Michael yanked the grate. It opened, and he climbed inside one of New York's many tunnels. Although out of sight and out of mind to the millions who live there and even more who visit, New York was honeycombed with underground passageways and caverns, some abandoned and some used every day to carry subway passengers, utility lines, sewage, and of course, Bebe's mythical water.

On narrow bands of iron that protruded out of the wall, Michael began his 670-foot descent below the surface and into complete darkness. The shaft that led from Tompkins Park to Water Tunnel No. 5 was originally constructed in 1913, and Michael hoped that the iron steps wouldn't break away from the crumbling walls and send him falling to the ground.

He stopped with each step, making sure that his foot was firmly on one before taking another. Michael listened for somebody above, certain that the men on foot had seen where he was going or the helicopters had spotted him. He heard nothing.

Michael kept on, lowering himself further into the dark. The air thickened with the smell of sewage and mold. Heat from the steam pipes raised the temperature in the narrow shaft with every step he took toward the bottom.

Finally, Michael touched ground. He allowed himself a second to relax and take a breath. He wondered how long he could stay in the tunnel, how long they would keep looking for him.

Michael got down on his hands and knees, crawling on the floor. He blindly circled the space below the ladder, reaching and feeling in the tunnel's muck, ignoring the rats that scurried through his fingertips.

"You have to be here." He reached into a pool of grease and mud. "Traditions never die."

Then he found it.

His right hand grazed the side of an old wooden milk crate, a gift from one urban explorer to another. He reached inside. It was filled with candles, most burnt down to an inch or two, but some were longer. Then he found the plastic bag.

He opened it and removed one of the boxes of matches by touch. He couldn't see them, but Michael could tell that the boxes were dry.

Striking one, an orange flame sparked and the match lit. Michael held it in front of him as his eyes adjusted to the sudden appearance of light. The small flame felt and looked like a miracle. He put the match to a candle, and the tunnel brightened.

When he first moved to New York from Boston, Michael had found a self-published 'zine at the Gotham Book Mart and Gallery. The 'zine was dedicated to the New York Underground. It was filled with black and white photographs, sketches, and maps interspersed with stories about the thousands of "mole" people who lived beneath the city. There were poems about abandoned subway stations decorated with elaborate mosaics and crystal chandeliers, and reviews of secret nightclubs underneath Broadway that had been built during Prohibition and were still in operation.

Most of what filled the pages of the 'zine were myth, but the water tunnel under Tompkins Park was true.

Michael removed his jacket. The temperature in the tunnel was near 110 degrees, and he felt the sweat begin to coat every part of his body in a gritty film.

He followed the dirty tunnel for roughly a half-mile. There, it split into two more narrow and even smaller passageways. Michael chose the tunnel on his right, and walked 150 yards to a door that looked like an old jail cell. A series of corroded bars,

each four inches apart from one another, sealed the passage-
way to the wider and more maintained tunnel on the other side.

Michael blew out the candle and put it inside a second
wooden milk crate near the door. Then, he reached his hand
through the bars. He closed his eyes, and tried to find the lever.
Once he found it, Michael said a brief prayer to himself, and
then lifted. The lever resisted. He lifted again and, this time, he
heard a click. The door swung open.

Just thirty feet more to a shaft leading up to the main Amtrak
station.

CHAPTER FORTY EIGHT

It was past midnight when Vatch finally made it home. The adrenaline was gone, no longer masking the pain. Each breath he took felt like he was inhaling needles through his broken nose. The swelling in his face had increased two-fold, and the muscles in his arms, back, and neck were exhausted.

Vatch wheeled across his sparsely furnished living room and into the second bedroom that he had converted to a home office. Vatch turned on the lights and went over to his desk.

He stared up at the photographs of Michael Collins. The kid he had been hunting for two years while everybody else at the bureau told him to let it go. Now, after getting close, Michael Collins had disappeared again. Rumors were flying of an investigation into him for firing his gun at an unarmed man on a busy street.

"Investigating me." Vatch shook his head. "Ridiculous."

If he had wanted Collins dead, he could have killed him, thought Vatch. Instead, all he wanted to do was freeze the situation. Stop the van, and keep Collins from going anywhere with a few warning shots. Nobody would get hurt, and nobody *was* hurt. It was just a few warning shots.

Vatch thought back to the white delivery van with no plates. It had to be the people who Collins had stolen the money from.

253

They knew he was in trouble, maybe had even gotten wind of the indictment, and wanted to get at him first. Or, maybe, they were only trying to help Collins escape, but that didn't make any sense. Collins had fought them. He didn't want to go.

Vatch reached around to the nylon bag strapped to the back of his wheelchair. It contained his trophy. He opened the bag and retrieved the only good thing that had happened that day. Just touching it made him feel better: Michael Collins' briefcase.

Vatch had interviewed many of the kid's former girlfriends who swore Collins cared more about that briefcase than he had about them.

Michael Collins had left the briefcase on the street when he ran. It was evidence that should've been bagged and kept in a storage locker somewhere, but Vatch wanted it for himself. His hands ran back and forth across the soft honey-brown leather, and then he unfastened the brass latch.

Inside, there was a three-ring binder. Vatch removed the binder and placed it on his desk, and then started to remove the other folders and clipped bundles of paper.

"Whatcha doin' ?"

Vatch jumped.

He turned and saw Anthony standing in the doorway.

"How many times do I have to tell you not to come in here through the window? Come to the door and knock. Knock on the door. That's what real people do. Only freaky kids go creeping through windows."

"Sorry," Anthony said, "my momma's working late, again, and I saw the light on from the. ..." The boy paused, noticing Vatch's face for the first time. "What happened to you?"

"Nothing." Vatch looked over at the clock on the wall. "You should be in bed."

"I'm not tired." Anthony walked further into the room, a look of concern. "You need some ice? I can get an ice pack for you."

Vatch shook his head.

"I'll be fine."

"I think you need some ice." Anthony turned and started to walk out of the room and toward the kitchen, but stopped after only a few steps. He looked back. "Did he do that to you?" Anthony glanced at the photographs of Michael Collins on the wall above Vatch's desk.

Vatch didn't say a word.

"I hope you get him."

"Me too," Vatch said. "Me too."

CHAPTER FORTY NINE

The ten-hour train ride from New York City to Montreal gave Michael time to sleep, but the sleep didn't come easy. He needed assistance from a half-dozen shots of Jameson to calm his mind. Once the sleep came, Michael crashed hard.

There was nobody else to disturb him in the Superliner compartment. He could be alone with the sound of wheels rolling over the tracks, a circle of sound that reminded him of the waves outside Hut No. 7 and the calm of the Sunset Resort & Hostel.

When he woke up, Michael showered in the world's most compact shower stall.

Feeling like a human being again, it was time to get rid of the platinum hair. He would have to go through customs in Montreal, and Michael needed something that more closely resembled the picture in his passport.

Wrapped in a bath towel, Michael stood in front of the sink and mirror. He reached into his green knapsack, and found the box of hair dye. He had purchased it the day before when he had originally gone gold. Michael removed the box, tore open the top, and then began to comb the auburn color into his hair.

He let it stand for ten minutes, and then showered again, watching the excess color flow down the drain. When the water ran clear, he knew that it was done. Next stop: Mexico.

The plane touched down in Cancun shortly after 1:30 p.m. Although everything had gone without a hitch, Michael was still on edge, worried that somebody would recognize him and that he would need to run.

Michael moved with the tourists, up the aisle, and then finally out the door. The instant he walked outside, he felt his bones began to thaw. The sun had never felt so welcome, and he allowed himself a single moment to let his guard down. He closed his eyes. The warm rays beat down on his face.

Michael descended the short flight of stairs onto the runway. He maneuvered through the terminal, out customs, and finally to one of the cabs lining the street. Every place Michael went, he kept looking for a way to escape, planning how to avoid the police, or, worse, one of Mario Deti's men.

"*Hola,*" Michael waved at a cab driver standing in a queue outside the airport. "Down the coast?"

"*Si,*" the driver smiled and patted the hood of his 1971 Volkswagen Beetle. "Runs good."

Michael climbed into the back and they were on their way. His return to Mexico wasn't smart, but he needed to come back. Even surrounded by memories of Andie Larone, Hut No. 7 was still his home. It would take a day or two for Mario Deti and the Professor to track him down, hopefully a little longer. And then, who knew?

The Volkswagen bounced along Route 307, which runs the length of Mexico all the way to the Gulf of Honduras. They left the fantasy resorts and shops of Cancun behind and headed into the vast open spaces of Mexico, miles of brush and scrub on one side with lush forests on the other. Occasionally, Michael caught a glimpse of the cobalt blue Caribbean water with its pristine reef below, or they would pass a tin shanty peddling produce or gasoline along the road, kids playing soccer in a dirt patch outside – glimpses of the real Mexico.

Michael leaned back into the seat. He tried to imagine leaving, trying to find another place to live. And then, for how long? Deti wasn't going to stop. $500 million was something worth some effort.

Michael felt a tinge of guilt, as he thought about Lowell Moore. Lowell was in just as much danger as Michael, but he didn't have the luxury of running away. He had the firm.

"Next turn off." Michael glanced behind them. There was nobody. "Take a left."

The driver slowed, and the car turned off the paved highway and onto a dirt road. The speedometer dropped to less than five miles per hour, as the cab navigated around potholes and debris.

Finally, the space opened and the jumble of huts and buildings comprising the Sunset Resort & Hostel were visible.

"You stay here?"

"*Si.*" Michael opened his green knapsack and removed some money for the fare. "This is it."

CHAPTER FIFTY

A four-inch gecko scurried under the bed when Michael opened the door. The hut was stale, so Michael opened all of the windows to allow the fresh ocean air inside. He took his knapsack off of his shoulder, and retrieved the photograph of the Irish revolutionary from inside. Michael set the picture on the nightstand.

The difference between a terrorist and a revolutionary, he thought, was that the revolutionary wins.

Michael turned away from the photograph, not feeling much like a revolutionary, and crossed the room toward the kitchen.

Hut No. 7 was approximately 650 square feet. On one side there was Michael's bed, nightstand, and dresser. There was no television, and certainly nothing plasma or "high definition." On the other side, there was a sink, an old 1950s Maytag refrigerator, small table, two chairs, and a hot-plate. These comprised the primary elements of Hut No. 7's kitchen.

The two "luxury" items were the tiny wedge-shaped bathroom (only three of the twelve huts at the Sunset had their own bathrooms) and a dusty record player that sat on the floor. Next to the player, there was a stack of vinyl LPs, primarily jazz with a few Cuban classics, like Sexteto Occidente and Lazaro Herrera. When he signed the lease, Michael had insisted that the record player and collection be included in the deal.

He opened the refrigerator. The interior was hollow, except for a six-pack of beer. That suited Michael just fine.

Michael took out the six-pack, walked back to his nightstand, opened the drawer, and removed a tattered copy of Burmese Days by George Orwell. He set the book and the six-pack on his bed, and then continued to rummage through the drawer for his sunglasses and a bottle of sunscreen.

His list for the afternoon and evening was fairly short, no sub-lists and no sub-sub-lists. It did not entail legal research, drafting memorandums, chasing down/running from members of the mob, or fighting embittered agents of the Federal Bureau of Investigation.

He would, instead: (1) change into his bathing suit, (2) get drunk, (3) read, (4) pass out, and (5) scream at the top of his lungs as the warm salty Caribbean surf crashed into him. Not necessarily in that order.

CHAPTER FIFTY ONE

The Professor removed the small piece of paper from his wallet. He unfolded it, read the numbers, and punched them into his cell phone. Four rings, and then an answer.

"Hey." He folded the paper and returned it to his wallet. "It's me."

"What did I say about calling here? You're not to call me here."

"Where is he?" The Professor ignored the rebuke. "We're in this together, you and me. Deep."

"You think I don't know that? I know that."

"Then where is he?"

A pause.

"Vatch got the fake names Collins uses on his fraudulent passports, don't ask me how. We ran a check through the FBI's computer system, and it shows a hit in Montreal, and then one at the Cancun airport."

"Back to the Sunset?"

"The Bureau is going through the State Department. They'll send some Mexican cops over to the resort to check it out."

"When?"

"Don't know. It's Mexican time combined with a diplomat's sense of urgency, so we're waiting. If they get him, they'll extradite Collins up here."

"All right." The Professor checked his watch, wondering if he could still get a flight out of New York. "Anything else?"

"Your boss still owes me money."

"I think he owes a lot of people money."

CHAPTER FIFTY TWO

With the assistance of three yellow pills of unknown origin, Michael slept without the intrusion of any dreams. He awoke the next morning to the sound of children's laughter. A boy and two girls danced around him with plastic shovels and pails.

When Michael attempted to sit up, he couldn't move.

The children's laughter became even louder. Then, the children ran down the beach, escaping the scene of the crime, each placing blame on the other, pointing, and laughing between friendly accusations.

Every part of Michael's body, except his head, was buried underneath a foot or two of sand.

"Need a hand?" A Mexican woman crouched down next to him. "Wiggle a little." She laughed. "You have to loosen it up with your hips."

Michael did as he was told, and within a few seconds he was free.

After he had brushed the sand off his legs, he held out his hand.

"Michael."

"Luise," she introduced herself, and the two awkwardly shook hands. "Can I get you anything besides your freedom?" She tilted her head toward the tray lying on the ground.

"You work here?"

"Just started." Luise picked up the tray. "Sammy needed help."

"Sammy Alverro?" Sammy Alverro was the man who made the Sunset run. He could do every job, from Andie's on down. Kermit must have left him in charge.

"I'm his niece," she smiled.

"It's a pleasure." Michael stared, taking her in. She wore a dark red linen top, and a loose blue skirt that rode low on her hips.

Luise turned.

"Maybe I'll see you around," she said as Michael watched her walk toward a family of naked Germans lounging underneath one of the Sunset's thatch umbrellas. Seemed like there was always a family or two of naked Germans at the Sunset.

CHAPTER FIFTY THREE

In a conference room on the fifth floor of the federal court-house, Brenda Gadd stood before the thirteen men and ten women who comprised the grand jury that would indict Michael John Collins. No judge, no defense counsel, and nobody from the public were in the room. It was just Brenda Gadd, a court reporter, and her jury. That was how it worked.

Gadd loved a grand jury.

Grand jury proceedings were conducted in secret with no in-tention of being a fair trial. The trial came later. Here, the jurors' only role was to listen to the evidence and decide whether it es-tablished a reasonable basis for the prosecutor to charge the defendant with a crime, not whether the defendant was guilty. No opposing arguments and defenses were heard and there was no cross-examination of witnesses. Openly biased jurors were not automatically excused, and defendants did not have the right to be present in the room and listen to the evidence against them. Theoretically, any errors that a grand jury made would be corrected at the actual trial. For now, this was Brenda Gadd's show. She was in complete control.

"I first want to thank each and every one of you for your ser-vice." Gadd folded her hands together in front of her. "When you were selected to serve on this jury, the judge talked to you about what you should expect, so I won't go over that again."

She smiled. Her pleasant, round, Mother Hubbard smile invited each of the jurors to relax, and, most of all, trust her.

"Although the law allows a grand jury to hear evidence over the course of three years, I don't think it will take you that long to reach a decision in this case." A few jurors laughed. Others nodded their head. The possibility of getting this done in a short period of time made them like Brenda Gadd even more.

"You are going to hear evidence related to Mr. Michael John Collins. He's been in the news recently, so I want to remind you all about the confidential nature of these proceedings. These safeguards are there to protect the innocent. It's at the core of our Constitution." Brenda Gadd loved to say that. It was all so very "stars and stripes and apple pie." Jurors ate that up.

"I have a series of witnesses to present over the course of the next several days. They're going to tell a story about a young attorney who made a mistake. A relatively small mistake at first, but then it turned into something much bigger. The FBI has been gathering evidence about this attorney for several years. Now it's time to ask you whether we have a reasonable basis," Brenda Gadd paused and smiled. "Or as lawyers call it, 'probable cause,' to charge him with a crime. I'm sure he has an excuse or two that would justify this behavior, but you only need to decide whether I should have the opportunity to charge him with a crime and ultimately have a trial to determine his guilt and potential punishment."

All of the jurors nodded their heads, fully on board with Brenda Gadd.

"My first witness is Agent Frank Vatch of the Federal Bureau of Investigation. He'll provide background information and a framework for the other testimony you will hear. You'll find that he's a hard-working, veteran agent who will be very informative."

At trial, no judge would allow Brenda Gadd to provide such an introduction for a witness, but in a grand jury proceeding, Gadd could do about anything she wanted.

"If I could have a moment, I'll go get Agent Vatch." Brenda Gadd walked to the door. She opened it, and stuck her head into the hallway.

Agent Vatch was waiting outside with an Assistant U.S. Attorney.

"It's time."

Vatch rolled down the hallway toward her, and into the conference room. Once Vatch was inside, Gadd looked at the Assistant U.S. Attorney and asked if there was any news.

"No," he said. "We're still working on the plea agreement with Andie Larone's new attorney."

"How close?" Gadd asked.

"Very close, probably get it finalized this afternoon or early tomorrow morning."

"Good." Gadd took a step back into the conference room. She started to close the door, but then stopped, adding, "We'll do Vatch today, dismiss the jury, reconvene tomorrow and do the priest, maybe Lowell Moore after a break, and then we'll have Ms. Andie Larone for dessert."

CHAPTER FIFTY FOUR

Michael spent the day sleeping and lying on the beach, punctuated by brief wanders to the bar for a bowl of chips and guacamole. He had been successful at keeping his mind away from New York, the people he left behind, and the ones who wanted him to return for all the wrong reasons.

When the sun started to set, Michael gathered up his things. He walked out to the rocky peninsula that follows a natural curve in the shoreline. It jutted a hundred yards into the water. The regulars had always called it "the Point," since a more elaborate name wasn't necessary.

Michael found a smooth patch of rock, threw down his blanket and pillow, and spent the next few hours watching the fishing boats come back into the distant harbor at Playa del Carmen and the cruise ships float by on their way to and from Cozumel.

A blink and the sky changed shades, from one color of blue to another, on its way to black, interrupted by brilliant streaks of gold and red. Watching the transition from day to night was the perfect way to relax and forget, but this time around forgetting wasn't so easy.

With Andie he was going through the five stages of grief and then back again. He closed his eyes and the memories came back in an instant. He thought about the hearing, the subpoenas, and Vatch. He circled through the facts and retraced. There had to be an angle that hadn't yet been played, a way for him to set a trap or at least convince Brenda Gadd not to immediately throw him in jail.

"Need a little company?"

Michael opened his eyes, looked up, and he saw Luise. She smiled. Her long black hair blew in the night breeze.

Before Michael said anything, Luise was sitting beside him.

"I got a pack of cigarettes, two Cokes, a bottle of rum, and a sandwich. The sandwich and Cokes are for you. The cigarettes and rum are for us, or perhaps just me."

"Thanks." Michael took the sandwich from her, and unwrapped it from the wax paper.

Luise pulled out a cigarette, tapped the end twice on the edge of the hard pack, and lit it.

They sat in silence, while she smoked and Michael ate.

"I thought you might need someone to talk to." She took a drag and exhaled. "But if you'd rather be alone ..."

Michael looked at her.

"No. It's good to have company sometimes." He was an extroverted introvert.

Michael finished the sandwich and opened one of the two bottles of Coke.

They sat and watched another cruise ship pass. Its fog horn filled the night and just as quickly went silent. Its lights got smaller and smaller as the distance grew.

Finally, Luise spoke.

"A broken heart?"

"That obvious?" Michael had always been terrible at poker.

"Woman's intuition." Luise retrieved another cigarette from the open pack next to her. "Plus my uncle filled me in."

Michael nodded.

"Sometimes people don't tell the whole truth." Luise lit the end of the cigarette, the end turning it bright orange. "Not because they want to hurt someone, but because they don't want to hurt anyone."

She opened the bottle of rum, and took a sip. She passed the bottle to Michael, and Michael gave Luise his bottle of Coke. They went back and forth like that, exchanging the Coke for rum, and then the rum for Coke.

"You understand," she said. "I'm sure you do."

Michael didn't respond.

"Did your Uncle Sammy know?" Michael took a drink. The rum burned as it went down.

Luise nodded her head with a trace of pity.

"She wanted to tell you, but ..." Her voice trailed, and they exchanged bottles again.

"She loved this resort. She was running out of options to save it." Luise rested her head on Michael's shoulder. "You see those lights down there?"

Michael looked at the hotel complexes, which seemed to get larger and closer every few months.

"The men who built them want this land, too," Luise said. "They don't care about the life that's here, the people or preserving the Point. They're pressuring the government to come down on Andie, assess fines for no reason, and push her deeper into a hole."

"I knew she was in debt," Michael said, which was only part true. He didn't understand or know how much debt she was in. Andie was independent, and talking about losing the Sunset was too painful for her.

"You can't stay here." Luise closed her eyes. "You have to go back, help her."

Michael kept quiet, and continued to watch the boats float by.

When Michael woke up the next morning, Luise was gone. His throat was rough, and his stomach felt like he had eaten the cigarettes rather than smoked them.

Michael stood, attempting to kick and stretch out the kinks that had formed on the hard rocks during the night.

He looked out over the Caribbean. The sun was just peeking up over the water and it had filled the sky with different shades of pink. He could already tell that it was going to be a hot, sunny day.

Michael picked up his blanket, and walked back along the rocks to the beach.

Somewhere along the way, he decided that the best remedy for how he was feeling would be to sweat out the smoke and alcohol.

Michael dropped his things off at Hut No. 7, purchased a few bottles of water at the main bar, and grabbed a kayak out of the boat house. Before the sun had fully risen, he was a mile away, gliding along the crystal blue water, just another fish.

CHAPTER FIFTY FIVE

Fifteen years in prison is a gift, considering the alternative."
Gadd avoided the direct threat of death. "I strongly suggest
that you advise Andie Larone to take it."

Taylor Goss leaned against the wall in the hallway outside
the grand jury room. He looked relaxed, confident.

"I want five," he said. "She's going to put the nail in Collins'
coffin, and I know you want Michael Collins more than her."

"True and not true." Gadd matched her adversary's confidence. "I do want Collins more than her, but she can't confirm
that he has the money. The nail in the coffin is that confirmation, which you say she can't offer."

"Right now." Taylor smiled. "She may be able to offer such
information in the future. You think about it, and I'll try and re-
fresh her recollection."

"Fine." Gadd held out her hand. "I have to get back to this
anyway." They shook hands, and then Gadd opened the door to
the conference room where the Grand Jury was waiting. "It's
just starting to get interesting in here."

Gadd walked through the door and closed it behind her. The
Mother Hubbard smile was back, and she apologized for the
disruption.

275

"Now where were we?" She looked at Father Stiles on the witness stand, then looked down at her notepad and back up again. "Oh yes, you were telling us about your conversations with Mr. Collins."

He shifted in his chair.

"No." Father Stiles bit his lower lip. "I wasn't telling you about my conversations. I was telling you that the conversations are confidential." He held up a Protective Order that the Catholic Church's attorneys had obtained from the Court, but there wasn't any judge in the conference room to enforce it.

"Right." Gadd continued, pretending that the court order was meaningless.

"You care a lot about Michael Collins, isn't that correct?"

"I do care about him."

"And you wouldn't want any harm to come to him?"

"I wouldn't want any harm to come to any of God's children." Father Stiles crossed his arms over his chest. "And particularly Michael. He's a bright young man, who was dealt a tough hand early on in his life."

Gadd nodded, but paused before beginning, again. The next series of questions were tricky. She needed to prove her point, but not come on too strong. Father Stiles was a priest after all. She didn't want backlash from the jury.

"Has Michael Collins contributed any money to your church?"

Father Stiles nodded.

"Yes, I believe he has."

"A large amount?"

"I don't know. We have an accountant. He may be better able to answer your – "

Slowly enunciating each word, Brenda Gadd interrupted.

"So you're saying that you are not aware of any large donations by Michael Collins to your church?"

"Correct."

"He's made none?"

"Yes."

"Michael Collins has made no large donations?" Gadd pinned the story down.

"I believe that to be the case."

Brenda Gadd seized on the word.

"Believe," she said, and then paused, letting Father Stiles' response to the last question, and the ones before it sink in. Silence often piqued the interest of jurors more than shouts.

Gadd took a step back toward her table and pulled out a stack of papers.

"You mentioned that the church had an accountant. I've actually spoken to that accountant." Gadd held the stack of papers out to the side. It was a subtle gesture to draw the jurors' attention to the paper without waving the evidence around.

Jurors trusted paper more than people. It was a fact. Psychologists had conducted studies of trials, both short and long. Regardless of the case, when the jury started to deliberate the first thing they looked at was the paper, the days or months of testimony were merely to refute or confirm what was on the paper.

Gadd took a step towards Father Stiles. She handed him the reports from the church's accountant, and then continued.

"I notice that three years ago, the church received fourteen thousand dollars in anonymous donations, correct?"

"I assume that's right, if the accountant said so."

"But then Joshua Krane was killed, Michael Collins disappeared, and then what happened to your anonymous donations?"

Father Stiles didn't answer, and any juror that hadn't been paying attention before was now on the edge of their seat. All eyes were on Father Stiles, anticipating a response that never came.

Breaking the silence.

"They went up, didn't they?" she pressed.

"I believe so."

"Believe?" Gadd said. "Or know?"

Father Stiles looked down at the papers in his hand, and then up at his interrogator.

"I know."

"In the year following Joshua Krane's death and disappearance of Michael Collins, the anonymous donations went up quite a bit, didn't they?"

"Yes."

"What were they?"

"I don't know, exactly."

Brenda Gadd grabbed the papers away from Father Stiles, and then pretended to read from the top page.

"Your anonymous donations went from $14,000 to $654,382, is that correct?"

"If that's what the accountant says, then that's correct."

"Does it sound correct?"

"Yes."

"And last year, the anonymous donations went from $654,382 to roughly $1.2 million dollars, is that correct?"

"I believe so."

"These donations saved your church from being shut down by the Archdiocese of New York, didn't they?"

"God saved our church."

"Right," Gadd said. "God and Michael John Collins."

She walked back to her table, set the stack of papers down, and shook her head.

"I have no further questions for you, Father."

CHAPTER FIFTY SIX

Michael didn't return to the Sunset until long after dark. The exercise had been good for him, but he still couldn't stop thinking about Andie and the case. There were things that just didn't seem right, although if asked to name one, Michael couldn't.

He pulled the kayak onto the shore, and then carried it back to the boathouse. Michael hung his life-vest on the rack, and put the paddle in a large barrel with the others. On his way up to the bar, he noticed a large, silver Airstream trailer parked at the end of the road.

New guests, Michael thought.

He walked up the steps, onto the deck, and into the bar. It was crowded with the usual mixture of retired vagabonds, college kids re-enacting the early days of Che Guevara, and people who were simply lost on a variety of levels. Michael found a seat at the bar. Sammy Alvarez saw him, and immediately uncapped a bottle of Corona and stuck a wedge of lime on top.

"Luise says hi." Sammy put the beer in front of Michael. "You be careful."

"Don't worry." Michael pushed the lemon wedge into the head of the bottle. "She'll be fine."

"I'm not worried about her." Sammy tipped his cowboy hat and raised an eyebrow. "I was talking about you."

"You hear anything from Kermit?"

"No," Sammy said. "Senorita Larone calls every day, but no Kermit."

Michael took a drink of beer, and then ordered a plate of quesadillas. Sammy wrote it down, and then he passed the slip of paper back to the kitchen.

"Anybody come around asking for me?"

"No." Sammy shook his head. "Should there be?"

"Hope not." Michael knocked twice on the wood bar in front of him.

As the evening went on, the bar started to empty and eventually only one other person besides Michael remained. He was an older man, probably in his early seventies. Too far past his prime to be a Deti hit man, Michael thought, but the old man kept looking at him. That made Michael nervous.

When their eyes met for the thirteenth or fourteenth time, the man said, "You look familiar." He had a thick New York accent.

"Must be mistaken." Michael glanced at the door.

"No." He shook his head. "I swear I've seen that face." The old man caught Sammy's attention, ordered two beers, and walked from his end of the bar toward Michael. Then, without asking, he pulled up a stool.

"If you're here to kill me, just say so."

The man laughed.

"I'm a bit too old for that," he said. "Maybe in my youth." He stuck his hand out, and introduced himself as Stanley "Big Stan" Pappas.

"You don't look so big."

"I've shrunk." Big Stan rubbed his nose and smiled, as Sammy placed two beers in front of them. "I worked the night beat for the N.Y.P.D. for thirty years," he said. "That's why you caught my attention. A lifetime of trying to remember a million faces." Big Stan opened his wallet and placed a few bills on the bar, and then picked up the bottle and took two long draws.

"Hard to turn off that switch." He burped and returned his wallet to his back pocket. "You just wait; I'll remember where I saw you before, just wait."

"Retired?"

Big Stan nodded. "Where you from, maybe I seen you back home?"

"Boston, originally," Michael said. "But I spent a few years living in the Vladick projects off Madison, finished up high school, and then got the hell out."

"I'm a product of beautiful Holmes Towers myself ... well, what eventually became Holmes, but Vladick ..." Big Stan brought the bottle to his lips. "Tough part of New York."

In a way that is only possible with men, they talked for an hour and a half about nothing particular and nothing personal. Topics went from the weather today to the weather tomorrow to the weather this month, and then this season. There were the usual suspects of sports, crooked politicians, and the eternal debate over whether the feelings experienced during an orgasm and a Number Two stem from the same portion of the cerebral cortex.

During this time, Sammy kept serving up the beers. The Sunset didn't have many rules, but so long as there were customers, the bar was open.

At three-thirty in the morning, Michael and Big Stan stumbled outside. Big Stan wanted to give Michael a tour of his Airstream, and Michael couldn't really think of any reason not to accept the invitation.

Big Stan opened the door to the large aluminum bubble trailer.

"This is a Safari 19. Others are larger, but after the wife died, this one just felt right."

They walked down the center aisle, and Big Stan pointed out the Safari's many features. He was especially proud of the television, located conveniently above the refrigerator, and then there was the shower directly across from it.

"Got my laptop hooked up right here so I can get all the news from back home off the ol' triple-W." They both stared at Big Stan's laptop computer, paying proper homage to the flat, black box.

"When you think about it," Big Stan surveyed his palace, "this is all the room you really need."

Big Stan opened the refrigerator and took out a beer.

"Another?"

"No." Michael started walking back down the trailer's aisle. "Better be heading off."

"Hold on just a minute," Big Stan said. "Only alcoholics drink alone, so don't go makin' me one."

Michael had walked to the door, but stopped, deciding to stay.

He followed Stan to the dinette in the front of the Safari, and they sat down across from another. Whether it was his well lubricated mind or something else, Michael decided that he could venture into areas more pressing than sports and poop. "You ever run into Mario Deti?"

"As a cop?"

Michael nodded, and Big Stan looked up at the ceiling as if he was searching for a memory floating around in the air above him.

"Not run into, exactly, but you'd hear stories. Why?"

"A friend."

"Good luck on that one." Big Stan laughed. "Your friend want a job or what?"

"Owes him money."

Big Stan nodded.

"Lots of people do." They sat for another minute or two while Big Stan drained a good portion of his beer. "How much?"

"A lot."

"Gambling?"

"Not sure," Michael said. "Not sure I want to know the details."

"Wise man." Big Stan raised his beer to Michael, and then took another sip. "So how much is a lot?"

Michael started to say, and then hesitated.

"Come on." Big Stan choked back another burp. "It's becoming increasingly unclear which portions of this conversation I'll remember in the morning."

"All right," Michael said. "$500 million."

Big Stan laughed. "And your friend's alive?"

"Very much so."

"Then he ain't dealing with the Mario Deti I know." Big Stan took another drink. "The mob biz isn't what it used to be and $500 million. ..." Big Stan shook his head. "Forget about it."

"So you're saying my friend doesn't owe $500 million."

"First, I'm saying Mario Deti doesn't have $500 frickin' million for your friend to owe him to begin with." Big Stan pointed at Michael. "Maybe fifty or a hundred million, at the peak, but he's got feds all over him now, people photographing and recording his every move. Think about it."

"Could be laundered." Michael tested him.

"Could be." He rolled his bloodshot eyes toward the ceiling again, continuing the search. "Could be a lot of things. But if it's true, your friend's dead." Big Stan ran his hand along his throat. "Deti doesn't fuck around. Even at his age, he doesn't fuck around."

"My friend, he's had his apartment trashed, threatening cards —"

"Cards?" Big Stan smiled and shook his head. "Greeting cards? The mob doesn't go around trashing apartments and sending spooky messages via Hallmark. They throw you in the back of a car, hook a couple electrical cords up to your nuts, and go until you are either dead or give them what they want."

Big Stan finished his beer.

"The toughest criminal to catch is the one who just does it," Big Stan said. "When you just do it, there's nothing there to investigate. Screwing around with this stuff you're talkin' about creates a trail. Deti is still out roaming the streets of our fair city because he's not that stupid. Your friend may be in serious shit, but it ain't with Mario Deti. I'd bet my left nut."

Big Stan got up from the table and stumbled back to the bathroom. He opened the small door, and turned toward Michael.

"You watch too many television shows," he said, disappearing into the tiny Airstream bathroom. "Beware the frickin' cards," he shouted, and then laughed.

Michael decided it was time to go.

"I'm heading out." Michael slid away from the table, and then stood up.

"Hold on." The toilet flushed, and Big Stan emerged from the bathroom. He looked at Michael and half-smiled. "Okay." He raised both hands in the air. "Big Stan now provides you his blessing and you may now leave."

He sat down on the edge of his bed, and then kicked off his cowboy boots and laid back.

"You have a real nice trailer," Michael said. "Thanks for the drinks."

"No." Big Stan closed his eyes. "Thank you."

As Michael reached the door, Big Stan's eyes opened wide and he sat straight up.

"I know where I've seen you."

Michael stopped cold, and looked back.

Big Stan pointed at him.

"The Post's website." He stabbed his finger at him again. "Yesterday," he nodded. "You're the. ..." Big Stan's eyes fluttered, as Michael went in and out of focus. "The lawyer." He smiled and lay back down, again. "I never do forget a face. Jesus H. Jehosephat, I'm good."

CHAPTER FIFTY SEVEN

There was little in life as wonderful as a cool shower courtesy of Hut No. 7 after a day of playing in the Caribbean and a night of drinking Coronas with some weird old man at the Sunset's bar. Michael let the water roll off his head and down his back. He thought about Big Stan and whether he was right about Deti. If Deti wasn't after him, then who?

Michael shut off the water, and stepped out of the stall and into the hut's small bathroom. He toweled off, located a pair of boxers and slipped them on.

He finished the remainder of his nighttime routine, and walked out of the bathroom and over toward the bed. It was then that he noticed that the room smelled like cherry tobacco. Every hair on his neck stood on end, and his heart rate spiked. The Professor had found him.

Michael was ready for the attack. He turned. His arms out, fists clinched, knowing that this was it.

Then the room lit up. Night became day as bright white light streamed through the windows from the outside.

"Stop, Senor Collins. Put your hands in the air." The deep voice boomed over a bullhorn from outside. Confused, Michael raised his hands up in the air as the commands continued. He had no place to run. "Keep your hands where we can see them, Senor Collins. You are under arrest."

Another voice just outside the door said, "You got the wrong guy. I'm not Michael Collins."

It was the Professor.

"I told you, I'm not Michael Collins."

Still unsure, Michael slowly put his hands down and crept toward the window. With the tips of his fingers, he raised the blind an inch and looked outside.

Hut No. 7 was surrounded by five Mexican police cars, each with their headlights on high. The space was bathed in light. A dozen men stood with their guns drawn. They were pointed at the Professor, just three feet in front of the hut's door.

"I'm telling you that this is a mistake." The Professor's eyes darted from side to side as four men approached and placed him in handcuffs. "My name is Dwight Keiffer. I have my papers in my back pocket. You can take a look for yourself."

The officers led the Professor over to the man with the bull-horn, who was presumably the Police captain. The captain set the bullhorn down on the hood of the car, and then he proceeded to pat down the Professor.

The captain started near the Professor's ankles and worked his way up one leg and down the other. Then, he felt around the waist of the Professor's windbreaker, pausing, and then feeling the area around the pocket.

"Gun?"

The captain reached into the jacket's front pocket and removed a Glock pistol. The other police officers started to talk among themselves. The captain set the gun down on the hood of the car next to the bullhorn, and reached into the Professor's back pocket.

He removed the passport and wallet, and read the documents silently to himself. The captain turned toward the crowd that had formed behind the police cars, and called for Sammy Alvarez to come forward.

Sammy emerged. He walked up to the police captain, with Luise just a few steps behind. In Spanish, the captain asked Sammy if the man standing before him in handcuffs was Michael Collins.

Sammy Alvarez hesitated, and then nodded. "*Si.*"

"That's him," added Luise.

"*Bueno.*"

The Police captain ordered the officers to take "Senor Collins" back to the police station while he called the embassy in Mexico City.

The Professor protested as he was hustled toward the waiting police car.

"This is ridiculous." The Professor started to resist, but the officers pushed him hard into the back seat. "What are you doing? Where are you taking me?"

The car door slammed shut, and one by one, the motorcade of police turned and drove away from the Sunset as the crowd of tourists dispersed.

CHAPTER FIFTY EIGHT

Dwight Keieffer. Michael wrote the Professor's name down on the back page of one of his paperback novels, and then he shoved the book into his green knapsack. He ran to the bathroom, gathered up his toiletries and put them in the bag. Then he went back into the room and grabbed his clothes off the floor.

Michael stuffed the clothes inside, and took the picture of his revolutionary namesake off of the nightstand and packed it away.

"That's it." Michael swung the knapsack over his shoulder. "How long do you think we have until they figure out they have the wrong guy?"

"At least two hours," Sammy said. "They have to take him to the police station. That's about forty-five minutes, and then the captain isn't going to want to admit that he arrested the wrong man, so more back and forth."

"Okay." Michael took a breath, taking a second to think. They would be looking for him at the Cancun airport, so that was out. He needed a way to get across the border without going through customs. "How long to the border by car?"

"You don't want to do that." Luise shook her head. "*Policia* love stopping tourists and hustling a bribe."

"All right." Michael thought for another second, running through his options. There was always the bus, but he would stand out, never blend, and there weren't any train connections in this part of Mexico. "What about the airport at Playa del Carmen?"

"Never been there," Sammy said, "but it's all private airplanes, corporate jets."

"Perfect." Michael started walking toward the door. "Can one of you take me?"

"I can." Luise smiled.

"No." Sammy put his hand on his niece's shoulder, not liking her intentions. "I'll take him. You stay here and watch things until I get back."

"Fine," Luise said with a pout. Then the three of them walked out the door. Luise walked up toward the Sunset's bar and office, and Sammy and Michael walked down toward Sammy's truck.

"It's the white F-10." Sammy pointed at the Ford pickup truck parked next to a shed a hundred yards off the main road. Michael climbed in the passenger side, and Sammy got behind the wheel and cranked the engine over. A couple of tries later, the engine started and they were on their way.

"Airport has to be closed at this hour." Michael looked at the clock on the truck's dashboard. "Maybe we can find a hotel where I can crash until morning."

"Sounds good." Sammy put the truck into reverse. "It'd be best if I left you anyway, in case the police come back."

"What are you going to say?"

"That it was late and I was drunk." Sammy turned the wheel, and shifted the truck into high gear.

"But you aren't."

"I will be." Sammy laughed. "As Senor Kermit says, 'By the time they come back, I'll be one very drunk *muchacho*.' "

CHAPTER FIFTY NINE

Michael found a vacant room in a rundown cinderblock motel across the road from Playa del Carmen's private airport. He paid cash for the room, signed nothing, and found himself in a lumpy bed watching the digital numbers on the nightstand clock gradually increase from 4:32 to 9:15. A count occasionally disrupted by moments of sleep.

He got up when he heard the first jet fly thirty feet over his motel room. It was hard to miss. The windows rattled, and the bed shook. Either the airport was open or a jet just crashed into the hotel's parking lot.

Michael grabbed his green knapsack and walked out of the hotel room into the morning light. He crossed the street, and then went through a small parking lot filled with limousines and imported vehicles, all black and spotless, and then finally into the airport's small terminal.

As soon as the glass doors slid open, a man in a white linen suit and tie came toward Michael. By the way he was dressed and the gun strapped to his hip, it was clear that the man was both security and concierge. "May I help you, senor?"

"Yes." Michael reached into his pocket and retrieved two hundred dollars. "I'm looking for a flight." He passed the money. "Any assistance you could provide would be appreciated."

"Of course." The suited man casually placed the money in his pocket. "A private flight?"

"Very."

"Simply wait in our lounge and I can see if there are any pilots available."

As directed, Michael walked through the marble entryway to a plush lounge. Thick red carpet covered both the floor and walls. The room was furnished with egg-shaped chairs and oversized ottomans upholstered in white leather, which surrounded a series of black onyx tables.

The '70s had returned, Michael thought, and unfortunately it appeared to be on purpose.

He picked up a copy of the Economist magazine off of the table, sat down, and began flipping through the articles. Michael found one that caught his interest. An article by Nobel-prize winner Joseph Stiglitz related to the creation of an international bankruptcy tribunal for third-world countries.

"Excuse me, senor."

Michael looked up. The concierge/security guard was standing with a squat man in a red jacket and pilot's hat.

"I believe Senor Chavarro will be able to assist you."

The pilot sat down across from Michael.

"I was told that you were seeking a private flight."

"That's correct," Michael said. "I'm not interested in waiting in lines at the border."

"*Si*," Chavarro said. "Private." Then, he lowered his voice. "Where do you want to go?"

Michael started to answer, and then paused. If ever there was a chance to truly escape, this was it. Anywhere he wanted to go, this man could take him.

"I go to Cuba," Chavarro said. "Columbia, Virgin Islands, Chile," he continued. "From there we can arrange a flight to Europe or Asia on a larger plane."

"No." Michael shook his head. "New York. I want to go to New York."

Chavarro nodded. "A more difficult trip."

"I understand." Michael reached inside his green knapsack and handed Chavarro fifty thousand dollars in cash. "Down payment for the gas."

CHAPTER SIXTY

S hortly after Michael sat down in one of the cabin's eight leather seats, Chavarro came out of the Gulfstream G 550's cockpit.

"Almost ready to go." He walked down the aisle holding a pair of folded gray pants, matching shirt, and baseball cap. "I'll let you know when we're twenty minutes away from Key West International."

Chavarro handed the pants, shirt, and hat to Michael.

"Customs requires us to stop at the first available airport once we cross the border to get inspected." He looked down at the clothes. "I need you to change before we land. A man from the ground crew will wheel the stairs up to the plane and come on board. After he comes inside, leave and walk around the outside of the airplane, inspecting it, you know. I need it to look good for the security cameras and the men watching in the tower." He paused. "The Immigration and Customs Agent will come on board, we'll talk, he'll take a look around and then leave."

"What about the real ground crew?"

Chavarro dismissed the question.

"We do a lot of business in Florida, senor," he said. "I know the ground crew and the agent that works this airport well.

When the agent leaves, just come back inside and we'll finish the trip. Should get in before the storm hits." He smiled and patted Michael on the shoulder. It was as if he made this trip every day, which he probably did.

"I'll have a certificate that we already went through customs, so that won't be an issue in New York. We'll land and you can go."

Chavarro turned, and began walking back to the cockpit. Along the way he pointed to the airplane's minibar.

"Help yourself to whatever. The business center in the back also has a phone and computer with internet access, if you need it."

"Thanks."

"You paid for it, senor," Chavarro said.

When the plane leveled off, Michael took out the paperback novel that he had shoved in his knapsack, but the novel wasn't to read.

He unfastened his seatbelt, and walked to the business center in the back of the plane. The "business center" was actually just a standard desk stocked with office supplies, a computer and a phone.

Michael checked his watch, and figured that he had about forty minutes before arriving in Key West. Plenty of time. Michael turned on the computer, waited for it to boot, and then logged onto the internet.

"All right, Professor, let's see who you are." Michael opened the book, and turned to the back page of the novel where the Professor's name was written. He typed DWIGHT KEIEFFER into the search engine. He got hundreds of hits; none of them relevant. Then he tried a different approach.

Michael typed the name in, again, but placed quotes around it, and then added "New York City." He pressed enter, and this time only twenty-five webpages popped up on the screen.

Michael scrolled down the list and then stopped: Guardian Security and Investigations, L.L.C.

The name was familiar. Michael remembered it from billing statements he had submitted to the court while still an associate at the firm. Wabash, Kramer & Moore used Guardian Security. Sometimes the work was official, but more often it was off-book, meaning that the information was sought, but no questions would be asked and no records would exist.

Guardian Security was filled with former FBI, New York cops, and even ex-CIA.

Michael clicked on the link, and up came a listing of Guardian's investigators and a brief biography. Halfway down the list, there was the Professor's name – Dwight Keieffer: Fifteen-year veteran of the Federal Bureau of Investigation, White Collar Crime Unit, specializes in asset and background searches, corporate investigations, civil litigation, executive protection, electronic surveillance, and missing person investigations. Mr. Keiffer was an honors graduate of Penn State and held a masters degree in psychology from Wake Forest University.

Michael got out of his seat, pacing as the pieces started to fall into place. For the first time, Michael felt his odds of survival increase and the scope of conflict narrow.

He should have known that, as Big Stan said, Mario Deti doesn't send frickin' greeting cards. And, if not Deti – if Deti was just a cover story, a myth – then Lowell Moore was one of the few who had the resources. Plus Moore had the connection to Keiffer. But why?

Greed was the first thing to pop into Michael's head. Nothing ever seemed like it was enough for Lowell Moore. The firm could never be too big. He could never have too many awards on his wall or wins under his belt, and he could never have enough money. But this all seemed like too big of a risk for just extra cash. There had to be more.

Michael picked up the phone and dialed information.

"I need the number for Taylor Goss & Associates in New York please." He waited, and then a computerized voice recited the number. Michael pressed the pound key to be patched through. Then a click, and the phone rang.

"Goss & Associates."

"Yes," Michael said. "I need to talk to Taylor Goss right away, it's an emergency."

"And you are?"

"A potential client."

"And your name?"

"That's not important. Get him on the line."

The receptionist hesitated.

"I'm sorry he's in court right now, can I take a message?"

Michael rolled his eyes. It was the oldest excuse in the book.

"I know that he isn't in court, so just get him." Michael paced the cabin. The phone pressed hard to his ear. "It's regarding Andie Larone. Tell him that."

"Please hold." An instrumental version of the song "Sexual Healing" by Marvin Gaye piped through the line.

Then, "This is Taylor Goss, may I help you?"

"It's me."

"And who might that 'me' be?"

"Your co-counsel in the Larone matter."

Goss didn't say anything at first.

"Wait." Michael heard Goss set the phone receiver down on his desk, and then the sound of the door to his office close shut. A few seconds later, he was back on the line. "I'm obligated to advise you that it's in your best interest to turn yourself in. Understand?"

"For now that's not happening, but thanks for the tip."

"You know I can't represent you," Goss said. "So what do you want?"

"Has Andie entered into the deal yet?" There was silence. "Just tell me if she entered into the deal."

"No," Goss said, "but she will."

"You have to give me a few days. Things are happening that I can't get into, but I think I understand – "

"I'm not waiting," Goss said. "It's not in my client's interest to wait for you."

"It is in her interest," Michael said. "I'm going to prove she's innocent."

"How?"

Michael didn't have an answer just yet.

"I'm working on it."

"Tell me what you plan to do," Goss said. "I can't just ask her to wait because you tell her to. I need more."

"Ask her."

"No." Goss was getting impatient. "I'm not even going to tell her we spoke. She's confused right now, and this would only make it worse."

"You have to."

"Goodbye, Michael," he said. "And don't call here anymore. I can't help you."

CHAPTER SIXTY ONE

As the plane's wheels touched down, Michael looked up from his notepad. On it, he had drawn a timeline, starting with the Joshua Krane murder and ending with the discovery of the Professor's identity and his connection with Lowell Moore. He thought about gaps in the timeline and missing information, questions that still needed answers.

He needed an event, a trigger. Greed couldn't be characterized as an event. Greed was just an emotion, and it was far too simple of an explanation.

The plane jerked to a stop, and then began taxiing to the end of Hoboken Airfield, a private airstrip on a patch of drained wetlands about a quarter-mile from the New York Giants' football stadium.

Chavarro's voice filled the cabin via the airplane's intercom system. He gave a summary of the trip, miles and average speed. Then he reported the current time and outside temperature, followed by a warning about a storm coming in that night.

Great, Michael thought. Another jacket to buy.

The engines whirred down to a stop, and Michael saw a ground crew start to scurry around the plane through the window. Above them, the sky was a solid gray wall, punctuated by a few black birds circling near the top.

305

Chavarro opened the cockpit door.

"You're all set, senor." He walked down the aisle toward Michael. "After I get fuel, I'm heading back."

"Thanks." Michael extended his hand and the two men shook. "I assume there are cabs outside."

"The charter service called a limousine," Chavarro said. "He'll take you where you want to go."

"Appreciate that." Michael took a final look out the window, and then shoved the notepad into his knapsack. He slung the knapsack over his shoulder and stood.

Chavarro led Michael down the aisle toward the door.

He grabbed the large lever on the airplane's door, and then pulled it down as two large bolts were lifted up and the door opened.

Cold air rushed into the cabin, and Michael paused. It wasn't, however, the frozen gust or the raw smell of coming snow that made him stop. He realized that his timeline of events had been too narrow. His analysis started too late.

"Everything all right?"

Michael looked at him. "*Maltow.*"

"Pardon me, senor?"

"*Maltow.*" Michael repeated it with a broad smile, knowing that the name made no sense to the pilot. "*Maltow* was the trigger," he said. "Just need to find out why."

CHAPTER SIXTY TWO

Michael didn't take the limousine that the pilot had arranged for him. He wanted anonymity, and he didn't accept favors from strangers, at least not anymore. Michael walked past the suited chauffeur standing next to the black GMC Suburban, and waved at one of the yellow taxis waiting across the street.

The taxi pulled around, picked him up, and within thirty minutes they had arrived at the sleek W Times Square hotel. It was the hotel where Michael and Kermit had moved after the Professor trashed their room at the Helmsley. Michael didn't know whether Kermit had changed hotels or not, but since the room was still under Michael's name and more importantly, still secured with Michael's credit card, he figured that Kermit was still there.

Michael rode the elevator up to the twenty-second floor and got out. He walked down the hall, and removed the unreturned key card from his wallet.

"Here we go." Michael slid the key through the magnetic card reader. A small, red light turned to green, and Michael opened the door. A foul odor escaped into the hallway. It was a combination of incense, pot, stale pizza, sweat, body odor, and permanent magic markers.

The shades in the room had been drawn closed and every available surface was adorned with tiny white candles. The sound of Coltrane filled the room.

"Kermit." Michael proceeded around random articles of clothing, fast food containers, and dozens of empty cans of Red Bull Energy Drink. "Kermit." Then Michael saw him.

Kermit hung upside down in the bathroom doorway with black magic markers in each hand. He was buck naked except for the pair of gravity boots that suspended him above the floor and the tin foil wrapped around his head.

"You okay?"

"Don't block the view." Kermit motioned for Michael to move to the side. "I'm almost there."

Michael looked at the far wall where Kermit stared intensely. A half-dozen poster boards filled with mathematical equations were taped to it. Kermit's brow furrowed, and then released. "Nope." He shook his head. "Lost it, *mi amigo*."

Kermit pulled himself up to the metal bar that had been screwed into the door's frame, lifted himself, and then dismounted. A few weeks ago, he had been a drugged-out Nadia Comaneci. Now the descriptor "naked" could be added to the string of adjectives.

"When was the last time you left this room?"

Kermit looked around, his eyes glazed.

"The numeric galaxy was out of alignment, *mi primo hermano*." He made the sign of rain falling to the earth, and then light exploding from the heavens. "Had to force myself to piece it all back together, again, for the good of us all."

"Did you do it?"

Kermit stared at the poster boards.

"Close, very close." Then he looked at Michael and smiled. "That must be why you're here. You came back, because the numbers started to get lined up again."

"Possible." Michael picked one of the empty pizza boxes off of the desk and placed it by the over-flowing garbage can. "Can you still help me out?"

Kermit hedged.

"I don't know. Got lots of work to do."

Michael looked at the poster boards.

"I need you out there helping me, not trapped in here."

"You getting back together with Andie?"

"I don't know." Michael answered honestly.

"Then I can't help you." Kermit walked toward the window and relit a half-dozen candles.

"I need my old friend," Michael said.

"Well, she's an older friend." Kermit moved to the candles on the television set, and started to light those. "You haven't really heard her out. Just left us. That breaks the K-Man's heart." Kermit took his black magic marker and drew a circle on his bare chest. "Right underneath here, man, lays a broken beat-beat boom-boom."

"What do I need to do?"

"Hear her out." Kermit said. "And hear me out. That would be a start."

"All right." Michael looked around. "And what about this?" He pointed at the poster boards, and then the candles.

Kermit scratched his head. "Well, there are certain things that are prohibited by the prophet Dr. Moo Yung Song, but if I were to go to the bathroom, say in a minute or two, and at that very moment an act of God were to open up the window and somehow dispose of certain little pieces of paper that are also filled with certain little digits." Kermit tipped his head to the side as the thought worked through his clouded mind. "The K-man would be very grateful for the fresh start."

Michael looked at Kermit and nodded.

"I can sense an act of God coming on."

CHAPTER SIXTY THREE

A large screen hung from the ceiling of the crowded conference room.

"When was he apprehended?" Gadd asked, and the United States Ambassador to Mexico responded. The audio coming from the speaker in the center of the table was slightly out of sync with the video picture on the screen, giving the effect of a poorly dubbed foreign movie. "Why has it taken so long to contact me? I've got a grand jury investigation going on here."

Gadd looked at Vatch across the table, while Tammy Duckstein rolled her eyes.

"We had to confirm that we had the right man." The ambassador's tone was proper New England. The private boarding school education and direct hereditary line back to the Mayflower was obvious.

"And do you?"

"We believe so," the ambassador said, "although he is quite larger than the height and weight listed on your information sheet."

"What do you mean by larger?" Condescension dripped from every word Vatch spoke. He hated the elites in every form.

"I don't know." The ambassador shrugged. "Just bigger that's all, but we had a confirmation from the man working at the resort that this was, in fact, Michael Collins."

"What about the photographs we sent you?" Gadd asked. The mood in the room, which had been relaxed and excited only moments ago, started to tense.

The ambassador shook his head. "I'm not aware of any photographs."

"Electronically," Vatch said. "I e-mailed all sorts of photos electronically."

"I'm sorry." The ambassador now started looking nervous, himself. "I'm not aware of any photographs, electronic or otherwise."

"Hold on." Gadd leaned over to the young assistant sitting next to her. They conversed, and then Gadd looked back at the ambassador. "We're going to fax you one right now." She whispered more instructions to the assistant, and then he disappeared into another room. "You've spoken with the man, correct?"

"Yes," the ambassador said, "of course I have. This was designated a high priority."

"And he didn't have anything to say?"

"Well, he was most adamant that we had apprehended the wrong fellow, but they all say that. We can't. ..." The ambassador turned toward the fax machine beeping and buzzing on the credenza behind him. "Here it is."

They watched the ambassador, as he waited and watched the fax machine. Finally he pulled a piece of paper out of the tray.

The ambassador's frame shrunk as he studied the faxed photograph of Michael John Collins. "Oh, my." He shook his head. "This isn't right at all."

CHAPTER SIXTY FOUR

Pretty lame ride." Kermit ran his hand across the dashboard of the newly purchased baby-blue Toyota Camry. $3,000 cash, a handshake, an agreement to delay filing the paperwork with the Department of Motor Vehicles for thirty days, and the car was his. "This ain't nothing like the El Camino, my friend, that Camino *tener cojones*." Kermit reclined the seat a little. "Where is this place, anyway?"

"We're getting close." Michael clicked on the dome light above them so he could see, and then he checked the map. "Should be right up here." He signaled, and then turned into a dimly lit subdivision.

Snow had begun to fall, not heavy, but the flakes combined with the limited number of street lights made it difficult to navigate.

"So let me get this straight." Kermit pressed a button to lock and unlock the door, repeatedly. "Mario Deti, the mobster guy, was a story? He really isn't connected to this at all. Moore, the geeky L-Man, was making it all up?"

"That's what I think." Michael glanced at Kermit, and then back at the house numbers. "He needed the money back, but didn't want me to know it was him. He knew I had heard the rumors about Krane, so he let my imagination fill in the gaps."

"At least that's what you think."

"Mobsters don't send greeting cards and trash hotel rooms."

"And who is this broad?"

"She's not a broad," Michael said. "Her name is Rhonda Kirchner. Went to law school together, started at the firm at the same time."

"Okay." Kermit stretched his long arms a few inches from the back windshield, and then yawned. "An esquire of the female stripe."

Michael slowed down to five miles per hour, trying to read the house numbers and determine whether they were going up or down.

"Whoa." Kermit's hands went from stretched behind his head to straight out in front of him. "You gotta stop man."

Michael, who had been trying to read house numbers, slammed on the brakes, and the car slid to a stop after only a few feet.

"Something's going on." Kermit looked at the police barricade in front of them.

"Something." Michael felt the knot begin to form in his stomach, again, and the screws in his head weren't too far behind. He turned the car around, and found a place to park a few blocks back. "Wait here. Keep the car running in case we have to clear out in a hurry."

"I can't come with you?"

"I need you to stay here." Michael picked up his recently purchased baseball cap and red plastic-rimmed reading glasses. "Lots of cops around." He buttoned up his new wool pea coat, and then got out of the car, putting the hat and glasses on once he was outside.

Michael walked up the sidewalk, past the police barricades, and then over to a group of neighbors huddled across the street from Rhonda Kirchner's house. He stood there for a few minutes, and then turned to the man standing next to him. "What happened?"

"Rhonda," he said, "a tragedy." The man paused, wanting to continue, but knowing that in the spirit of good taste he should allow the conversation to unfold more reluctantly.

"Tom returned home from work with the two kids. Opened the garage door, pulled inside, and saw that Rho's Volvo station wagon was running." The neighbor looked around to see if anybody else was listening, and then continued. "That should have been a warning, but Tom didn't put it together until little Bethy pointed at the car and asked why mommy was sleeping."

"How long's it been?"

"Ambulance came and took her about two hours ago." The neighbor nodded toward the ambulance across the street. "Heard they were about finished."

"Suicide, case closed."

"I guess." The neighbor shrugged. He didn't understand the statistics.

According to Johns Hopkins University, lawyers were more than three and a half times more likely to suffer from major depression than the general population. The National Institute for Occupational Safety and Health found that lawyers were more than twice as likely to commit suicide. It was the perfect way for Lowell Moore to get rid of a problem associate who was asking too many questions and interested in the wrong types of things.

Michael broke away from the crowd, and crossed over to the other side of the street.

"Tom." Michael waved. "Tom Kirchner." He walked up the driveway toward a man who resembled the person in the picture that Michael had seen in Rhonda's office.

"Yes." Tom looked at Michael, weary, his eyes bloodshot. "Can I help you?"

"I'm a friend of Rhonda."

"You are?"

"Yes," Michael said, a little too quickly. Skepticism crossed over Tom's face. "I worked with Rhonda at the firm."

"Didn't think she had any friends there." Tom's feelings about the prestigious Wabash, Kramer & Moore were clear.

"Well, she had me," Michael said. "Do you mind if we talk?"

Tom looked at his watch. Then he looked at the small crowd of neighbors still standing across the street, each of them wishing that they, too, had come over to get fresh information.

"I have to see my kids. They're at Grandma's house right now, but I need to see them."

"Understandable." Michael took a step away, and then decided that he couldn't wait. He needed information tonight.

"You mind if I use the bathroom?" Michael asked. "I drove all this way when I heard the news." He shrugged. "I'm embarrassed to ask, I really am."

Tom looked annoyed, but he was too tired to argue.

"It's up the stairs and to the left."

Michael thanked him. He went inside, and headed up the stairs. He felt awful about what he was about to do, but didn't see any other choice. He was convinced that *Maltow* was the key to understanding what had happened, and that *Maltow* would give him the information that he could use to get Andie out of jail and maybe even save himself.

Instead of taking a left, Michael took a right and walked into Rhonda's home office. He knew she had to have one. When each associate started at Wabash, Kramer & Moore, the firm provided a $5,000 "grant" for the associate to furnish and set up a home office. That way the associate didn't have any excuses for not billing several hours every night before they went to bed. Michael still remembered the memo announcing the program, the "Wabash, Kramer & Moore Flex-Schedule," whatever that meant.

Michael went inside and closed the door behind him.

He immediately went to Rhonda's computer and turned it on. The computer chimed as it powered up, and then a request for a login name and password appeared on the screen.

Michael swore under his breath and moved on.

He walked to the file cabinets, and flipped through the research files, sample pleadings, and copies of recent correspondence. Nothing.

Then he went back to the desk and opened the narrow pencil drawer in the middle. There wasn't much, but off to the side there was a stack of business cards bound together with a black clip. Michael picked up the stack, and shoved it in his pocket.

Then he opened the lower drawer on the desk. There, in the middle, was a green hanging folder marked "*Maltow.*"

Michael pulled it out of the drawer, and was flipping through its contents when Tom entered the room.

"What the hell are you doing?"

"I was just looking for a file we were working on together." Michael lifted the folder up so that Rhonda Kirchner's husband could see it.

"My wife died today." Tom's fists clinched into a fist. "It was that firm that – "

"I'm so sorry." Michael started walking toward the door. "I just wanted the file."

"You have three seconds to get out of my house," Tom said as Michael passed him. His eyes were watered. He was about to explode, and Michael couldn't blame him. "Three seconds."

Michael hustled out the door, shoving the file under his coat. "I'm sorry," he said, as he headed down the stairs, not waiting for a response.

###

In the rental car, Michael turned on the ceiling dome light so that he could see.

"Whatcha got? Whatcha got?" Kermit rubbed his hands together.

"We'll soon see." Michael opened the folder.

Inside, there were memos written by him, pleadings, discovery, correspondence, and of course, the settlement agreement. Michael skimmed over the documents, trying to allow the memories of the case to come back to him, but there were few.

The *Maltow* litigation was going on at the same time that Joshua Krane was being investigated. He had worked on the *Maltow* case, but Lowell had handled the teleconferences with the client and opposing counsel. Michael had just written the briefs.

"I don't see anything." Michael shook his head. "There has to be something in here, but it all looks so typical. It's just a case."

"Let me see." Kermit held out his hand. "I'll put my keen intellect to work."

Michael passed him the file, and removed the stack of business cards from his pocket. There were probably fifty cards in the stack. The first dozen or so were colleagues at Wabash, Kramer & Moore, with the home number and address for each handwritten on the back.

The next series of cards were personal. One was for a housekeeping service, another for a nanny placement agency, dry cleaning, grocery delivery, and so on. It was a team of service people who did everything around the house while Rhonda was trying to meet her billable hour requirements.

Towards the bottom of the stack, there were the cards from opposing counsel. The title of the litigation was handwritten underneath each of the counsel's name, and on the back, Rhonda had written notes about each attorney's personality and responsibilities in the litigation. It was a technique that every associate at the firm was taught when they first started.

Finally, at the very bottom, Michael found a familiar name. "Of course," Michael thought. "That only makes sense."

The business card was simple, black and white. The only graphic was the seal of the State of New York, and the rest was contact information for Tammy Duckstein, Staff Attorney, Departmental Disciplinary Committee for the First Department. On the back, Rhonda had written Tammy Duckstein's home number and address. They had been meeting and talking after hours.

CHAPTER SIXTY FIVE

Tammy Duckstein got up from her couch, and was walking toward her kitchen when there was a knock on the door. She looked at the clock. It was past eleven. Her daughter was out, but she had a key. Probably lost it again, Tammy thought. Her daughter was constantly leaving things at her father's house as she was shuttled back and forth every other week.

"Just a second." Tammy turned off the television and crossed the room.

She got to the door, unlatched the dead bolt, and then opened it. "You could have called, first, sweetie," she said. "It's late and I could have already gone to. ..."

"Rhonda Kirchner is dead."

Michael had rattled off a variety of instructions, which Kermit didn't remember, but that was the most important one: Tell her about Rhonda. "The fuzz say it was suicide, but don't believe the Man on this one."

"Who are you?" Tammy looked past Kermit to see if anyone else was there, and started to close the door. "Who told you where I live?"

"I'm friends with a guy you're looking for. You've been wanting to talk to him."

"Collins." Tammy's eyes narrowed.

"He isn't with me." Kermit held up his set of car keys, and then jangled them in front of her. "But he wants me to take you on a ride."

"Why don't you just tell me where he is and I can take myself?"

"No go, Princess Kay of the Milky Way." Kermit slipped the keys back in his pocket.

"Well, I'm not going anywhere with you. You're a complete stranger."

"Fine." Kermit turned and began walking down the steps. "This is all like, a take-it-or-leave-it deal." Kermit walked to the sidewalk outside Tammy's brownstone. "Last chance, senorita."

"Hold on." Tammy stood in the doorway, thinking of options, running through the list of things she could do, most of which she shouldn't. "Can you wait here and let me gather my things?"

"And let you call the cops? My instructions are to let you get a coat, and that's it." Kermit pointed at his eyes. "You're never to exceed the scope of my two 20/20 peepers."

"What?"

"Out of my sight." Kermit pointed at his eyes, again. "I'm not supposed to let you out of my sight, pretty lady." Tammy looked back at the inside of her apartment. She knew she should just let the strange man go, and then call Vatch. Let the FBI know that Michael Collins was back in New York, let the real cops chase the bad guys.

"I'm starting to freeze." Kermit stomped his feet. "What's the decision, counselor?"

CHAPTER SIXTY SIX

Kermit allowed Tammy Duckstein to slip on another pair of jogging pants, a turtleneck, and a heavy sweatshirt. Then, he allowed Tammy to get her jacket and purse. The cell phone was removed. All she had was her wallet and keys.

They rode in silence to East 59th, and then took a left on the famed Fifth Avenue. Driving past Central Park's children's zoo, the conservatory and Cedar Hill, Kermit pulled over.

"Go to one of the benches over by the Reservoir." Kermit pointed. "He'll find you, and if you try to make a call or take a detour, he says he'll see it happen and disappear."

"Okay." Tammy nodded, grateful to be getting out of the car.

"Good luck, lady friend." Kermit unlocked all the doors, and Tammy opened the passenger-side door and stepped outside.

Once in the street, Tammy started to thank Kermit for the ride out of habit, but then stopped. She was going insane. Tammy closed the car door, and Kermit sped away, leaving her alone.

Tammy walked across the street, and headed into the park on one of its many paved walking paths. Central Park was quiet and deserted. Most people were already holed up in their apartments or houses, preparing to get hit by the full front of the coming storm.

She eventually found a bench overlooking the partially iced-over Reservoir. Tammy brushed away the recently fallen snow, and sat down on the cold wood. It wouldn't be hard for Michael Collins to find her. She was the only person there.

Tammy waited, not minding the quiet. She could let her mind wander, trying to remember the last risk she had taken, the last time she had broken the rules. Nowadays Tammy lived through her daughter, who was supposedly sleeping over at a friend's house that night. Tammy was afraid to ask if that friend was a boy or a girl.

A pack of runners decked out in spandex sped past, and then an old man walking a dog.

Once they were gone, the park quieted again.

At a quarter past midnight, Michael appeared beside her and sat down. Without turning his head, he spoke.

"I'm hoping you have some answers for me."

"There's a warrant out for your arrest." Tammy stole a glance at the young man that she only knew through memos and photographs. "You should turn yourself in."

"That seems to be the consensus."

She kept her eyes forward, watching the snow fall. From a distance she hoped it would look just like two strangers sharing a park bench. Vatch could be out there watching, she thought. That would be a disaster.

"All right." Michael leaned back, stretching his legs out in front of him. "I go first."

"Okay." Tammy tried to calm her nerves and pretend like this was just part of the job. "Then I get some answers from you?"

"It's a deal."

"It's a deal, then." Tammy took a breath, and then brushed away some of the wet flakes that had landed on her cheek. "I work disciplinary. You know that, but what you probably don't know is that the job is routine. The same infractions occur all the time, maybe a fact or two changes, but it's the same stuff. The same questions. Every day, one of the staff attorneys is assigned to answer the phones and field these questions, and that's how I got *Maltow*."

"You answered the phone."

"That's right." Tammy nodded. "It was an associate from Wabash, Kramer & Moore."

"Rhonda Kirchner."

"Yes, I later found out who she was." Tammy swallowed hard, and then continued. "So I get this call, and we don't get calls from Wabash, Kramer & Moore or about Wabash, Kramer & Moore. None of the big boys are ever on our radar, but this associate starts telling me about the *Maltow* case."

"What about it?"

"At first, just background. That it was a big patent infringement case that the firm had involving the pacemaker battery."

"Well, sort of," Michael said. "Our client, Dr. Maltow, invented a pacemaker battery that could be recharged without surgery. You just put this machine over the heart and it sends a million tiny electrodes through the skin and recharges the battery. The only indication that it happened would be a little redness for a day or two. Every pacemaker sold worldwide uses this technology, and in turn, should pay Dr. Maltow a royalty."

"That was the allegation."

"Right." Michael agreed. "There was a debate about whether the patent truly claimed the new technology that was being used or whether the patent was so old that it had expired. We filed the lawsuit in the spring, I think, just as the statute of limitations was about to run against the three biggest pacemaker companies in the country."

"But it was also in the midst of the Joshua Krane litigation, at least that's what Rhonda told me."

"It was a crazy time," Michael said. "I would start a brief at five in the morning, work all day, and have thirty pages, edited and proofread, by midnight. I was billing fifteen to twenty hours a day, sleeping in my office. It's hard for me to imagine how I did it."

"What has Lowell told you about me? What did he say I was doing?"

Michael skipped over the "bitch" part.

"Told me there was a complaint about *Maltow*. That he didn't understand it, because the client was happy. It was a good settlement, and that if I didn't talk to you the case was going away."

"But he couldn't order you not to talk to me, because that would be obstruction."

"Exactly."

Tammy tested him.

"What did you think about the settlement agreement?" She watched, wanting to believe his innocence. But was he somebody that could be trusted? Certainly nobody in her office or the FBI thought he was.

Michael thought back to his days toiling as an associate. He could say that he was miserable, but that wouldn't be accurate. He was in his own world, then. He believed the firm's own hype, sacrificing a life that he didn't even know was possible until he met Andie.

Michael shook his head, coming back to the question.

"I didn't think much about it, other than it was big."

"$300 million."

"That's right," Michael said. "If it went to trial it would be in the billions, but $300 million was a fair settlement, given the risks."

"A lot of firms would kill to get a piece of that settlement."

"Other firms aren't Wabash, Kramer & Moore," Michael said. "We do the multimillion-dollar cases every day. We won't even take a patent case that's under $20 million."

"Were you in the *Maltow* settlement discussions?"

"No." Michael stomped his feet, trying to keep the circulation going in the cold. "I didn't negotiate the thing. I was just a scribe."

"Meaning?"

"It was in the midst of *Krane*," Michael said. "You have to understand that compared to *Krane*, *Maltow* was a boring case. No press coverage. No magazine covers. My focus was on *Krane*, that's all, and *Maltow* was just a case that I helped Lowell out on. I'd draft the memos or discovery, but Lowell had the client contact and he also took the lead with opposing counsel."

"Is that normal?"

"Depends on the case. Has a lot to do with client preference."

"So you didn't negotiate the settlement?"

"No." Michael shook his head. "But, why does that matter?"

Tammy decided to lay it out. What did she have to lose? She turned to Michael, looking at him until he turned to her. When she had his attention, Tammy spoke.

"It was a fake. That's why."

CHAPTER SIXTY SEVEN

Michael looked at Tammy, but didn't say a word. He had no doubt that she was telling the truth, but he couldn't understand how. How could a lawsuit be faked? There was so much paper and correspondence, it didn't make sense.

He felt the sudden need to move, get the blood that had thickened in the cold flowing again. Michael also wanted to make sure there wasn't anybody watching him. His eyes scanned the still, dark silhouettes, watching for a shape to change.

"Can you stay just for a few more minutes?"

"It's cold," Tammy said.

"I know." Michael stood, then he pointed. "Belvedere Castle is down that path. I'll follow behind. There's a bench near the top of the hill."

"Do you think people are watching?"

Michael scanned the edges of the park.

"You never know."

Tammy got off of the bench and started walking. Michael waited, and then followed from behind. They walked along the trail that ran parallel to Fifth Avenue, toward the Metropolitan Museum of Art. Lit from the ground, the building's stone facing glowed white, with the falling snow casting odd shadows on its face.

It took another ten minutes before the castle came into view. Belvedere Castle rose out of the gray Manhattan Schist, the second highest point in the park. The dark outline of the miniature castle overlooking the Great Lawn was simultaneously the most natural and unnatural structure in the park, and maybe in the whole city.

They followed the trail leading up to Vista Rock, but stopped short at a bench nestled in a grove of leafless London plane trees. Tammy sat down, and Michael sat down next to her.

"I'm not convinced." Michael was playing devil's advocate.

"That's fine. You don't have to believe me, but I've got enough to go forward with a formal inquiry to the board."

"Against Wabash, Kramer & Moore?"

"That's right." Tammy left out the part about the case and files being taken from her, the reluctance of her supervisor to even consider it, and the high likelihood that she will be fired if anyone ever learns about her current meeting.

"I talked to the defendants, and they don't have any record of ever being served with that lawsuit and they have no record of paying any money toward any settlement fund. And the court also doesn't have any record of the lawsuit, not one scrap of paper."

Michael shook his head.

"I must have filed a half-dozen motions in that case."

"Did you?" Tammy smiled. "Or did you just sign the motions and give them to your legal secretary to file?"

"What about the letters that I'd get from opposing counsel, the briefs they would file?"

"Faked. I have copies of some of the correspondence and motions, but the attorney for the Defendant told me he had never seen them before. He signed an affidavit stating he never worked on the *Maltow* case and I have a handwriting expert ready to testify that the signature of defense counsel is a forgery."

Michael leaned back and tried to remember any personal meeting with opposing counsel or any specific conversation, any deposition, any court appearance, anything that would make the case real.

"You were just a scribe," Tammy said. "Lowell would file the papers for you, or rather pretend to file them. And Lowell would talk to opposing counsel, not you. He would make the appearances in court, and you sat behind the computer and did the work."

"Why?"

"I don't know," Tammy said. "I think I know, but not for sure."

"All right," Michael said. "Let's hear it."

"Okay." Tammy looked at Michael. Her confidence was growing, and for the first time someone was actually listening to her theories. She was being taken seriously.

Tammy took a breath, and then punctuated every word: "He missed the deadline."

"What?"

"The lawsuit needed to be filed and served by a specific date, and Lowell Moore missed it. You had everything ready; and he just forgot or got busy or something. You said yourself it was crazy with the *Krane* investigation. I think he just made a mistake, a mistake that would have ended up costing the firm millions of dollars in a malpractice lawsuit and who knows about the firm's reputation."

Michael thought about it for awhile. The reputation of the firm, it was the one thing Lowell was interested in more than money itself. The firm was his legacy, his identity.

"What does Lowell say?"

"Lowell says you did it," she said. "That's how he's going to testify tomorrow morning at the grand jury."

"How would I pay a $300 million settlement out of my own pocket?" Michael asked, but before he finished, Michael already knew the answer. "Joshua Krane."

Tammy nodded.

"Agent Vatch loves that theory. Thinks you had a nervous breakdown after you missed the deadline and were too proud to admit it and take your lumps."

"So I murder my client and shoot myself in the face?"

"No, Reginald Thompson shot you in the face."

"And this disgruntled shareholder and I are somehow partners."

"Agent Vatch thinks so," Tammy said. "But Thompson wasn't a shareholder. That's just what was reported in the newspaper. He was former FBI, worked at a place called Guardian Security. Ever heard of it?"

Michael thought of the Professor.

"Yeah, they do work for the firm."

"Right, so Agent Vatch seems to think you two cooked up the scheme together, and then you double-crossed Thompson somehow."

"I was bleeding to death in the car at the time. Doesn't he get that? How could I double-cross the guy?"

"Maybe you have another partner." Tammy rubbed her hands together, trying to generate some warmth. "Anyway, I think it's more likely that Lowell took the money out of the firm's general account or maybe an escrow account for a larger client. Then he started shifting the money around, paying one settlement agreement with another to cover up the shortfall. All he has to do is show me the audited bank statements to prove I'm wrong."

"But he won't."

"Correct," Tammy said. "If the audited financials come back clean, then my theory falls apart."

"But if we get the financials and it shows that Lowell has been playing a shell game with the money, it'll establish a motive for Lowell killing Krane and prove that I didn't just take the money from Krane's secret accounts to fund this settlement agreement in the *Maltow* case."

"Right," Tammy said, "but nobody's interested in my theory or investigating your old firm."

"You think I can get them?"

Tammy avoided the question.

"A chance to clear your name, move on with your life." Tammy looked up at the castle's turret and stared. "But I can't know about it or direct it. It's something you just have to do."

"Is it something Rhonda Kirchner tried to do?"

There was a long silence, and then Tammy said what Michael already knew.

"She tried."

CHAPTER SIXTY EIGHT

Kermit picked Michael up at a 24-hour Dunkin' Donuts a block from Rockefeller Center.

"How did it go?"

Michael climbed inside the Camry. "I don't know." He shut the door. "Good, I guess."

"Guess?" Kermit shifted the car into gear, and then merged into traffic. "I thought all the secrets were going to be revealed by the mistress of the night, no?"

"I got the answers about *Maltow*, but. ..."

"What?" Kermit looked at Michael, and then turned back to the road in front of them. "But what?"

"I still need to visit another friend."

"It's late, *mi amigo*," Kermit said. "I gotta get some shut-eye."

"We have to do this tonight."

"They're going to be asleep," Kermit said. "You know? Sleep? That thing which we both need to have in order for our super-hero strength to be preserved for our daily fight for justice?"

"We have to do this now." Michael pointed at the approaching stoplight. "Take a left up here."

Kermit mumbled to himself, and then signaled for a left.

"Whoever it is, they ain't going to be coming to the door this late at night. Fact of life."

"I know." Michael organized the thoughts in his head. "I don't want my good friend to come to the door. I don't even want him to wake up, at least not right away."

"A surprise."

"Kind of," Michael said.

CHAPTER SIXTY NINE

He turned on the small light sitting on the nightstand. Then Michael pulled a chair up next to the bed and sat down. He held Vatch's loaded gun in his hand and stared down at the man who had been nothing but a thorn in his side whenever their paths seemed to cross.

It began when Michael took Vatch's deposition as a first-year associate. Vatch could barely control himself as Michael tore apart every piece of evidence that Vatch had purportedly collected against Michael's client. Michael poked holes in Vatch's theories, challenged Vatch's opinions with prior testimony he had given in other cases, and called Vatch out on every assumption.

Then there was Vatch's partner. Michael had never met her, just read the obituary. But he knew that he had come close to death that night. The headline in the paper could have just as easily described four dead as it had described the three: Joshua Krane; his killer, Reginald Thompson; and the female agent that was killed in the confrontation with Thompson in a nearby alley.

But here they were. After listening to Tammy Duckstein, Michael needed to talk to him, hear what he was thinking, and this was the only way. The police were looking for him, and Michael couldn't call and make an appointment.

He coughed and stamped his foot on the floor a few times.

Vatch didn't move.

Michael coughed, again, and then prodded Vatch with his foot.

Vatch rolled onto his side, pulling the cover up and grumbled.

"Anthony, too early to play cribbage. Back to bed."

Michael prodded Vatch a little harder this time.

"Francis." He prodded, again. "Wake up. I need to talk to you."

Vatch rolled over. His eyes opened, and then shut again.

"It's me, Michael Collins."

At the sound of Michael's name, his eyes opened wide. Initially there was panic. Michael was afraid Vatch would start screaming, but the panic soon turned into an icy stare.

"Collins." Vatch pushed himself up into a sitting position. "I underestimated you. Didn't think you had the guts."

"I want to talk to you."

"Well I want to kill you." Vatch looked at the gun, and his tongue flicked in and out. "I could have, outside the courthouse, but I didn't. Won't make that mistake again."

"That's nice," Michael said, "but right now, I want to talk." He noticed Vatch looking for his wheelchair and phone, which had both been taken into the other room. He was trapped. "You really shouldn't leave your window unlocked. Basic security."

"Anthony."

"What's that?"

"Nothing." Vatch shook his head.

"So I noticed your little shrine." Michael nodded toward the other room. "Kind of sick, really. You need a vacation."

"Fuck you," Vatch said. "This is over, Collins. We aren't having a conversation anymore. You want to shoot me, fine, but this is over."

"I get to decide when it's over." Michael looked down at the gun and took off the safety. "And for right now, I'm talking." He raised the gun, pointing it at Vatch's head. "So, I know that Reginald Thompson, the guy who killed Krane and left a little piece of shrapnel in my face, was former FBI, worked at Guardian Security. That's new information, withheld from the newspapers, but would've been nice to know. I was a victim after all. It could have caused me to ask questions sooner, maybe avoided all this, but in your wisdom, you kept it to yourself."Then, I find out that Dwight Keiffer, another guy who has tried to kill me, is also former FBI and also works at Guardian Security. In case you forgot, he's the man who the Mexican police caught creeping around with a loaded Glock."

"Then I look back at Helix Johannson," Michael said, "and I realize that the reason he's killed isn't because of Andie Larone or anyone else. He's killed because the FBI blows the surveillance. Incompetence at the bureau isn't surprising, but that's a lot of connections to the bureau. Don't you think?"

Vatch didn't respond, and Michael leaned closer, still with the gun raised.

"So I begin to wonder if you're setting me up, if you're in on this too, trying to pin everything on me so that you and whoever else can get a nice, cushy gig at Guardian Security and a retirement package financed by Lowell Moore and the firm."

Michael stood up. He was in the zone now. Talking out loud was helping him make the connections real, and was raising new ones.

"So I break in here and see what I can find. I find all sorts of things in your little files over there. Namely, that you had the same suspicions as me about Guardian and a bad egg at the bureau, but the higher-ups have ignored your memos and ignored your research. They don't want to investigate the moles in their ranks, don't want to know about the agents who sell a little information on the side to make ends meet, or maybe do something extra, like pretend to botch the Helix Johannson surveillance and then knock the guy off themselves."

Michael lowered the gun.

"I know that Lowell is going to testify against me, but I'm telling you that he's the one you want."

Vatch flicked his tongue, followed by a half-bent smile.

"I know what I want, Collins, and I want you in prison."

"You're not even going to investigate the other possibilities, are you?"

"There are theories," Vatch said, "and then there are theories that I can prove. I'm not going to make the perfect be the enemy of the good. Maybe Lowell is involved, maybe he isn't, but I can't prove that either way. All I know is that I have a theory and the proof to get you, and that's what we're going to do."

Michael shook his head.

"No." Michael bent over, and picked up his leather briefcase. "I'm changing your plans." He glanced down at the briefcase, and then back at Vatch. "Thanks for keeping this safe for me. It has a lot of sentimental value." Michael started walking backwards toward the door.

"And thanks for copies of those internal memos about investigating the connections between the FBI and Guardian Security. Somehow Brenda Gadd forgot to produce those to the defense in the initial round of discovery. But now we know they're going to come to light, don't we?"

Michael backed out the door.

"Goodnight, Francis."

CHAPTER SEVENTY

Gusts of wind howled outside, as morning snow continued to fall down, layering three inches of white powder over an inch of dark New York City slush.

"I hope to have you out of here rather quickly." Gadd's Mother Hubbard smile was back in full force. "The weather doesn't seem to be cooperating with us, so we'll adjourn for a few days after the next bit of testimony."

Brenda Gadd stepped forward.

"Is everyone ready to begin?"

The jurors nodded their heads, and then Brenda Gadd signaled to a bailiff to open the Grand Jury room door.

"The United States would like to call Lowell Moore to the stand."

Lowell walked down the center aisle, past Brenda Gadd, and then up into the witness stand. He raised his right hand. The court reporter administered the oath and then Lowell Moore sat down. He looked comfortable, but also kept an air of power and wealth. Unlike a lawyer during a trial, he knew that his job wasn't to have the jury identify with him. As a witness, he needed to command authority.

"Mr. Moore, you've been sworn and you are under oath. Do you understand that?"

341

"I do."

"Good." The two exchanged pleasantries, and Brenda Gadd asked Lowell Moore softball questions about his education and background. Then she moved into his life as a founding partner of Wabash, Kramer & Moore, starting as a law firm of only three attorneys and now employing more than 1,500.

"And Michael John Collins." Brenda Gadd took a step toward him. "He was an associate at your firm?"

"Correct, for about six years."

"And then what happened?"

"Well," Lowell looked briefly at the ceiling. "That's really something that he would be able to answer better than me, but I have my theories."

"Okay." Gadd leaned in, as if the two were sharing a secret. "Tell us."

"Michael Collins was one of the best associates at our firm, and that's not easy. It takes sacrifice and motivation, and most importantly," Lowell turned to the jury, "there isn't any room for error."

The jurors were listening, after the first several witnesses they had begun to recognize what parts of the testimony were important. This was important.

"Michael was putting in a lot of hours," Lowell continued, "and we had a lawsuit to file. It was big lawsuit. Statute of limitations was about to run out."

"What does that mean?" Brenda Gadd asked. "For those of us who aren't fluent in legalese."

"All right." Lowell became the mentor and teacher again. "There's a timer attached to every potential lawsuit. Let's say you fall down on the ice outside the courthouse, for example. As soon as you hit the ground, the clock starts running. Or let's say you have a contract to buy a house and the seller backs out of the deal at the last minute. As soon as the seller backs out, the clock starts running. Maybe the clock runs for a year or maybe the clock runs for six, depends on the type of case, but when the time runs out, you no longer can file a lawsuit. It may be the best legal claim in the world, but if you miss the deadline, you're out of luck. That's the statute of limitations, and it was running out on one of our firm's biggest cases."

"The *Maltow* case."

"Yes." Lowell nodded his head. "The *Maltow* case." He then launched into a carefully rehearsed description of the patent dispute and Dr. Maltow's pacemakers. "It was a billion-dollar case. Nearly every pacemaker sold in the world had one of Dr. Maltow's rechargeable batteries."

"And so what happened?"

"I was busy with another piece of litigation involving Joshua Krane and Krane Engineering, so I let Michael handle the filing of the *Maltow* lawsuit."

"And did he?" Gadd asked.

"Did he what?"

"Did he handle it?"

Lowell shook his head.

"No, I thought he did and it appeared as though it had been filed on time, but I later discovered that no lawsuit had ever been filed."

"How can that be?"

"He faked everything. The correspondence, the motions, even the Judge's Orders related to discovery disputes. It was all a fabrication." Lowell paused, to draw attention to his conclusion. "Even the settlement."

"How much was the settlement?"

"$300 million." Lowell let the number speak for itself. The rocking had stopped and jurors sat still, listening. "A big win for our client, obviously, but the reality was that this settlement agreement was also a fake."

"But you got a check for $300 million," Gadd said. "That kind of money can't just be withdrawn from an ATM."

"No." Lowell shook his head, gravely. The disappointment in his protégé was clear. "That's why I didn't discover it until much later. The $300 million was a wire transfer, and I believe that it was Michael Collins who wired the money into the firm's account."

"Where does an associate at a law firm get that kind of money?"

"Well," Lowell paused and turned again to the jury, making eye contact with each one. "In this case, I believe that Michael Collins stole it from Joshua Krane."

He waited for Brenda Gadd to ask another question, but when she didn't, Lowell continued.

"Shortly before the money was wired, Joshua Krane was murdered. I believe that Michael Collins arranged for that murder, took Krane's bank account numbers, and wired the money into the firm."

"Then what happened to Mr. Collins?"

"That's an easy one." Lowell laughed. "He disappeared."

CHAPTER SEVENTY ONE

A thick piece of bulletproof glass separated Kermit Guillardo from Andie Larone.

"I have a favor to ask." He took the receiver away from his ear for a second, looked around the room, and then continued. "You know I never ask for anything, so this a big deal in the life of the K-Man."

"That's not exactly true," Andie said, "but what's going on?"

Kermit glanced up at the security cameras. Then he thought about the men who sit on the other side of the room's mirror, listening to prisoner conversations.

"I can't get into everything at the moment, but it's about the plea bargain."

Andie shook her head.

"It's done. I've already made up my mind. I'm taking the deal."

Kermit looked up at the cameras again. Then he lowered his voice to whisper.

"I'm not telling you what to do. We go back far enough into the dark, dark past for me to understand that's a no-go. What I'm asking," he looked at the mirror running the length of the back wall, and then back at Andie, "is that you delay," he said.

"Just hold-off for twenty-four hours. Blame it on the snow, blame it on the sun, blame it on me, whatever. Just hold off."

"The hearing is scheduled for this afternoon," Andie said. "I've already signed the papers."

"Doesn't matter." Kermit shook his head. "A certain former resident of Hut No. 7 tells me that – in order to be final – you gotta stand up in the court and accept it in front of the judge."

"I don't think so, Kermit." Andie looked away. "I have to take care of me. Okay?"

"I know you do." Kermit pointed at her. "You know what else the K-man knows?"

Andie shook her head.

"The K-man knows that you love him. And the K-man knows that he loves you. And I think, as a matter of mathematical fact, that such an equation equals you giving the guy twenty-four hours."

Andie leaned back in her chair. A tear rolled down her cheek and she wiped it away, but others came.

She closed her eyes, processing, and then finally a nod.

"You'll wait?"

Andie nodded, again.

"Twenty-four hours."

Kermit started to get up, but Andie raised her hand before Kermit hung up the receiver. He stopped.

"What is it?"

"Tell Michael that I love him." She rubbed her nose, and wiped the tears away. "Tell him that." She nodded, becoming more sure of herself. "He should know that, but tell him any-way."

CHAPTER SEVENTY TWO

Snow had piled up eight inches, and wind snapped each new flake against Michael's exposed and reddened face. He ducked inside the church. The large, heavy wood door closed behind him, exchanging the outside fury for the peace of the empty sanctuary.

Michael looked up at the rows of stained glass windows that lined the outside walls, each told a story of faith, punishment, and redemption. That's all religion was, Michael thought, regardless of denomination. A universal truth that promised heaven in some form to everyone, provided they had faith in something, anything.

He walked down the center aisle to the front of the church. The pulpit was adorned with purple vestiges, three cuts of fabric hung down between intricately carved square columns of dark wood. Michael raised his hand up and down, and then over in the sign of the cross as he walked to the side.

Twelve rows of twelve candles were lined below the marble statue of Saint Thomas the Compassionate. Saint Thomas was one of the few disciples whose biography of Jesus couldn't actually be found in the Bible, because the scribes thought it revealed a Jesus Christ that was too human, too filled with doubt to be lifted up as the actual word of God. The masses needed a world of right and wrong, rules and punishment. The true words of salvation, according to Saint Thomas, offered none of that.

Michael picked up a long wooden match and lit it.

He picked up one of the small, red glasses containing a candle. He held the lit match near its wick and waited for a flicker. A flame appeared, and Michael put the candle back down in its place, saying a prayer and asking for a blessing.

He walked over to the confessional, pulled back the heavy, black cloth, and sat down inside.

"Forgive me Father for I have sinned."

"How long since your last confession?"

The sound of Father Stiles' voice comforted Michael, and gave him even more clarity about what he needed to do for both Andie and himself.

"Too long." Michael bowed his head. "It's been too long since my last confession." Then he told his story to Father Stiles for the first time. It was unedited and uncompromised, from the moment he was shot to that morning with Frank Vatch. Everything.

"Forgive me."

"God forgives," said Father Stiles, "and I forgive, but do you forgive yourself?"

Michael thought about the question.

"No."

"Then that's the place start."

"I need your help," Michael said, "in more concrete ways."

"I can't do that."

"I need to clear Andie's name. To do that, I need to prove that Lowell set her up. I need to show that somebody out there had a motive and resources to do it."

"And the motive is you?"

"Lowell faked a settlement and has been shifting money from one escrow account to another for the past two years, figuring out a way to bring me back. Duckstein says that the bank statements and financials are in Lowell's office. The statements will show the transfer of money, at least that's what Rhonda told her. And I don't have much doubt that the logs and security video for Andie are up there too."

"Michael, that's not my role," Father Stiles said. "I've already crossed the line with you." He paused, shaking his head. "Too often, I'm afraid, I've crossed that line. I can't risk this church and my work for this. Testifying in front of the grand jury shone a light on that."

"I'm not asking you to go with me." Michael looked at Father Stiles through the fine privacy screen of the confessional. "If I get these financials, I can prove that I didn't steal Krane's money and write a cashier's check, myself, to settle the *Maltow* case. That's what they're all saying I did. That's the motive. That I got the money, and faked the settlement to cover up my mistake. But, if the books don't add up, if it shows that the firm is $300 million in the hole and Lowell Moore has been transferring the money from one account to another, I can move on and Lowell becomes the focus."

"And the assault charges related to that federal agent?"

"They'll be pled away in exchange for my testimony against Lowell," Michael said. "I've thought this through. I can move on."

"You know that's not true," Father Stiles said. "You may have proven you didn't fake the settlement, but you still took the – "

Michael cut him off, he couldn't hear those words.

"I need your help. Rhonda Kirchner's funeral is tonight. I'm just asking that you go to the funeral, and call me when Lowell Moore arrives and when he leaves."

"Michael, I can't….I can't be an accomplice to this."

"An accomplice to freeing an innocent woman and helping a friend? You can't be an accomplice to that?"

Michael watched the silhouette of Father Stiles. Father Stiles ran his hands through his hair. His head down, then he raised it up slowly, and then back down, again. There was anguish and conflict in his movements.

Michael was ready to take back his request when Father Stiles mumbled a brief prayer. Then, Father Stiles turned toward him.

"What phone number do you want me to call?"

CHAPTER SEVENTY THREE

The windows of Café Krolle were fogged three-quarters of the way up to the ceiling as the coffee shop's antique roaster hummed and crackled in the corner. The roaster's arm swept the pan in a circle, turning the toasted beans and filling the small and crowded room with a distinct smell of espresso and dark bittersweet chocolate.

Michael adjusted his tie. It was the first time he had worn a suit since Andie's hearing. It didn't feel right. He took off the jacket and laid it on the stool next to his, then Michael rolled up his sleeves.

Setting his recently reclaimed briefcase down on the counter next to the computer, Michael sat down. The counter ran along the café's large window that overlooked the street. On the other side of that street, there was Hopper Tower and the offices of Wabash, Kramer & Moore. Michael glanced up at the clock: 6:55 p.m. Rhonda Kirchner's funeral service was scheduled to begin at 7:30 p.m.

Lowell Moore wouldn't attend the visitation, but he was obligated to attend the service. His obligation wouldn't be rooted in guilt, but appearance. Lowell understood that his absence might prompt questions, and he didn't want questions. Not when he was this close.

351

Michael opened his briefcase and removed the photograph of his revolutionary namesake. He propped it up next to the keyboard. It was an effort to get some inspiration.

Michael clicked the web browser, and after the menu came up, he punched in the bank's website address. He typed in his code and transferred money from one account to another. Then, he logged on to his private e-mail account. This was not Hotmail or Yahoo, nor was it free. In fact, Michael's private e-mail account wasn't advertised at all. The host offered very private, very confidential, encrypted communication services to a select number of clients. The manager of Hoa Bahn's had arranged for it shortly after Joshua Krane was murdered and Michael was released from the hospital.

He typed in another series of passcodes and usernames, and then finally Michael was able to access his messages. He clicked through each, most were financial account summaries. Then, Michael typed in the e-mail address of his banker and attorney in Switzerland.

Michael confirmed to the banker that he was authorized to make the offer to purchase the Sunset Resort & Hostel. The offer was to be made in the name of a newly incorporated company, and his identity was to be kept private. If the offer was not accepted and Michael did not respond within ten days, the money was to be sent via cashier's check with instructions to Bayer's Banc of Playa del Carmen, the bank that holds Andie Larone's mortgage. Michael typed, "Just pay off the debt, give her the money."

He logged out of the email program, and pulled up the website for British Airways. He clicked through a few screens, checked his watch, and then booked a direct flight to Amsterdam that departed JFK in two hours for Kermit Guillardo.

Michael confirmed the flight information and the seat in first class, and then searched for another flight. He chose a direct flight to Switzerland that departed in three hours, entered the billing information, and then moved on. Mexico City in four. Hamburg in five. Paris in six. Cape Town in seven. Montreal in eight.

He then logged off the British Airways website, and chose flights on Northwest out of LaGuardia and United out of JFK.

Every hour Michael had provided Kermit Guillardo at least three options that, hopefully, he wouldn't need. As for Michael, he had made the decision to stop running. He wasn't going to be a runner any more. Michael had decided to get into Lowell's office and stay there until he found what he was looking for, and, if he didn't find it, he would keep looking until he was caught or killed, whatever came first.

Michael printed out the confirmations for Kermit, and stuck them in his briefcase just as his phone rang. Michael picked it up.

"Hello," he said.

It was Father Stiles. Lowell had just arrived. The start of the funeral service was going to be delayed because of the weather, but everything was moving forward.

"Okay." Michael looked through the window at the Hopper Tower across the street. "I'm going."

He hung up the phone, glanced up at the clock, and then logged out of the computer. He put the photograph of his namesake back in his briefcase, and then called Kermit.

"We're ready." Michael slipped on his jacket with the phone still pressed against his ear. "I'll meet you in the alley."

CHAPTER SEVENTY FOUR

The snow fell even harder than before. The few cars and trucks that tried to drive in front of the Hopper Tower slid and slipped, and ultimately left deep tracks behind. Michael put on a brown felt fedora and his red glasses, a silly disguise, but the best he could do. Then he crossed the street and ducked into the alley where delivery trucks loaded and unloaded office supplies, furniture, and paper to the Hopper Tower's tenants.

The baby-blue Camry was stopped halfway down the alley. Its lights were on and smoke billowed from its tailpipe.

Michael rapped on the window, and Kermit rolled it down.

"You know what to do?"

"Using these peepers to peep the perps." Kermit pointed at his eyes, and then grinned. "I'll circle the block and call you if I see any cops or our arch nemesis enter the compound."

"Right." Michael turned his cell phone to vibrate. "Let's do this," he said, more to himself than to Kermit, while reaching into his briefcase.

Michael removed the printed airline confirmation sheets.

"These are for you." He handed the papers to Kermit. "You see anything, call me, and then get the hell away. I don't want to see you thrown in jail."

Kermit took the printouts from Michael, and set them in the seat behind him. Then, he put the car into park and suddenly got out of the car.

"Love you, dude." Kermit grabbed Michael and put him into a massive bear hug. "You and Andie are like the sun and moon, and I'm like that stuff that's, like, secondary to those things. You know?"

"I know." Michael patted him on the back. "Love you, too. Now put me down."

CHAPTER SEVENTY FIVE

Cold out there tonight." Michael brushed snow off of his long, felt trench coat, and offered the security guard a confident smile. As Michael walked up to the desk, he held his head high, confidence was going to be the key to pulling this off.

He reached into his back pocket and removed a gray security pass card for the Hopper Tower's elevators, and silently prayed that the tech support hadn't gotten around to canceling his access to the building. Surely Lowell would have submitted the request to cancel immediately, but tech support at Wabash, Kramer & Moore wasn't unlike the tech support in every other business in America. They operated with a different perspective of both time and urgency.

Michael picked up the clipboard and wrote down the name of another associate he had pulled off of the firm's website, and then walked past the security guard without asking for permission. He didn't need permission. After all, he worked at one of the biggest and best law firms in the country. He also happened to be in a hurry.

Michael walked to the elevator. He pressed the "up" button, and a set of elevator doors at the far end of the row slid open. A bell rang and the light above the doors lit up.

Michael walked into the elevator. He pressed the pass card against a gray magnetic reader; then punched in the number of the tower's top floor and held his breath. As the request processed, Michael felt a cold bead of sweat roll down his back. Finally the floor number lit up and the elevator began to move.

The famous Wabash, Kramer & Moore foyer was empty and dark. The only noise that could be heard was the distant hum of a vacuum cleaner somewhere on the floor. All the legal assistants and the paralegals had gone home. All of the attorneys were also gone, unusual for this early in the evening, but it was Rhonda Kirchner's funeral.

If handled in the normal manner, which it most certainly was, the firm would have circulated an e-mail to all associates and partners. The e-mail would appear no different than other firm announcements, such as a new hire, a birth, a wedding, or an anniversary. It would provide the who, what, when, and where of the funeral service. No descriptions of Rhonda as a person or a mother would appear, nor would it be revealed that she had been fired by Lowell Moore or provide the cause of death.

To encourage attendance at Rhonda Kirchner's funeral, the final paragraph of the e-mail would note that the executive committee had authorized a specific administrative file to be opened. Time spent at the funeral could be billed and counted toward each attorney's required number of billable hours per month. In a fitting tribute, the meaning of Rhonda Kirchner's life would be quantified and evaluated as part of the cost of doing business. She had been reduced to the ten digits of a Wabash, Kramer & Moore billing code: 14.2F64.0050 (Misc. Administrative-Kirchner Funeral).

Michael passed the copy room, and then a series of cubicles. He walked by one empty attorney office after another, until he arrived at Lowell's office at the corner of the building.

He looked back and didn't see anything or anyone.

Michael looked in the other direction and saw only a large, blue cleaning cart at the far end of the hallway.

Lowell's office was in front of him.

Michael took two steps inside, and turned on the lights. He shut the door and felt his pulse quicken.

At night, the view was spectacular. Hundreds of outside lights dotted the windows that encased the large room like a planetarium. It was easy to be hypnotized, but there was work to do.

Michael took off his jacket and set the jacket and his briefcase down on Lowell's table. Then he walked toward a row of file cabinets on the other side of the room.

He pulled the first drawer. It slid open, and Michael scanned the headings of each folder. Then he pulled the second drawer, and then the third.

Michael moved down the line of file cabinets, looking for financial records or anything related to Andie, but no luck. The file cabinets only contained copies of correspondence and pleadings. It was the paper that every lawyer shuffled every day.

He got to the fifth file cabinet and pulled the top drawer, but it didn't slide open. The lock in the upper right corner had been pushed in.

Michael looked on the top of the cabinet for a key, but it wasn't there. He then went to Lowell's desk. Michael opened the drawers, faster now, looking for a small key to open the cabinet. Then he stopped.

There was a bulge underneath an open magazine on Lowell's desk. Michael picked up the magazine. A ring filled with small keys was underneath.

He ran back to the file cabinets, put a key into the hole, and turned. The lock popped out, and Michael pulled open the top drawer only to find personnel files.

"Hell-o." There was a knock on the door, and the woman repeated herself. "You working?"

"Ah ..." Michael hesitated. "Yes, busy."

"Garbage?"

Michael thought about how he should respond.

"Yes." He looked for the garbage can. "Come in."

A large Hispanic woman in her late fifties opened the door, crossed the room and retrieved Lowell Moore's garbage can. She took it out into the hallway, and then emptied it in her large blue cleaning cart.

She returned the garbage can to its place, and then said, "Open or close?"

Michael didn't understand.

"Door," she said. "Open or closed?"

"Closed." Michael felt his cell phone vibrate as she left, closing the door behind her.

Michael flipped open the phone, and pressed a button.

It was Father Stiles. Lowell Moore had gotten a phone call in the middle of the service and left. He tried to follow, but lost Lowell on the freeway. It looked like he was coming back to the office, but Father Stiles didn't know. He was trying to catch up with him.

Michael turned off the phone, and scanned the office again. He checked his watch. Eight minutes had passed.

Michael knew the documents had to be in the office. Lowell wouldn't trust them to be stored anywhere else. But where?

Michael sat down in Lowell's chair and took a breath. His eyes scanned and re-scanned the room. Maybe Lowell had a safe behind one of the paintings – Michael stood – or maybe not.

He remembered Lowell's comment about Hooten, taking over the old man's office when the firm "trimmed the fat."

Michael walked over to the door to Lowell Moore's private bathroom and tried the handle.

It was locked.

Then, Michael took a step back and saw a small silver keypad next to the door. Bathrooms usually don't have security.

Michael pressed 1,2,3,4, and then the pound key. The light on the top of the keypad beeped and flashed red. The door remained locked. Michael pressed the zero key four times, and then pound. Then, zero six times. Red. Red.

"Think." Michael needed numbers: birthdays, anniversaries, social security numbers, they were all possible. But Michael didn't know them and didn't have time to find out. He checked his watch, again. He wondered if Lowell even remembered his anniversary date after three marriages. Maybe it was written down on a piece of paper on his desk.

Michael felt his cell phone vibrate again.

It was Father Stiles. He had caught up to Lowell in the Lincoln Tunnel. Michael had ten minutes.

He hung up the phone, and tried to focus. Closing his eyes, Michael tried to think. "Come on. I need this."

And then, it came to him.

Michael slowly and carefully punched in the numbers: 1-2-0-3-2-9.

He paused. That had to be it, he thought, and then pressed the pound sign.

Michael saw the yellowed statement and the check hanging in Lowell's home office so clearly in his mind: Paid to Lowell H. Moore, Esq. in the amount of $1,203.29. It was the amount paid by his first client, the first one to ever pay his bill.

The light flashed to green, and Michael opened the door.

The bathroom was no longer a bathroom. It was another small office equipped with a computer, telephone, and a second set of file cabinets.

Michael walked inside. He pulled out the top drawer, scanned, and then pulled out the middle drawer. Nothing.

Last, Michael pulled out the bottom drawer and started flipping through the folders. Half way through, Michael found the financials.

Each year was separate, and about an inch thick. Michael didn't need to look at them. There would be plenty of time for that later. He pulled out the last three years, stuck them under his arm, and then fingered through the rest of the cabinet.

Wedged in the very back, there was a large white envelope. Michael pulled the envelope out and looked inside. It contained the sign-in logs from the First National building, and the time-stamped video of Andie entering and exiting.

Michael checked his watch. It would be close, but he still had plenty of time to get out. He turned and headed for the door, but only made it a step.

Patty Bernice stood in the doorway. Her friendly face and rosy cheeks were nowhere to be seen.

"Hello, Michael." She pointed the gun at his chest. "I never did trust you." She paused. "Always a little too eager for my taste."

CHAPTER SEVENTY SIX

Michael remembered the driver of the white van's voice, the woman screaming at the Professor to hurry. It was Patty Bernice. He should've recognized it.

Patty cocked her head to the side, but the gun remained pointed at him.

"I told that to Lowell, tried to warn him, but he went on and on about me being paranoid and about what an asset you were to the firm."

Patty shook her head.

"But look at you now, stealing confidential information from us, information that could jeopardize the integrity and reputation of Wabash, Kramer & Moore."

"Patty." Michael tried to take a step forward, but Patty raised the gun, stopping him short. "What are you doing?"

"You know how many hours of my life have been spent dedicated to this firm?" Her eyes blinked; a nervous twitch. "I was here at the beginning. I was the one who had the magic touch, finding those cases that no other firm would take, but I could turn them into gold."

"Patty," Michael said. "Lowell's been shifting money around. There's a hole that he's trying to cover – "

"You don't think I know that?" Patty laughed. "I'm every bit as smart as you. In fact, I'm smarter than every attorney in this place, except for Mr. Moore, and even then, sometimes I wonder."

"Patty." Michael repeated her name, hoping to connect. "Put the gun away."

She shook her head.

"Lowell doesn't have the guts to do this. He doesn't like to get his pampered little hands dirty."

"It's gone too far."

"Why did you do it to us?" Patty asked. "There was a simple plan to fix a simple error related to the filing of the *Maltow* lawsuit. It shouldn't have happened, but it did, an oversight on my part, and I had a plan to fix it. The *Krane* money was just sitting there, and if we didn't take it," she shook her head, "the government was just going to flush it away."

"Patty." Michael tried, again, to take a step toward her, but stopped when Patty's grip tightened on the gun.

"Lowell loved the plan, called me brilliant." Patty took a step back, out of the doorway and gestured for Michael to follow. "All we needed was those account numbers. Thompson would do the carjacking. He would meet me in the alley, give me the numbers, and then I'd take care of Thompson. That was how it was supposed to go ..."

"Except he didn't have the numbers."

"Except you took the numbers," Patty said. "You took the money that was supposed to help the firm out of a little jam." Patty led Michael to the French doors leading out to the balcony overlooking the street below.

Patty gestured to the ground.

"Set the files down and open the doors."

Michael, unable to think of anything else, did as he was told. An opportunity had to come. Where was Father Stiles?

He rose back up, and looked out the glass doors to the terrace now filled with mounds of fresh snow.

"What are you waiting for?" Patty nodded toward the space behind him. "Outside."

Michael raised his arms and looked at the door.

"Okay." He opened it and cold air filled the office in a rush. The pictures rattled from the wind and the walls moaned from the sudden change in temperature.

Patty gestured for Michael to step backward, out of the office and onto the terrace. The wind picked up again, and Michael felt the needles of icy sleet cut into the back of his neck.

"We had Dwight track you down." Patty shook her head. "You have to take risks to succeed in this firm, Michael." She shouted to allow her voice to be heard above the howling wind. "That's something you never really understood. You need to bend the rules, and not ask how or why, just do it and get the reward."

"That's what Rhonda was," Michael said, "a risk taken so that a problem would go away."

Patty shrugged her shoulders.

"Not much of a risk, and neither is this." Patty lowered her voice an octave and pretended as though she was reading a news script. "A young man caught stealing from a local law firm, takes his own life after his accomplice confesses to the crime and takes her own life just one day before."

"It won't work." Michael's back was pressed against the railing. The wet of the snow had already sunk through his shoes and the entire lower part of his pants.

"You have to jump now." Patty took a step closer to Michael. It was her first step onto the terrace. "But don't think I won't shoot you if I have to."

Then Lowell Moore arrived.

"Patty!" Lowell shouted. "What are you doing?"

When she turned, Michael lunged at her. His hands wrapped around her wrists, trying to lift the gun up and away from him. Patty kicked twice as Michael struggled to pull the gun out of her hands.

Lowell ran toward them.

Patty looked at Lowell, and Michael jerked her as hard as he could. Her grip loosened on the gun, but then she jerked it back. Michael tried again, but this time he lost his footing on the ice.

He let go of the gun, and grabbed Patty as he started to fall, pulling her down with him.

She screamed, and the gun went off as they crashed into the cold. Michael's head hit the stone terrace, and everything went black.

CHAPTER SEVENTY SEVEN

Kermit heard the gunshot. A bell attached to the building started to ring, and then Kermit heard the sound of police sirens.

"Holy smokety-smokes." He shifted the car into gear and sped out of the alley. He got about a block away, and turned on the overhead dome light.

While trying to keep the Camry under control in the wet snow, he studied the printouts that Michael had given him. Kermit was trying to find a time and an airport that would work, but it was dark and he was having difficulty reading the sheets.

He dropped one on the floor. When Kermit bent down to pick it up, the Camry slammed into the back of a silver minivan. His head hit the bottom of the steering wheel, and then jerked back from the blow.

Kermit stumbled out of the car, as the driver of the silver minivan got out to examine the damage. She looked at Kermit.

"You're bleeding," she pointed. "Your head."

Kermit touched his forehead, and then looked down at the red blood on his hand.

"Gotta do something, bleeding's not a good thing." Kermit closed his eyes, trying to regain his focus as throbs of pain shot through his neck and bounced around his head.

When Kermit opened his eyes, the pain suddenly shifted and roiled down his spine, causing him to slip. He fell to the ground.

"Are you okay? Stay down."

Kermit shook his head.

"I have to go." He looked away from the woman, and then saw it. The sign bathed in a soft fluorescent yellow. It was The 365 Day Store on West 34th. It was the numbers that caused the magic: 3-6-5.

There were an infinite number of possibilities in those digits, two odd, one even. It promised to provide a numeric equilibrium to set the order straight.

Kermit got up. The woman tried to stop him, but he continued on toward the store.

"I'll be back." He waved her away. "I'll be back."

Kermit went into the first aisle near the checkout and examined the shelves of candy and chips, specifically the various prices. There were so many prices to choose from, too many.

He finally decided on a Butterfinger (.67) and a Kit Kat Giant ($1.09). He picked both off of the shelf, and walked up to the register. Only one other person was in line. He waited, holding his snacks in one hand and covering the bleeding cut on his forehead with the other.

"Rough night?"

The cashier looked at Kermit, as Kermit placed the candy on the counter. Car horns sounded outside the door. Traffic was backing up. More horns outside, and then the klip-klop of two horses.

The cashier finished ringing up the purchase, and Kermit paid. He left the change and the candy bars on the counter, and ripped the receipt out of the cashier's hand as he ran toward the door.

"Hey you forgot your stuff, man." The cashier was yelling, but Kermit didn't stop.

When he got outside, a police officer had already dismounted his horse, and was examining the accident scene.

"This your car?" The officer pointed at the Camry, while his partner spoke with the driver of the silver minivan. Kermit hesitated at first, but then nodded his head.

"Well, you're causing all sorts of problems." The officer walked around to the back of the Camry to get the license plate number. He wrote it down, and then finished scratching out a preliminary police report and citation. "You're going to have to move it." He looked at the line of cars behind them. "Like now."

A beep, static, and then a dispatcher's voice came out of the officer's radio.

The officer picked it up as dispatch repeated the 411.

He signaled to his partner.

"We gotta go." The officer turned back to Kermit, actually looking at him for the first time. "You know you're bleeding?"

"Yes, sir."

The officer walked closer, examining the cut.

"Doesn't look too serious." He handed Kermit the citation. "Get that taken care of." He looked in the direction of Hopper Tower. "We have to respond to this call."

The officer turned away, and then hurried to his horse. His partner was already mounted and waiting, and soon they disappeared into the heavy winter snow.

Kermit looked down at the ticket.

It was Citation No. 0346405000 written by Officer Badge No. 2389 for a violation of New York Municipal Ordinance 257-24 regarding Toyota Camry License AEX-891 for a total fine due of $63. Getting in a traffic accident was evidently illegal in New York City.

Kermit stared at the citation a little longer. Then he saw the numbers move and rearrange as the traffic ticket began to glow in his hand. It was happening. For the first time in over thirty years, it was finally happening. His fluency in the language of numbers, a childhood gift that he had taken for granted during the first twenty-two years of his life, was coming back to him.

The air outside was freezing, and the snow was coming down harder than ever before. But he felt warm and light, as the numbers continued to move.

"A little more."

Then the digits on the ticket reached their cosmic pre-destination, a perfect equation staring back at him:

$$\frac{(0346405000/2389)}{891} + (257\text{-}24) - 63 = 100$$

Kermit looked down at his receipt from The 365 Day Store, generated by Employee No. 126, for a Butterfinger .67 and Kit Kat Giant $1.09 for a sub-total of $1.76 and .1020 tax for a total of $2.03. The receipt vibrated in his hand and radiated the same yellow glow as the police citation, then the numbers began to move gracefully in front of him, floating in space. Slowly at first, but then the movement picked up speed, until finally stopping in a beautiful, linear sequence:

$$\frac{(3\text{x}65) + (176\text{-} (67+109) + (10/2) - (0(18/6))}{(12/6)} = 100$$

Numeric equilibrium had been achieved.

CHAPTER SEVENTY EIGHT

Father Stiles' face came in and out of focus as he knelt over Michael.

"You banged your head pretty bad out there." He pressed a piece of gauze against the small cut on Michael's forehead. "Cops are here already. An ambulance is on its way."

"Files?" Michael asked, unable to form the full question.

"We got 'em." Father Stiles smiled.

"Kermit?"

"Stay down." Father Stiles put a gentle hand on Michael's chest, keeping him still.

Michael closed his eyes and turned his head to the side. He rested there for a minute, maybe ten. Then he opened his eyes and saw Patty Bernice being led away in handcuffs, her dress torn, her hair wet and messed.

Two paramedics came over to him.

"You want to take him now?" He was talking about Michael. The paramedic lowered the stretcher, its legs folding beneath itself as the stretcher went down to the floor.

"Might as well. No point with the other."

Michael was lifted onto it, and they began to wheel him out of the office.

He jerked and bounced. His head throbbed. He felt himself about to slip back into unconsciousness, when he noticed Agent Frank Vatch with a crowd of officers and detectives huddled near Lowell's desk. They were looking down at the floor, talking casual, like it was no big deal. Then Michael looked.

Lowell Moore. His right leg was unnaturally bent back. His arms out wide, like a tilted airplane. And then there was his chest. Lowell Moore's chest was a mess of churned up bone and tissue, blood and hair. His white starched shirt was open, and it appeared to be dipped in a bright shade of red paint.

"You have to rest, Michael." Father Stiles replaced the bandage on Michael's forehead with a fresh piece of gauze. "Everything is alright, now."

EPILOGUE

As the moonlight skimmed across the water outside Hut No. 7, Michael's fingers traced the lines of her body. He started at her knee, then up to her hip, the edge of her breast, and then finally the back of her neck. He rubbed her shoulders, and Andie edged her warm body back into his, falling back asleep.

Michael had lost track of the number of times they had made love in the past twenty-four hours. It was like he was a teenager again, snuck away with his one and only sweetheart on a camping trip.

He closed his eyes and listened to the waves lap against the Sunset's white, sandy beach. Sleep came easy, and he was thankful that the images waited a few hours before they made their return. The flashes and spins – the frames and images random – until the memory ended where it always ended.

"Wait here." Krane unlocked the passenger side door and grabbed his briefcase. "Should only take a minute."

"Fine." Michael watched as Krane got out of the BMW Roadster and walked up to the Bank of America building. Krane took out a card, swiped it through an electronic reader, and then opened the door.

Through the glass doors, Michael could see Krane stop at the security desk, show some identification, and then he was waived through to the elevator.

Michael looked at the small digital clock inside the BMW. It was a quarter past two, only the latest in a string of seventeen hour days. He stopped going home a few weeks ago, and simply crashed on the leather sofa in his office. He showered at the club.

Michael looked back at the building. Krane still couldn't be seen so he drummed the steering wheel to keep himself awake, turning on the stereo to break the silence.

$500 million, Michael thought, sitting there in a bank account. He tried to calculate how many hours his mother would have had to work at minimum wage cleaning office buildings to accumulate that much money.

Michael looked back toward the bank, and then in his rear-view mirror. He thought he saw something. Maybe it was the FBI. Krane had to be under 24 hour surveillance, Michael thought, there's no way he'd be let out of their sight.

Another minute or two passed, and Michael began to get nervous. Maybe Krane was having second thoughts. Lowell would be furious if he backed out.

Michael pecked through the hundreds of radio stations populating the New York dial, searching for a decent song. He finally settled on an old Mellencamp tune, but turned the radio off when Krane emerged from the bank building.

He opened the car door, got inside, and Michael shifted the BMW into gear.

The roadster pulled away from the curb.

"It pains me." Krane shook his head. "Absolutely hurts."

Michael looked over at Krane, but didn't say anything. His briefcase was open at his feet, and he was holding a white envelope out in front of him.

"This was the legacy." Krane looked down at the standard, white envelope, which contained the account numbers to access over $500 million. "My kids and their kids and so on would all benefit because of this." Krane shook his head. "And now the government gets to piss it away on some feel-good after-school program."

Krane held the envelope out to Michael.

"Take it. Makes me sick just to think about it, much less hold it anymore."

Michael took the envelope containing the account numbers and passwords.

"Your kids would like the money." Michael slid the envelope into his suit jacket's breast pocket. "But I think they'll also like seeing their father a free man again." Being a lawyer also meant being a salesman. Keep the client happy with the deal, at least until it's signed and approved by the judge.

"Maybe you're right." Krane locked the briefcase. "Or maybe the kids would rather have the money." He laughed and Michael shifted the car into neutral as they rolled toward a red light and stopped.

A man on the sidewalk began to cross in front of them.

Michael turned toward Krane.

"Well, you know your kids better than – "

The windshield shattered and glass sprayed the interior of the car. Michael pressed down on the gas pedal as far as it would go. It was instinct. The BMW's engine roared as the RPM needle hit red, but they didn't move. The car was still in neutral.

Another shot, Michael looked at Krane and screamed, but nothing came out. Krane's head was half gone. A third shot into the chest and Krane's body jolted forward.

The thin figure outside the car moved quickly from the front to the side. A fourth shot was fired into the passenger side window as a hand reached in to unlock the door and grab Krane's briefcase. That was when Michael felt a searing pain and wetness on his neck. He realized that he'd been shot, and then nothing.

Four days later, Michael woke up in a hospital. Another week, and his discharge nurse handed him a garbage bag filled with the clothes that he was wearing on the night of the incident. The envelope was still in the suit jacket's breast pocket. The police and the FBI never looked.

Michael sat straight up in bed. His sheets and pillow were drenched with sweat.

"Michael?"

"It's fine." His heart still pounding. "Go back to sleep. It's nothing."

Andie rolled over, and fell back asleep.

Michael got out of the bed, and found his boxers and shorts on the floor near the door. He slipped them on, and then stepped outside.

Cool, salty air came off the Caribbean water, and Michael tried to take as much of that air in as he could.

He walked through the other guest huts, toward the beach. A series of thatch umbrellas dotted the shoreline, and Michael walked to the small hut at the end of the line. Inside, there was a cooler stocked with beer.

He grabbed a Corona and opened it, then he took a lemon, sliced out a wedge and squeezed it into the bottle's neck. With his thumb over the opening, he slowly tipped the bottle upside down and watched as the wedge floated upward.

Michael took a drink, and then walked out to the Point that jutted a hundred yards into the small bay. He took another deep breath, sat down, and stared back at the shoreline.

Hut No. 7 sat among a dozen others. It was basic shelter, but it was his.

Michael finished his beer and walked back. Instead of going directly to his hut, Michael walked to the Sunset's cantina and main office.

He stepped up onto the empty deck, and then into the bar. The alcohol was safely under lock and key, but everything else was open.

Michael walked into the lobby, around the front desk, and finally into the back office. He turned on Andie's computer, and waited for everything to power up and log on to the internet.

Michael clicked, and finally got to the appropriate screen. He typed in his password, and checked his email. There were three messages. The first one was from Tammy Duckstein. He clicked and a small window opened:

> *Michael, hope you're doing well. I still want to talk to you about the financial reports. Internal investigation is coming up with a lot of connections to Guardian Security. Dwight Keiffer pled, and has agreed to testify against the agents and Patty Bernice. Vatch is still after the money. Do you think Patty took it?*

It was late, and Michael decided that he would respond some other time or maybe never. The past was the past. He clicked, and another message flashed on his screen.

> *Ms. Andie Larone has accepted the offer of Highland Investors, Inc. for 50% of the shares in the Sunset. I signed the partnership agreement as secretary and treasurer of Highland Investors, and I have forwarded a copy of the partnership agreement to your address. Your anonymity has been maintained. Please let me know if there is anything else I can do for you. This transaction should be reflected in your account's current balance.*
>
> *Sincerely,*
> *Art Mittesonne*
> *Account Services, First Swiss*

Michael clicked on the third and final message. It was from Kermit Guillardo.

> *Yo man, thanks for the loan. Hanging in Amsterdam and helping the grieving widow. Val says howdy-doody. The numbers are aligned and in balance. Later, bro-ha, be back in a month. –K*

Michael minimized the e-mails and pulled up the home page for Rutthanson Bank of Bern. He typed in his account information and password. A few seconds went by as the bank verified the information, and then a menu appeared. Michael chose English as one of the language options. The screen refreshed, and he clicked the button for current balance.

A new screen appeared, and he scrolled down to the bottom.

AVAILABLE BALANCE: $473,152,915.19

His hand moved the mouse, again, ready to click and shut the computer down. Then, he paused.

He looked at the account balance, and then Michael clicked on Kermit's email. He looked back at his account balance, and started to laugh.

Numeric equilibrium had been achieved:

$$(4(7+3)-15)2) + ((9+1)-5)(1+9)) = 100$$

Thank you for reading "No Time To Run."
Don't wait to read the exciting sequel, "No Time To Die."
Available Now

44399201R00214

Made in the USA
Lexington, KY
30 August 2015